"But," Atamar ch... are to enjoy this tr... what we have done. ...
means."

"A soul," said Lura. She was unhappy, thinking of the squandered camel-driver. Lura was a deep thinker, not a quick one.

"Boss, there are *six* of them!" objected Gerial. "Six of them! One out of six is all we need, and that's nothing. We could have one signed, sealed, and halfway to Hell before breakfast tomorrow. Look, I've been giving these babies the once-over, and it's going to be like picking windfalls, rotten-ripe for the tumbling."

"An embarrassment of riches," said Atamar, "can sometimes mean poverty. We may lose sight of the forest for the trees. Grasp all, lose all."

"With all due respect, my lord," said Melisan, "you'll bore those mortals all the way to Paradise before we can nab a single soul."

"Bore them?" Atamar was indignant. "*I* am boring?"

"Let's put it this way, mighty one," said the golden-haired succubus, languidly fanning herself with one wing. "You just might have invented the Eighth Deadly Sin there. Thou shalt not cliché."

ESTHER FRIESNER

Here Be
Demons

ORBIT

AN ORBIT BOOK

First published in Great Britain by Sphere Books Ltd 1990
First published in the United States of America by
Ace Books, a Division of the Berkeley Publishing Group, 1988

Reproduced, printed and bound in Great Britain by
Cox & Wyman Ltd, Reading

ISBN 0 7474 0552 2

Orbit Books Ltd
A Division of
Macdonald & Co (Publishers) Ltd
Orbit House
1 New Fetter Lane
London EC4A 1AR
A member of Maxwell Macmillan Pergamon Publishing Corporation

**FOR
DAVID VIERLING
AND
KIRK WAGNER**

*I am bound to call them gentlemen;
I am pleased to call them friends.*

Prologue

THE WIND BLEW out of forever and into tomorrow. It was a dry wind, a desert wind, and it blew the names from things and it blew the shapes out of memory. It spread wings of gold, hot and glaring in the forge of the desert, and covered the camp and the village, the temple of the sacred prostitutes and the huts of the monastery, the bones of donkeys and of men. At times it shrieked, at times it sighed, at times it held its breath, waiting to see what would happen. It blew out of a sky hard and blue as an enamelled basin. There was no word of power capable of sealing up that scorching breath.

The demons brooded, perched on the spar of livid rock that poked impossibly out of the heart of the desert. The sun warmed them and the wind lifted their folded wings. They clung to the rock with naked claws and waited. In the sky, the silver needle of a passing jet was the only thing that dared to move, mirrored in yellow eyes. The demons, the rock, and the wind.

PART I

1

In the Footsteps
of the Caesars

"IT's YOUR MOVE," said Atamar. He tossed the dice to Gerial,
who snaked out his tail into a pretty double-loop and caught
them easily.

"Show off," mumbled Lura. She was making drawings
in the sand with the blood of a lizard. She was mediocre as an
artist, and like her mortal equivalents made up for lack of
talent by rationalization. Right now she mentally blamed
Gerial's trick with the dice and his tail for distracting her from
her drawing. No wonder her scene of depravity was no more
erotic than a visit to Grandma's house.

She was about to cover her effort with a fresh layer of sand
and start over, when a slender shadow fell over her and a
voice made loathsome by centuries of companionship said,
"That stinks."

"Who gave you a degree in art appreciation?" demanded
Lura, shooting a look of sulphurous hatred up at the golden-
haired succubus hovering above her on leathery wings.

"I don't need a degree to know what stinks, and that
stinks," maintained Melisan, coming in for a landing. "What
a waste of good blood! I haven't had a decent drink in years,

5

and here you lie wasting it on trash that couldn't seduce a Boy Scout.''

"Oh, come now, Melisan," Horgist murmured sleepily, opening one saucer-shaped eye. It was the only one he had. "It's only lizard's blood."

"What did you think I was expecting? Half a pint of Château Rommel?" snapped Melisan. "We are down to lizard's blood, for Dis' sake! And we're lucky to get that. I'm not about to have this slut wasting it on scribblings."

"I caught that lizard myself, so I am free to do whatever I want with it," sniffed Lura, placing a protective hand over the vial of chipped Phoenician glass that held her treasure. "If you're so thirsty, catch your own."

"We're supposed to share what we catch!" shouted Melisan.

"Yes, that's what you always say when it's a matter of divvying up someone else's prey, but who did I see crouched behind old Quintus' cell with a four-inch tail sticking out of her mouth?" countered Lura.

Horgist sighed and lumbered to his flabby feet. This was fast escalating into one of the classic Lura vs. Melisan free-for-alls. He had only roused himself to try to restore peace, but the situation was out of his control. All he wanted to do was sleep. You didn't get bored in dreams.

"Atamar," called Horgist groggily. "Atamar, they're at it again."

Atamar jerked his head up sharply, annoyed at the interruption. The fineness of his features cast amorous shadows across the rock where he and Gerial gamed. There was no god of beauty, no Adonis, no Apollo, no Tammuz of the ancient world that could compare or compete with him. He was flawless, perfect, designed by a loving hand solely to be adored. But the tattered wings of a bat clapped together in the hot air behind him, and he reeked of dung.

"May the desert swallow them, and their sisters!" he swore, striding down from the rock. He siezed them both by the hair and shook them like puppies until icy tears ran from their eyes. Satisfied, he flung them away and went back to his match with Gerial.

"It's all your fault," hissed Melisan as she shook sand from her wings. Lura groaned in answer. Atamar had a strong arm. She had slid one hundred feet across the desert floor on her naked belly. She stung in places she would not give Melisan the satisfaction of mentioning.

The game had lost the exciting spark of immediate combat by the time Atamar resumed his seat. Gerial was tumbling the dice in his left hand and scraping his tusks with his right. Atamar made a disgusted face. Years had lost all sense of time and even centuries were beginning to blur, but still he could not abide the idea of being exiled in the company of Gerial.

"If there were such a thing in the hierarchy," he had once told the blue-skinned horror, "I would say that you are the patron demon of revolting personal habits."

"Sorry, boss," Gerial had beamed an apologetic reply. It would have sounded more sincere if he hadn't belched loudly between words. Atamar gagged and gave up.

Gerial passed him the dice and lolled back on the rock, picking at his navel with the tip of his tail. He was proud of that tail, and prouder still of his navel. Most demons made do without them. Furthermore, no one would have noticed Gerial's special ornament if not for the most recent visit of their old friend Murakh.

Murakh meant good times when he came. Murakh meant news of the underworld and the otherworld and the outerworld. There was no knowing when to expect him. He delighted in surprising them, and he never failed to bring a heavy load of gifts for his unfortunate colleagues. It was Murakh who noticed Gerial's navel, and thereby won the blue-skinned demon's adoration for half past eternity.

"How about that?" Murakh had exclaimed when they all stretched out on the rock to enjoy the sun. "Gerial's got a belly-eye."

"Hmm?" remarked Lura. She was feeling sleek and sated. Murakh wasn't like the three male demons who shared her punishment. They had gotten bored with her body long ago and left her alone. There is no more depressing fate for a succubus. Her only comfort was knowing that they'd stopped fumbling Melisan first.

"Look there," said Murakh, pointing with one gnarled brown claw. The navel was flattered and winked at him. "Do you know what that means? It's a sign of mortal birth. Old Gerial started out as a mortal."

"Do tell," yawned Horgist, trying to steal back into his dreams. "Do tell."

The news shocked no one more than Gerial himself. He had to admit that he could not recall ever being mortal, but as Murakh pointed out, mortal memory can't stand the pressures of demonhood. Some of the most illustrious hell-hounds had been mortals, but you'd never know it to look at them now.

"Nor to look at you now," added Murakh, mentally toting up Gerial's fine set of inhuman features: blue skin, jutting tusks, serpentine tail. "Whatever you did, I wish you'd re-member it. It must have been a winner."

Thinking about Murakh depressed Gerial. His overlord, Atamar, wasn't interested in the game any longer. Horgist was asleep, as usual. The succubi were sulking. It was a moment like innumerable other moments in the centuries of their exile, a moment that held emptiness forever.

"I quit," said Gerial. "I'm going to read."

It was a lie, a contemptibly white one, uttered for form's sake and fooling no one. It was common knowledge these days that Gerial nourished an unrequited passion for one of the more vapid-eyed video stars, a Mohawked canary whose tapes he ran and re-ran courtesy of the VCR Murakh had provided.

"Go to the abyss and be done with it," snarled Atamar, throwing the dice away. He hoped to lose them, if only to give himself the task of carving a new set from bone. In his sullen mood, he waited until Lura came back to her aban-doned drawing, then licked out his tongue and snapped up the flask of blood, draining it before her eyes. "Any complaints?" Atamar grinned.

"I was going to give it to you anyway," Lura shrugged. What good would complaints do? Atamar was their named lord, and so he had always been. So he would always be, until the term of punishment ended.

Her easy surrender enraged him. They were a fine pair, Lura and Atamar. He could even remember feeling such deep lust for her that he had taken out his feelings on the willing Melisan. Then, drained of the most volatile impulses, he intended to ask her to share a roosting place with him alone. He dreamed of their future together, and of the brood of demons they might raise. But time passed, and he still had to resort to Melisan, and he still could not drain quite enough of his lust, and it was bad manners to rape your intended mate while proposing to her, and Lura still claimed she liked her freedom. He would never know whether she meant that or was just saying it to cover the fact that she had no apparent allure for him.

"What do you mean, have I ever considered roosting?"
she tittered while he strained to keep his questions sounding
indifferent. "What for? I wouldn't want my children to be
brought up in this bog, without the chance for a proper
education. Remember what Murakh said. Education's the
thing these days."

He tried not to remember Murakh. It conjured up visions of
Lura in his arms, the tight braids of her raven hair tangling
his wings like a thousand small iron chains.

"Besides," Lura went on, stroking herself with her tail in
a most provocative way, "What do you care about my roosting intentions, Atamar? You pay me less attention than you
give to the rock. Didn't think I'd seen you at it, eh? Or are
you trying to find out what Melisan thinks by asking me? If
you want to roost with her, go to it at your pleasure. Only
don't raise too many younglings, will you? One Melisan is
more than enough for me." With that, she had flounced back
to Horgist's absentminded embrace.

Years followed years, and Atamar no longer needed to
slake his passion for Lura on Melisan. The time was ripe, he
thought. He had caught a glimpse of the fair succubus gazing
at him hungrily, for he was still the only demon who had not
touched her. Yes, it was a propitious time.

Until that triple blasted camel-driver came wandering across
the sands and ruined it all.

She had wandered far from the rock and found the louse-
ridden old Arab snoring against his camel's side. Her touch
awakened him, and he thought he had died in his sleep and
gone straight to the Paradise reserved for faithful servants of
the Prophet. For was this not one of the divine houris who
await the pleasure of Mohammed's servants? A few moments
later, in Lura's arms, he was doubly convinced that he was
happily dead. A moment past that, he was right. In the midst
of his ecstacy, when he called out in thanksgiving to Allah,
Lura sank her pretty teeth expertly into his carotid and gorged.

It killed romance.

Melisan found her the next morning, practically purring in
her sleep. She was hauled before the assembly where she
protested that she had saved them the camel. Wasn't there
blood to spare? Why was Atamar looking so furious? What
was he saying about stupidity? He ordered her to remain
behind while the others went to drain the camel.

"—anyone stupider than you! Slut! Noseworm! Greedy-gut!"

"Atamar, there is plenty of blood for—"

"Idiot! And tell me, is there also plenty of soul?"

"Oh," said Lura. In her joy at spotting the old camel-driver she had forgotten about that little matter. Lizards were scarce, and she had been longing for a treat. "I forgot."

"Well, you'll have plenty of time to remember," snarled her overlord. His illusions were shattered, his dreams destroyed. He had lusted for her body, but loved her for her mind. To share a roosting place was forever. There is no divorce in Hell. And he *would* not spend eternity with an airhead.

"Come with me," he commanded. He lead her behind the rock and had her in the sand. Lura was delighted. If this was to be her punishment, she would see to it that she offended the law more frequently. But Atamar's heart was dust.

The memories still hurt him. Doing things like stealing her flask of drawing-blood were his petty revenge. It irritated him when he got no response. He was jealous of Melisan. Lura fought with her all the time. Their quarrels were tiresome, but they made a few bright spots in the endless days.

"Atamar! Atamar!"

Gerial's bellows split the heart of the desert. The purple shadows of distant mountains on the horizon shimmied on the waves of his voice. Panting and gasping, trumpeting his overlord's name, Gerial loped over the sand on all fours, his tail streaming out like a pennant behind him.

"Oh, my," sighed Horgist, slitting his eye open and rolling onto his side. "Now what?"

"There!" Gerial shouted, bouncing up and down on the rock and pointing wildly into the west. "You'll be able to see for yourself in a second! Oh! what I'd give for wings! Look, Atamar, all of you! Look!"

Atamar spread his wings majestically and flapped them twice to rise three stories high above the rock. He looked into the west. Melisan, too, rose up beside him, flittering and stumbling in the air like a drunken mayfly. She saw what he saw and felt tears of joy searing her cheeks, leaving red welts like lashes.

"Men," she breathed.

"Men," agreed Atamar. "And they come this way."

2

Go Marmota, Inc.

WHEN THE LEAD jeep crested the fifth dune and hung like midsummer firefly in thin air before jouncing down, Dr. Randolph Hack swore and lost his glasses. He also lost the use of one kidney, or at least he felt he had, but glasses cost money and kidneys come free.

"Stop the jeep, you," he growled, poking the whey-faced youth who played chauffeur.

"What's wrong, Doctor?" the young man asked nervously. He hated being touched unexpectedly, and Dr. Hack's constant series of jabs to the arm had frazzled his nerves to cracklings.

"Dropped my glasses. Signal the others. Have to find them," the sandy-haired sage communicated. The other jeeps came chugging over the rise and smoothly down the other side, where they pulled up beside Dr. Hack's chariot.

"Everyone else drives like a sane person," Dr. Hack grumbled half-aloud. "I'm the only one stuck with a dimwitted daredevil at the wheel." In a classroom voice he announced, "Attention, everyone. I seem to have dropped my glasses in the sand. This will be a good opportunity for all of you to see how much you've learned about archeologists needing a good eye. No, not you, Geordie. That wouldn't be fair to our new partners." He motioned for the tall, sun-bronzed driver of the second jeep to stand by him.

The four who were left set to their task half-heartedly. They'd had a long drive and were yearning for the cool of the evening and a quick basin-bath. By tomorrow the fourth jeep would join them, laden solely with tanks of water, and there would be showers for all hands. But first they would have to find those glasses.

"Come on, now. This shouldn't be too hard," coaxed Dr. Hack, sounding like a mother hen plagued by a coop full of cretinous chicks. "It's not as if you'll have to dig through the seven layers of Troy. Think about it. They're made out of glass. Glass sparkles in the sun. Look for the sparkle."

"Look up yours," said Amanda. She said it very, very quietly, so that Geordie would not hear. He didn't think she knew such language.

"I found them, Doctor!" caroled Faith, waving a pair of horn-rimmed glasses overhead. She held them by one earpiece and the good doctor uttered a short prayer that she wouldn't snap it off. He couldn't count the digs he'd headed for Marmota Travelrama, Inc., Tours of Distinction for Young Adults, and yet it seemed that he'd spent each one with adhesive tape holding his glasses together.

Faith toddled proudly over to Dr. Hack's jeep and handed him her find. The old doctor flashed his benevolent smile and restrained the urge to pat the girl on the head and give her a doggie treat. Faith was no one's fool, but she still made him think of an especially addle-brained fox terrier he'd had as a boy. She was just as small, just as curly-headed, just as eager to please, and twice as bouncy.

Hands off, Randolph, said the small, still voice of Marmota, Inc.'s official Manual of Tour-Leader Morals. Rule One: Never touch the clients. Rule Two: Absolutely no physical contact. Rule Three: Not even if they're drowning. Go get a pole and fish them out. Rule Four: Love doesn't last forever; lawsuits do.

"Thank you, Faith. Well, everybody, we don't have far to go now. Don, why don't you let Amanda drive for a while? Faith, you can ride with Geordie. Steve, you can drive the lead jeep for me." Dr. Hack smiled to himself. This Steve kid was the smoothest of smooth drivers, and Dr. Hack only had one kidney to spare.

"Ohhh, Dr. Hack, I simply cannot drive one of these things," moaned Amanda, toying prettily with her wheat-blonde hair. "I mean, I can do all right on the road, but here in the middle of absolutely nowhere, I'm sooo afraid I'll have an awful accident. Please, couldn't someone else drive?"

"Fine, Amanda. Don can drive."

"Oh, but he just got finished driving *your* jeep for ever so long! It's not fair to him," Amanda cooed. Don Swann gave her a look of sopping adoration.

Dr. Hack sighed. "Then you ride with Steve. He hasn't been driving for hours." There goes my second kidney, he thought. Well, maybe he'd get Faith to drive his jeep.

Amanda opened her huge brown eyes wide and looked on the verge of tears. Under the shadow of her pith helmet her rosy lips were trembling.

"Amanda?" asked Dr. Hack. "Is something wrong?"

"No," the answer strangled on suppressed sobs. "Nothing. It's—it's nothing. I'll share a car—I mean, a jeep—with St—St—*Steve*!" The floodgates burst.

Dr. Hack slumped wearily back against the side of his jeep while everyone else gathered around Amanda to comfort her. The metal was red-hot from the sun, so his slump was not a long one. What was it with these kids? What did Amanda have against Steve? Dr. Hack studied the lad and found no trace of any obvious faults. His smile was pleasant, neither cynical nor bitter. His looks were clean-cut, if a trifle bland. You could even say he was handsome. You could never say he looked like a born degenerate.

Well, you never know. Dr. Hack had supervised enough Marmota Travelramas to realize that. Who knows what Steve and Amanda had been up to in the hotel at Cairo? Furthermore, who cares? Dr. Hack's job limited his worries to the tour, the dig, and whether or not the girls got pregnant.

"Professor," Geordie Burns' warm baritone discreetly interrupted Dr. Hack's train of thought. "I wouldn't mind it if Miss Rhodes continued in my jeep, sir. I'm not tired."

Tired? Dr. Hack's private demon laughed aloud. That one looks so bloody healthy that you'll have to pistol-whip him to sleep. Which isn't a bad idea, damn him.

"All right, Geordie," Dr. Hack said. "You see to it. I'm too tired."

"I understand," said Geordie, patting the archeologist on the back. As assistant leader, physical contact between Geordie and Dr. Hack was allowed by Marmota, so long as it stayed manly and did not provoke gossip among the clients.

Dr. Hack found himself in his seat while Steve took the wheel. "At least you're a better driver than Don," the old digger remarked grudgingly. It didn't do to let these kids get too full of themselves. "One more joy ride with him and I'd be a goner. Thank God you signed up with Marmota at the last minute."

Steve's smile glowed warmly. "Nice of you to say that, Dr. Hack. It was my father's idea, but I'm glad to be working for you. You're a good man."

Praise from a young snippet always made Hack edgy. He grunted vague thanks, then more audibly said, "Drive on." Behind them came Geordie and Amanda, and bringing up the rear was Faith and Don. The tatty map rustled in the wind of their passing as Dr. Hack juggled its infinite folds and his clammy compass. Just five more miles, according to the map, and they should see a distinctive spar of black rock which marked the site they were seeking. They cleared another mound of sand and saw nothing but further mounds.

If we don't find that blasted rock soon, I'm going to say we're there anyway, Dr. Hack swore to himself. What difference will it make to this load of ninnies? They want experience on a real dig, they'll get it. Who says every dig has to be a success? God knows, I've led enough that gave failure a bad name. Let them sift sand for a while, then get them back home again. Give them a taste of reality for their money.

You are holding the compass sideways, fool. Bear left.

Dr. Hack jumped in his seat, or perhaps it was only a small bump in the sand that made the jeep jounce so fiercely.

Left, moron, the hot wind whispered in the doctor's ear. Haven't you tasted enough failures in your life? One more will finish you! Bear left.

"B—bear left, Steve," stammered Dr. Hack, poking the boy's arm. It lacked the force of former jabs, but Steve obeyed. The jeep crested a modest slope of sand and the lone black rock grinned a crocodile's welcome to the caravan that had found it at last.

3

Tempting on the Old Camp Ground

DR. HACK SAT on a camp stool in his tent and went over the paperwork for the expedition. The oil lamp cast liquid shadows across a handful of mangled application forms, maps, and Xeroxed copies of relevant background material. Marmota Travelrama, Inc., was a highly mechanized and efficient organization, especially when their tours were supposed to deliver a gratifying, stimulating, educating, satisfying experience to the client.

"Makes it sound like a damned whorehouse," said Dr. Hack. "And I'm the pimp."

Dr. Hack unfolded a tattered handbill and smoothed it out on top of the motley pile already covering the folding table before him. It was the old Marmota Travelrama, Inc. advertising circular. He had found it thrust into his unwilling hand by a buxom coed on the campus of the last college that had seen fit to hire him.

MAKE YOUR VACATION AN EXCAVATION!
Meet new friends and old relics in an atmosphere
of Class, Culture, and Intellectual Expansion.

Noted archeologists guide each group.
Digs now organizing for North America, South America,
Meso-America, Europe, Africa, and the Holy Land.
MARMOTA TRAVELRAMA, INC.

"No doubt about it," said Dr. Hack, folding up the hand-bill and sticking it back in his wallet. "They've met the old relic already." The sound of Amanda's honeyed voice drifted into the tent, underscored by Geordie's resonant tones. "And they're doing their damndest to make new friends," Dr. Hack remarked coldly.

Outside, the moon rained silver on the flank of the black rock. It was a cold night, the way all desert nights are cold, but where the moonlight touched the sleek surface of the impossible rock, it seemed to call up a wave of warmth and golden light, and an illusion of shadows.

"Did you ever see a prettier night, Geordie?" asked Amanda, leaning nearer. Geordie looked even taller and stronger by moonlight. He smelled of wood and leather and the sun, and his smile was a line of errant moonlight drawn earthwards.

"There's nothing like seeing the desert by night for the first time," he said to Amanda. "The real desert, and not just what they've left of it near the cities. I've come here with about nine different tour groups, and each time it's like the first, seeing the desert by night."

"Oh, dear, but it *is* soooo cold," whimpered Amanda, her large eyes woebegone. She shiverred once, for effect, and waited for him to take the hint.

"There you are," said Geordie, proudly passing her his heavy wool shirt. "I'm always prepared for emergencies. You see, I know what to expect in the desert."

"He's mine," said Melisan, perched on Dr. Hack's tent-pole.

"No way! I saw him first," said Lura, switching her tail back and forth like a cat ready to spring.

"Wingless worm," laughed Melisan. "He'll be mine before you take a step towards him! Why should he wait for you when he can have me?"

"He," said Atamar, coming up stealthily behind them, "sleeps alone this night. Orders."

"Spoil-sport!" cried Melisan. "Quencher! I wasn't going to drink him, like some people I could mention!"

"If that's a dig at me, I'll tie your wings around your scrawny throat for you," replied Lura pleasantly.

"You will stop fighting," stated Atamar, freezing the bickering succubi with a single look. "You'll come with me and join the meeting. It looks as if I am the only one among us who is sane enough to realize what's happening. We are not going to lose this opportunity the way we lost the last one."

"Hmph!" snorted Melisan as they trailed after Atamar. "He acts like he's so high and mighty, so smart. You'd think he wasn't just as much to blame for what went wrong the first time. Yes, and the second time as well! But just look at him and you'd think butter wouldn't melt in his mouth!"

"Oh, I think it would," suggested Lura.

The demons gathered together in the dark lee of the black rock and waited for their overlord to declare the meeting in session. They cast no shadows by sun or moon, but in the darkness behind the rock you could see tiny tongues of lambent green flame, like corpse-lights, hovering above the sand behind each demon. Horgist opted to remain asleep until the meeting began. Gerial was rooting between his toes to pass the time. The succubi sat tailor-fashion, the better to expose their charms to full view. Atamar knelt in an attitude of deep meditation, his wings loosely wrapped around his magnificent torso for warmth.

"Colleagues," he said at last.

"Comrades," corrected Gerial. His amendment was hissed down unanimously.

"Colleagues," Atamar began anew, "the day of our freedom is approaching, and the keys of Dis are as good as in our hands."

"Hear, hear," snored Horgist.

"My brothers—and sisters—there is no need for me to review our sad plight," said Atamar. "We have had far too many centuries of exile here, on the borders of oblivion, for any of us to forget why we are condemned here. Though we have come close to obtaining our goal, close buys no ice cubes in Gehenna. We have often provoked our prey to the *intent* to sin, to the *point* of sin, even to the *commission* of sin"—here he looked meaningfully at Melisan, who hid her blushes with her wings—"but what is required to obtain clear title to a mortal soul is more. There must be sin committed and unrepented. Let it be one mortal sin or all seven, the principle remains the same: no repentance. Oh, regret is allowed—a chasm yawns between regret and repentance—but never enough regret for our dupes to admit that what was done was wrong.''

Lura raised her hand. "How about the contract?"

Atamar shrugged. "A formality, though a good one to have on hand if you're dealing with a lawyer. Use the standard form if it will make you feel better. Use whatever you like, but use it in the furtherance of our cause! Even as I speak, thousands of our more fortunate fellows are crisscrossing the globe in search of souls. Their journeys take them before kings, potentates, and the perfumed courts of emperors!''

"Horse patties," said Gerial. Atamar took this as a comment on his pungent personal aroma and interrupted his speech to conjure down a rain of horse patties onto Gerial's azure skull.

"As I was saying," Atamar resumed, "we all know why we are here. But I say unto you, brothers and sisters, these many centuries of our torment shall end. Yes, they shall end, and we shall be brought home once more. Home, I say, home to the hearth that spawned us and the warmth that nurtured us. Verily, I say that we shall be welcomed back in triumph, and the streets of Dis shall echo with the cheers of our people, and the years of our suffering shall be as the blink of an eye.''

"Tell it, brother," said Melisan.

"But," Atamar changed his tone abruptly, "if we are to enjoy this triumph, first we must atone for what we have done. And you all know what that means.''

"A soul," said Lura. She was unhappy, thinking of the squandered camel-driver. Lura was a deep thinker, not a quick one.

"Boss, there are *six* of them!" objected Gerial. "Six of them! One out of six is all we need, and that's nothing. We could have one signed, sealed, and halfway to Hell before breakfast tomorrow. Look, I've been giving these babies the once-over, and it's going to be like picking windfalls, rotten-ripe for the tumbling.''

"An embarrassment of riches," said Atamar, "can sometimes mean poverty. We may lose sight of the forest for the trees. Grasp all, lose all.''

"With all due respect, my lord," said Melisan, "you'll bore those mortals all the way to Paradise before we can nab a single soul.''

"Bore them?" Atamar was indignant. "*I* am boring?"

"Let's put it this way, mighty one," said the golden-haired succubus, languidly fanning herself with one wing. "You just might have invented the Eighth Deadly Sin there. Thou shalt not cliché."

Atamar filled his lungs with air and blasted Melisan to the stratosphere. End over end she tumbled on the steaming geyser of his breath, then plummeted down to earth again, where he had conjured up a noseless nightmare that champed its double row of fishy teeth and gibbered madly for a nice, plump succubus to eat. Melisan screamed her head off, struggling to take wing before she should get within talon-range of the monster, but the force of her fall was too great. She smelled stinking breath and felt two rows of agonizing prickles maul her wings before she passed out.

She came to her senses flat on the sand with a terrible headache and an exquisite pain in her wings. "Boring, did you say?" smirked Atamar.

"Who, me?" wobbled Melisan, resuming her place in council. "Hell, no. Please go on. You're fascinating." She sucked at a raw spot on the tip of her right wing and kept quiet for the rest of the meeting.

"To proceed," said Atamar, "we mustn't make the same mistakes we made with Quintus and the Russians. Now, who can tell me what we did wrong with Quintus? Yes, Lura?" he beamed at the succubus who was waving her hand wildly, begging to be called on.

"We didn't follow through," she said.

"Quite right. We didn't follow through. What do we learn from this? Horgist?"

"Don't count your souls until they're hell-bound," said the demon around a yawn.

"Exactly. Now, what about the Russians? Gerial, I'm sure you remember them better than any of us. Why don't you tell the group what we learned from the Russians."

Gerial's eyes grew moist with happy memories of the Russian archeological expedition that had camped so near the black rock that on a calm night you could smell the mouth-watering fragrance of their hearty Slavic blood. He recalled also the thrill it had given him to hear them sing. The other demons disliked music, but Gerial had once been mortal. His love of music and his belly button were the only things that had come with him out of mortal life into demonhood. At any rate, they were the only mortal remnants within him that he knew of so far.

"We learned," said Gerial, "that it's stupid to waste time arguing over whose soul we should grab. There were twenty or so of them in the Russian camp, but we kept meeting in committee, trying to decide which one to go for first. While we were still debating our course of attack, they packed up and left."

"Which teaches us several things," said Atamar, eager to regain the spotlight. "First, since it has been shown many times that one demon is more than a match for one mortal, we did not need to act as a group. Second, any action is better than hesitation. If you see a soul in peril, don't come running to me for help. Snap it up yourself. And third, we must be vigilant. We could have kept the Russians here if we'd had sense enough to learn what they were after and give it to them. That," he finished proudly, "is the first thing I shall see to personally with this group."

"Whuh—?" snored Horgist, shaking off the edge of a bad dream and waking to find it was true.

"Who do you think brought them here?" said Atamar, looking pleased with himself. "Who lured them to the very spot where they'll find something so momentous, so significant, so startling, that they'll spend their lives here rather than leave it?"

"What is it?" demanded Lura. She hated secrets. Atamar knew this and kept deliberate silence, changing the subject just to torment her.

"So we are agreed, there shall be no bickering about whose soul to go for. Use your good judgment. There are five of us and six of them, so there will be no tussling over souls. Plenty to go around. And mind you, should we land more than one, it will be a feather in the cap. But one is really all we need. Dismissed!"

The desert floor exploded into scarlet flames in the shape of a pentacle. "Atamar's a sucker for a flashy finish," chuckled Gerial. He thought over Atamar's lecture. There was some good, solid advice embedded in the bluster. He would get right to work, pick out his man, and go about reeling in a soul. He reviewed the occupants of the four tents and decided on his quarry. There was a blue spark in the air when Gerial vanished, to rematerialize in the tent shared by Don Swann and Steve Ritter.

In sleep, the two young men looked angelic, but a quick dip into their dreams would show the real reason for those contented smiles. Gerial dwindled to the size of a gnat and buzzed across the gently rolling terrain of their faces, seeking the microscopic aperture just above the pineal gland that was the gateway to the subconscious.

A pastel tableau opened wide to welcome Gerial's descent. Somewhere a rock band was playing. Two-dimensional palm trees kissed an aqua backdrop where lend-lease flamingoes, cut-out white cardboard Cadillacs, and dubious types in stubble and slouched hats stood waiting. One of the dubious types was engaged in a lackadaisical round of mumblety-peg with one of the flamingoes, using a blade the length of Baja California. The bird made a bad toss and the shiv tumbled end over end to land in a pile of white powder the size of a small Christmas tree.

"Hey, man, you know what we do to birds who mess with El Geordo's stash?"

The flamingo went white. Its knobby knees struck up a reggae tattoo. The dubious types all smiled, a pack of wolves addicted to Gleem and good flossing habits. Twenty switchblades *snicked* as one.

There was a patter of delicate feet from offstage and the toothsome Amanda Rhodes, clad in a net bikini and spiked heels, came running in. She flung her arms around the doomed flamingo's neck. *"Oh please, please don't kill him. He won't testify, I swear it!"*

Her moving plea and excellent lung action appeared to soften the desperadoes. They backed off, making apologetic remarks in which figured reverent memories of their mothers and sisters. Amanda began to smile, the tension leaving her lithe body. The flamingo was relieved, too.

Suddenly, there was a roar, a streak of flame, and a miniature bazooka shell blasted the bird into three orders of Original Recipe. His weapon still smoking, his wardrobe a mix of snazzy street-lord and godless Nicaraguan Commie Fiend, El Geordo took command.

His hand shot out to seize the shocked and grieving Amanda. *"Hey, bay-bee, you hear the man? He say nobody fool with El Geordo's stash, he mean it!"* The accent was Speedy Gonzalez out of *Treasure of the Sierra Madre* bad guys. Gerial, pretty well baffled by the ways of the mortal subcon-

scious, wondered whether he might take this as a sign that
Don would sell his soul for Berlitz Spanish lessons.

Linguistic accomplishment was not on the dreamer's mind.
Though Amanda struggled, losing control of her emotions
and her bikini top at one go, the nefarious El Geordo had a
grip of iron. He sneered at her efforts.

*"Cool it, chica. You wanna live, you be El Geordo's
woman now. C'mon, honey, play nice and you gonna have
the happiest sinuses in all Miami! You don't, and . . ."* He
made the classic gesture of drawing a thumb across her
windpipe with a guttural *"SCHI-I-I-ICHK!"* He dragged her
over to the pile of white powder and tried to stick her face in
it.

A shot rang out. Amanda screamed. El Geordo dropped her
and reached for his Uzi. Another shot, and it flew from his
hands.

"Cojones de culebra!" the malefactor swore, sucking his
smarting fingers. *"It is . . . Don Swann!"*

And it was, the artfully rumpled white suit and three-day
growth of whiskers notwithstanding. It was Don Swann behind those Foster Grants, stepping out of that killer red sports
car, flashing a glimpse of well-toned muscle beneath that pale
turquoise singlet.

He also flashed a badge. *"Vice, El Geordo."* His voice
was deep and cool as a bayou bottom. *"You're busted."*

As a crowd of faceless supporting players arrived to hustle
off the snarling El Geordo, Amanda Rhodes expressed her
gratitude to her savior. The scene melted into a dimly lit Art
Deco boudoir with a bed whose headboard looked like the top
of the Chrysler Building. Amanda's nubile body was draped
with pink satin sheets. Don still wore his sunglasses, but little
else. Before Mr. Swann joined the lady of his fancy, Gerial
got a peek at what wishful dreaming had done to the boy's
natural attributes. If he couldn't nail the nerd on Lust, he was
a cinch for Bald-faced Lying.

"Almost as good as mine," came a sleepy voice behind
Gerial. It was Horgist, bored as usual. Don's midnight fantasy was small potatoes to him. In his more active days, he
had been an incubus, that well-known male equivalent of the
succubus whose job it was to tempt and seduce virtuous ladies
while their husbands were away. Queens had been his slaves.
Vestals had submitted to him without question. In spite of his
single yellow eye, in spite of the rubbery paws and flabby

body, Horgist had conquered them all. But in exile he had only his dreams.

Gerial could not refrain from stealing a peek at Horgist's most salient feature. To be honest, it was a marvel to behold and a permanent challenge to the Law of Gravity. There were times that Gerial wished he could swap Horgist his navel for it.

"You want this one?" asked Horgist. "Work's half done for you. Get him on Lust and Lechery and the rest is easy."

"Well," said Gerial, "Lust is more your specialty, old friend. There's plenty of souls to go for. Let me check out this fellow next door, okay?"

"Don't bother," Horgist stretched, trying to shake off his ingrown lethargy. "I've already been in there. Nothing."

"Nothing?"

"A blank. Pure white, with a pretty pattern of shifting multicolored clouds. Untouched."

"But—but he's smiling!" protested Gerial. "Innocent as a newborn baby!"

"That," said Horgist, "is just what he is. Stainless. At his age, too. I call it—" Horgist yawned cavernously—"a damned shame. Someone in the outerworld's not doing his job."

An innocent! The idea appealed to Gerial. What could be easier than corrupting an innocent, especially if he drummed up one of the succubi to help him? How much easier it would be to draw a landscape of sin on a clean slate than to have to pick and choose among a host of established sins, then nurture the chosen one into a full-fledged damnation.

The thought of drawing made Gerial think of Lura and her blood doodlings. "You can have this one, Horgist," he said magnanimously. "I'll go for the other one."

"Gerial," Horgist replied, actually wide-awake for the first time in centuries, "it was a great day for Hell when you were damned." He pounded Gerial on the back in a show of warmth and friendship. Getting Swann's soul would be a piece of cake, and then back to slumberland for Horgist, where his most impotent fantasies put poor Don's best efforts to shame.

"Kind of you, Horgist, my comrade. I'll just be buzzing along now." With a perfunctory bow, Gerial flew off and sprang full-grown from Swann's forehead. Behind him he could hear muffled squeaks and snuffles. Horgist was adding a few professional touches to Don's dream.

The amicable settlement and partition worked out by Gerial and Horgist was unique by nature. Out on the star-bright desert sand, Lura and Melisan were disputing in a markedly vigorous manner. Rolling over and over, sending up swirling dust-devils, each succubus was putting her heart into slaughtering her rival. Lura's belly still burned from her earlier skid across the sand, a weakness that Melisan delightfully exploited by further kicks and scrapes to the abdomen. For her part, Lura latched onto the more recent wounds in Melisan's wings, clawing and gnawing.

Nothing interesting lasts forever. The succubi released each other simultaneously and tumbled in opposite directions, coming to rest at last in the shadow of Geordie's tent. Purple spells of hatred and ruin blazed from their eyes to meet in thin air and shatter, hitting the ground with the clatter of a rain of old bones.

"Long-tailed dog," said Melisan.

"Short-tailed pig," replied Lura.

"Overbraided bitch."

"Tousle-haired trollop."

The hatred thinned and died. They were both tired. Silently they got up and came towards one another, each examining the bloody handiwork she had inflicted on her sister.

"I really rubbed your belly raw, didn't I?" Melisan said proudly.

"Not as raw as I got your wing, my dear," Lura giggled.

"What's so funny? It hurts!"

"Do you think my belly feels any better? I'm not laughing at you, Melisan. I'm laughing at us. If we keep wrangling for the soul of Geordie Burns, Atamar is sure to catch us at it, and he's got a heavier hand than any demon here. That's why he's our leader."

"Don't I know it," whispered Melisan, shuddering when she remembered that fish-mouthed creature he had called up for her punishment. "We'd better settle our differences now."

"Just what I'd suggest!" chirped Lura. "And I say that since we'll neither one of us back down—"

"Damned right."

"—and neither one of us trust the other if we flipped a coin or tossed dice for him—"

"True. You're almost as good a cheat as I am."

"—then I say let neither one of us have him."

"Are you out of your skull, or are those braids of yours

bound too tight?'' shrieked Melisan. ''Do you know what you're saying? It has been centuries since either one of us had a halfway decent lay. It has been centuries since either one of us had a lay, period. And now, with fresh meat dropped on our doorstep, you want us both to back off? You're a disgrace to succubi the world over, you are!''

''Melisan,'' Lura was very patient, ''I am not saying we should do *without*. But there are three other warm, living, breathing, capable male bodies within spitting distance of where we now stand. I merely propose that we content ourselves with them for our amusement, meantime doing our best to separate the female campers from their souls.''

''Us go after females? That's incubus work,'' objected Melisan, showing commendable solidarity with her union brethren. ''I don't poach on their preserves and they don't poach on mine.''

''Sweetie, I don't mean go after them with our usual tactics. That's too easy. Instead, we use our brains to garner souls. After all these years I'm itching to try something new. Will you go along with my idea?''

''I'll go along with it,'' grumped Melisan, ''but after all these years, I'm just plain itching.''

The light in Dr. Hack's tent was extinguished. The noble man of science was going to bed. Conscientiously he removed, smoothed, folded, and stored his daytime clothes. The light of the moon knifed through the flaps of his tent to play a wedge of brilliance across his pallid, freckled forearm. He hastily covered his naked skin with a pair of blue cotton pajamas. He was a freak, and he knew himself to be one. Eight summers of leading Marmota Travelrama tours through the desert, and he never tanned. Nor did he burn. The fishy skin that covered his lank limbs would freckle, giving him a stippled effect, but nothing more.

''Eight years at three tours per summer at two weeks actual fieldwork equals forty-eight weeks of sun, and I still look like an ad for coffins,'' said Dr. Hack to the desert.

And very soon you will need one, the desert replied.

Dr. Hack started, then shook his head as if to dislodge water from his ears. ''Great,'' he remarked. ''Not only have I been driven to talking to myself, now I'm giving myself depressing answers.''

Depressing answers for a depressing life, said the desert.

There was no mistaking that the soft, persuasive voice

came from somewhere outside his head. Dr. Randolph Hack
scurried to the flap of his tent and thrust his beaky nose out
into the gathering chill of the desert night. The lights were
out all over camp except in the other single tent where
Geordie Burns lay propped on his cot, reading a book. His oil
lamp cast a thick shadow of him in perfect profile against the
canvas wall.

"Go to sleep already, damn you," muttered Dr. Hack.
"Can nothing tire you out? All day in the jeep, driving—and
with that little miss limpet clinging to you all the way—then
pitching camp, digging the khazi, cooking dinner . . . Won't
you ever drop?"

Those who do not drop, said the desert, might be pushed.

The sound arose from the sand, as if every golden grain of
it cast off a drop of malice. The full disc of the moon shone
down on the silver splendor of the desert, and the shadow of
the black rock echoed with chittering voices, like a conclave
of whirring bats.

"Who are you?" breathed Dr. Hack.

We know each other, replied the desert.

"I must be losing my mind," the bewildered archeologist
told himself. "The sun doesn't touch my skin, so it must've
gone straight to my head. I'd better ask Geordie for some
help." He started towards the warmly glowing tent on slippered
feet.

Go, then, and give him the final card he needs to destroy
you, spat the desert.

Dr. Hack stopped. He took a deep breath and tried to go
on, but bitter laughter laced with scorn wove a barricade that
did not dare to pass.

"I'm just over-tired, that's all," he remarked to the stars.
"You know, I'll bet that's it. Not enough rest can do that to
you. I'm going back to bed."

He waited for an answering whisper. There was none.
Sighing with relief, he went back into his tent, lay down on
the cot, and found comfort in dreamless sleep.

The tips of legendary wings bloomed out of the sand and
unfurled like sorcerer's weed. Then Atamar himself rose up
with somber majesty and let the moon caress the perfect ivory
of his face. White flesh, black wings, white stars, black
night, he was the desert, white sand, black rock.

"Sleep, good man," said Atamar, smiling at the huddled
shape within the darkened tent. "I will lead you slowly down

the path I wish you to go. I have time . . . I have had too much time not to know when a gentle hand is wanted. Too quickly, and I might frighten you away. Yes, I mark you for a good man, Dr. Hack, though a sad one. You have your scruples, though life has given you plenty of reasons to doubt them. I could almost feel as sorry for you as you do for yourself. I come near to pitying you. You have made your own life a series of self-torments. What more can we do to you? I would spare you, if I could, or hope for your escape.''

Atamar's smile twisted. ''Ha! There's a rare thought. Mercy from me? Maybe you're not the only one who's had a bit too much sun, Dr. Hack. Sleep now. Sleep. We will have a good deal to discuss in the morning.''

4

Ex Libris Quintus

DR. HACK FELT better in the morning. He got up early and ran through a few exercises left over from his college days. They were supposed to quicken the blood. He supposed they did, but they also made his translucent skin come out in red patches. Some wise-mouth kid on his last Marmota tour had remarked that the old gomer (sic) must be allergic to exercise. Being put on khazi detail took a lot of the starch out of that smartass.

The camp was stirring. Geordie, stripped to the waist and glorious in a pair of khaki shorts, came bounding in from a morning run across the sands. Amanda took one good look at him and insisted that she prepare breakfast for everyone.

"Just because I come from—well, I guess you'd call it an aristocratic family—" she giggled modestly, "doesn't mean I can't cook. I'm terribly domestic."

Terrible was an apt choice of words. The things Amanda did to eggs would remind you of Herod's famous Slaughter of the Innocents. Everyone tried to look polite about it, but Faith sized up the situation and decided that there had to be a better way to start the morning.

"Here, Amanda, let me do it," she said. "I know you're very domestic, but even my Mom screws up scrambled eggs after over thirty years of marriage. Pass me that pan."

Geordie, the only one man enough to dare a bite of Amanda's disaster, quickly scraped out a hole in the sand and gave the remains decent burial. "I could do with a second helping, Faith," he grinned.

"Ow!" Amanda squealed, leaping to her feet and sending a frying pan full of hot grease spinning in Faith's direction. The curly-haired girl rolled aside just in time. "Oh, now see what you made me do, Faith!" Amanda wailed, clutching her right index finger. "You grabbed that pan away from me and made me burn myself. Oh, it hurts!"

Geordie sprinted off and back with the medical kit while Faith grimly retrieved the frying pan and wiped the sand out of it. She produced plate after plate of beautiful scrambled eggs, a veritable albuminous symphony, but Geordie was busy bandaging Amanda's finger and his eggs were cold by the time he finished.

"Cold or not, they're great," he said, patting Faith on the back in spite of Marmota Morals. Amanda poked her portion twice with a fork, to make sure the eggs were dead, then said she felt a little funny from the first mouthful. She took another long session with Geordie and the first-aid kit while the others cleaned up after breakfast.

When the dishes were done and all was calm, the Marmota team settled down to await their leader's traditional early-morning lecture. It was about as rousing as a warm Nembutal milkshake, but it was unavoidable.

Unseen, unnoted, a wisp of thinly blue air shimmered through the desert heat, trickling down into the sand behind Steve. Out of the corner of his eye, Gerial observed his comrades doing the same roundabout sidle-up, for the demons were invisible to mortal eyes only. Horgist poured a blubbery puddle of himself into Don's lap and awaited results. Lura and Melisan darted back and forth between Faith and Amanda. The two succubi looked just like perplexed browsers in the world's grandest bazaar, perishing to purchase, unable to make up their minds.

Only Atamar remained aloof. He eschewed more dramatic means of approach to his chosen victim, merely striding across the sand to stand behind Dr. Hack, wings furled.

What a demon the chief was! A pick-of-the-litter hellhound

of purest pedigree. Long days at a loose end had made Gerial
forget just how masterful his appointed lord could be. Some
revolting residual bit of mortal nature made Gerial a sucker
for high drama. He gazed at his master with sincere admiration.

Then he saw the unthinkable happen. Gerial's prey Steve
had been talking to Faith. Now he turned his placid gaze in
Dr. Hack's direction . . .

And looked right at Atamar. There was no mistaking it.
The demon towered above Dr. Hack's head, the angle of
Steve's face aimed his eyes directly at the demon-lord. At
first Gerial couldn't believe it. It had to be a fluke. Tentatively he probed the back of Steve's mind, seeking the daydream that must have made the boy's eyes wander at hazard
and stare off into what he *must* see as thin air.

Within Steve's mind, Gerial found no daydream. He found
Atamar, image-perfect, and with the shock of that contact he
fled. He did not linger long enough to see Steve casually look
away the instant before the chief demon became aware that he
was being watched.

After several "hmphs" and throat-clearings, Dr. Hack began a short talk about the wonderful world of Archeology
today. First he tried having his pupils sit on the sand at his
feet while he reclined in a safari chair, smoking his pipe and
looking very much the tweedy scholar. It didn't work. Even
sitting at Dr. Hack's feet, Geordie Burns still dominated the
group. It was the last thing Dr. Hack had in mind. He
suddenly decided it would be more picturesque if he perched
on a ridge of the black rock and they sat on the sands below,
the better to turn their eyes heavenward and receive his pearls
of wisdom.

Once settled, he took a deep draw on his briar and began:
"My friends and co-workers, here we are at last, the site of
our dig. I'm sure you realize that Marmota Travelrama, Inc.,
is far superior to any comparable work-study program for
young adults, if only because Marmota never treats you like
children. Other excavation tours take their clients to sites that
have been previously developed, but only Marmota gives you
the exciting opportunity for not just excavation, but *discovery*!"

"And now, back to our program," whispered Amanda.
Don choked back a giggle and tried to edge closer to her. She
gracefully shifted away from him and closer to Geordie.

"Now I don't like to brag," said Dr. Hack. No one believed him. "I don't like to brag, but did you know that it

was a Marmota summer excavation in the heart of France that unearthed the remains of a Gallic temple?''

Some temple, thought Dr. Hack. A crumbling wall and a big flat stone where some Roman Legionary scrawled CAIUS DOES IT WITH SHEEP, and they call it a ruined temple.

"How thrilling," remarked Amanda. "And were you leading that expedition?"

"Um—no. My specialty is Near and Middle Eastern archeology. In fact—"

"Oh," said Amanda, cutting him off. "I see." She looked smug.

The little bitch'll probably get pregnant on me, too, thought Dr. Hack, champing on his pipestem.

"So as I was saying," he went on, dabbing at the beads of sweat on his brow, "you can expect almost anything on a Marmota tour. You may be wondering why we've come all this way into the desert where there isn't a sign of human habitation for miles. Ah, but that is *now*, and we archeologists are more concerned with *then*. My assistant, Mr. Burns, who is currently a part-time assistant professor at Princeton—" There!—"will be the first to tell you that today's desert wastes were yesterday's bustling metropoli."

"Oh, wow," gaped Don. "We're gonna dig up a lost city?"

"Ah—no. To be honest, there was a small city assumed to be in this region, which was once a secondary trade-route. But we are not going after that. Instead, I ask you to cast your imaginations back to the fourth century. How many of you have heard of St. Anthony?"

Steve raised his hand. "Didn't he go into the desert and start the first monastery?" he asked.

Dr. Hack favored Steve with his finest governess-to-precocious-child smile. No one could patronize like Dr. Randolph Hack.

"That is almost correct, Steve," he said. "St. Anthony was a third-century Christian who went into the solitude of the desert for prayer and meditation, in order to cleanse his soul. When word of this got around, other devout believers followed his example. They sought him out and asked him to give them his rules of living. So in a way, St. Anthony did establish the first monastery, a male religious community following a certain set of rules. That would make St. Anthony the world's first abbot, too."

"Whoopee," said Amanda under her breath.

"Now I remember!" Faith cried, bouncing again with zeal to contribute to the discussion. "He was the one they tempted! I saw the picture by Bosch. The temptation of St. Anthony. The devil tried to tempt him with everything he had, but St. Anthony resisted and won."

"Double whoopee," remarked Amanda. Privately she believed that anyone fool enough to come into a wasteland like this voluntarily was crazy. Good old St. Anthony caught a touch of sun, more than likely, and all of his diabolical visions were the fever-dreams of sexual repression. Amanda was steadfastly against sexual repression. That was why her mother insisted she either go on this dumb Marmota tour or spend the summer locked in the house, her room, and a chastity belt combined.

"Are we going to dig up something connected with St. Anthony?" asked Don.

"Ha! You're making this sound as if we're newspaper reporters," said Dr. Hack. "St. Anthony was of the third century. We are concerned with the fourth, for that was the time at which St. Anthony's biography was written by another saint, Athanasius, and we have reason to believe that this biography influenced many aspiring Christians to follow the example of Anthony and seek salvation in the desert. Quintus Pilaster was one such man."

"*Who*?" the eager, upturned faces asked in chorus.

Dr. Hack smiled down upon them from the seat of wisdom. It wasn't often that he had the chance to flaunt his knowledge.

"Quintus Pilaster," said Dr. Hack, "is one of the mysteries of the ancient world, like the lost continent of Atlantis. His name crops up in the writings of several of his contemporaries, besides which he has left us a fragment of his own. . . ."

Don felt his eyelids begin to grow heavy. It was still fairly early in the morning. The heat was not oppressive, and he knew he hadn't had a big breakfast. Maybe he'd overexerted himself in that dream last night. Covertly he slewed his eyes towards Amanda. If she only knew! The things they'd done! The variations on a theme! Hellfire, some of their antics were stuff he'd never suspected could be done with the unaided human body. Looked as if the psychologists were right about the subconscious. Great stuff.

Funny, he had the disquieting feeling that if he closed his eyes now and stole a fast catnap, he'd have that same dream again, only better. Dr. Hack's voice was droning on and on about fragments and documentary evidence and ruined monastic communities, but Don thought he heard another voice snuffling in his ear, filling it with insidious promises of delight. Just close your eye, my boy, and dream.

With a violent shake of his head, Don snapped out of it. The whiplash effect sent his glasses sailing through the air. They fell smack into Steve's lap, and Steve was listening with total absorption to what Dr. Hack had to say. Don blinked like an owl and inched cautiously towards Steve. He didn't want to interrupt the doctor or make a scene. Amanda would want her man to be suave. In the sky, the sun resembled a single yellow eye that watched Don's every move and waited.

"For instance," Dr. Hack was saying, flashing a closely written index card out of his shirt pocket, "we have this tidbit from the *Annals* of Antoninus Aurelius, a fourth-century Roman courtier. Ahem . . . 'The Emperor seemed unconcerned by the old man's petition. Not even when he offered gold to fetch back his lost son Quintus would the Emperor heed him.' The writer then goes on to make some totally irrelevant descriptions of the Emperor's midday feast and concubines. Well, that should be enough for you to get a general idea of our evasive friend Quintus. And now, we shall take up our tools and begin the search."

With much stretching of stiffened limbs and much groaning, the assembled diggers got to their feet and gathered around Geordie, who was in charge of staking out the first experimental shaft area. Dr. Hack clambered down from his rocky perch and made sure that he was on hand to correct three out of every four orders that Geordie gave.

They did not accomplish great things that morning. Most of the cool hours had been wasted in the breakfast controversy and Dr. Hack's forgettable lecture. Then the fourth jeep, driven by an anonymous extra straight out of *Lawrence of Arabia*, showed up with fresh water and a bundle of letters that had been dogging the Marmota tour since Cairo.

They broke for lunch and sweltered in the tents for an enforced siesta while the sun sizzled the sky white. It was nice weather for devils. Five shadows detached themselves from the basalt heart of the black rock and crept furtively into camp.

Don lay on his cot all curled up in the fetal position. Horgist seeped through the pores of the canvas and melted over the sleeping mortal's body like a pat of butter. Don twitched once, then rolled onto his back while the grandfather of all salacious leers spread across his face. He moaned happily.

Gerial lingered invisibly in the air just above Steve's brow. He had no wings, but all demons possess certain limited powers of levitation. He had gotten over his earlier fright, putting it down to a bad case of performance jitters. It was an artistic as well as moral challenge to bring someone as pristine as Steve through the Seven Basic Steps to Total Turpitude (Dis Press, 7359 B.C.). Gerial knew he had better get under Steve's skin, and fast, but he had once been only human, and he would dearly have loved to see what erotic masterpieces Horgist was nursing inside Don Swann's thick skull.

"Amanda," gasped Don, shuddering with delight. "Amanda, you're insatiable! . . . Like what? . . . Like *that*? . . . Well, why not? Anything's fun the first time." His words dwindled to soundless mouthings and he rolled over to his stomach, filling his pillow with grunts, sighs, and minor shrieks of ecstacy.

"I should have held onto him," sighed Gerial, thoughtfully nibbling his claws. "Too late now, and so—" He poised on tip-toe right between Steve's eyes and sank into oblivion.

He came back to consciousness lying in a patch of muzzy gray shadow. Looking up, he saw Steve's face above him. The lad was smiling. "Are you feeling better now, Gerial?"

"You . . . know my name. But how can you?"

"Oh, I can't. No way. This is just a dream."

The blue demon shook his head hard enough to make his tusks rattle. It didn't work. Steve was still there, backed by a wash of light and a horizon that gleamed with the promise of great peace, greater wonders.

"Demons don't dream."

"Mortals do. In my dream, Gerial, you are mortal again."

Crabwise, trembling, Gerial inched backwards. He felt a cold beyond cold, the fear of worse things than pain. "I—I never wanted to be mortal again."

"In my dream you do. Dreams are such strange things, Gerial. Here." Steve stretched out his hand to the cowering demon. "Take it. Come with me. See what you can dare to dream by a touch . . ."

"NO!" With a roar that made the guy-ropes thrum on their

pegs, Gerial burst from Steve's head and rocketed right through the roof of the tent. It took many hours of serious rationalizing before he was willing to join his mates again, and even then he decided firmly not to tell them a word of what he had suffered. A dream? But demons didn't dream. They might delude themselves, if they liked, and that was as close to dreaming as they might come. The others would only laugh, and Atamar would order him back to his post in the hellish name of Duty.

He would not go back. Not into Steve's mind. Never, never . . . But what had awaited him beyond that luminous horizon? What marvels might he have seen if he had only dared . . . to dream? No. Demons didn't dream, and Gerial was all demon.

At least that was what he told himself.

In the ladies' tent, no one slept. Amanda had taken an instant dislike to Faith from the moment she set eyes on her in New York. There were times when she wanted to strangle the girl, but that was only when Faith seemed to accidentally thwart her, as she had over breakfast. Amanda hated to be thwarted.

Lolling on her cot, her two letters from home unopened on her pillow, Amanda watched amiably as Faith buried her pug nose in a musty volume on the early Church. It was, she thought, so nice of Lady Luck to give her Faith Schleppey as the only female competition for miles around. The girl was painfully cute, cute the way a toddler is cute. Bubbly. Vivacious. And had she mentioned wholesome? Wholesome enough to turn your stomach. In short, the competition was no competition.

"What are you doing?" asked Amanda.

"Checking for any references to Quintus Pilaster in here," answered Faith.

"Good Lord, why? Didn't we just get enough of an earful from Dr. Quack? Marmota must be paying him by the word. Oh, but I'm bored!"

"Why did you spend the money to come if you're so bored with archeology?" asked Faith. She herself was contemplating a major in the subject when she returned to college in the fall. Perhaps she would see about a transfer to Princeton as well.

Amanda's thoughts were running in the same direction.

One of the letters she was ignoring came from Frank Cabot, the main reason for her exile to this endless beach minus ocean. Her mother had surprised them together one luminous May morning, on the verge of doing the unthinkable.

"Amanda Rhodes," Mummy's tone was stern, "how could you?"

"Oh, for God's sake, Mummy," the exasperated pride of the Rhodes family snapped. "It's not as if he was New Money!"

New Money was as vicious a curse as any member of Amanda's set could hurl. She and her parents were transplanted Bostonians on Mummy's side, and Mummy had insured that Amanda be raised with the proper respect for the three sacred B's: Boston, Blood, and Breeding. Amanda's Daddy, on the other hand, was only sixth-generation American, and the really hefty money hadn't made it into the family coffers until his Grandpa yanked a bank out from under the thumb of a minor Winthrop.

Mummy never passed up any likely opening in a conversation with Daddy when she could insert a delicate stab at his New Money. She was awarded a comfortable amount of that same despised New Money at the divorce, but somehow it was purified by being her money, and therefore Old.

Amanda believed with heart and soul that the reason Mummy had shipped her off to Camp Misery was not for groping a Cabot in the gazebo, but for destroying the poor woman's faith in the morals of Frank Old Money Cabot.

"Mummy thinks Old Money stays virginal until symbolic blue-chip stock portfolios are exchanged at the wedding," said Amanda when she first spoke of her past to Faith.

"I didn't spend it. Mummy did," she said in reply to Faith's original question.

"Ah, yes. Caught you *in flagrante*. Now I remember."

"Caught me where?"

"Never mind, never mind," said Faith, going back to her book. Amanda withdrew into dignified pouting behind a dog-eared copy of *Shake Hands With Your Sensuality*, but soon gave it up for a globe-trotting issue of *Cosmopolitan*.

"I'll take the stupid one," said Melisan.

"Goody. I prefer smart ones. They can outsmart themselves and be down the Pit before the dumb ones remember how to make an X on the contract," snickered Lura.

"Why don't we see who lands hers first," challenged

Melisan, looking down her nose at Lura. Even without her wings, Melisan was taller than Lura, and more elegant. Good, sensible reasoning went behind the decision to send two succubi of different styles on every mission of temptation. If a man tired of Lura's kittenish ways he might stumble and fall when faced with Melisan's alluring sophistication. When they didn't fight, they were an unbeatable team.

"A wager?" Lura arched one brow coyly. "How much?"

"Since we'll be allowed to return home after we have the soul, you can be my handmaiden for one turn of the stars."

"Oh, let's make it really interesting," said Lura, twisting her tail around and around her fingers. "Loser has to come back up here for one turn of the stars. Alone."

Melisan looked uneasy. "Back here? So soon after getting free? I never want to see this place again!"

"All right, coward, then wager your wings. I've always wanted to fly."

Melisan hesitated, then clasped Lura's hand firmly in the secret sign. "My wings to your tail then. I've always wanted to scratch my nose when my hands were full."

The succubi dissolved in a peal of mischievous laughter and plunged into the girls' pillows to await their dreams.

Faith was the first to drift off. Lura was ready for her. She had discarded Lust straight off as too obvious a route to Faith's soul, having learned her lesson with the Russian excavation team. While the others bickered about their course of action, she had slipped off, hoping to bag a soul and redeem herself in Atamar's eyes for that camel driver.

She discovered that redemption did not come easily to a demon. There was one fairly young Russian, a man named Vlad, who seemed to be the group's shining light in matters academic. Lura decided to sneak into the fellow's subconscious and graphically demonstrate that books were not the only things concealing fun between soft covers. She would use the dream to soften him up—only figuratively speaking—and then make her move in the flesh. She would tempt him, seduce him, sate him, make him howl for more . . .

She made him howl, all right. Lura never did learn the Russian for "conniption fit," but Vlad had one anyway, before the dream even got warmed up. He launched into a polemic about Intellect being more important to him than Body, sweating bullets as he orated, and sprang from his cot into the mess tent, where he had to be restrained from packing certain portions of his person in dry ice.

No. Never go for Lust overtly with the smart ones.

She set up a book-lined faculty office, painted gobs of ivy against the mullioned windows, stuffed Geordie Burns into a Scot's ransom of tweed, disguised herself as Amanda Rhodes, who lounged shamelessly in one of the leather armchairs, and allowed Faith to enter.

"Come in, Miss Schleppey." A pipe materialized in Geordie's hand, a last-minute addition. *"I have something rather serious to discuss with you. It's about your paper on octopoid motifs in Early Minoan pottery shards."*

Faith had been regarding Amanda suspiciously, but at Geordie's words she became all happy-scholar zeal. *"Oh, I'm so glad you liked it, Professor Burns. I—"*

"I did not say I liked it—" her face fell *"—although I did."* Hope returned. *"Indeed, I liked it the first time, WHEN AMANDA RHODES SUBMITTED IT LAST WEEK!"*

In the demon-orchestrated tumult that followed, Lura led Faith down every possible path of intellectual humiliation, and always with Amanda Rhodes riding high, claiming honors rightfully Faith's while simultaneously exposing the poor girl as dilettante, plagiarist, parrot, and *poseuse*. With the fine illogic of dreams, scenes shifted at will, until Faith found herself in a dark alley, filthy and in rags, begging Amanda to give her a pittance, the tattered copy of Cliff Notes for *Silas Marner* which the cruelly mocking Miss Rhodes held just out of reach.

"Why should I give this to you?" Lura spoke for Amanda. *"I'd hate to waste it on a . . . pseudo-intellectual."*

The ultimate insult! The carving knife was in Faith's hands, a gift. She launched herself at Amanda—

And stopped. *"Honestly,"* Faith said, chucking the knife into a nearby trash can. She looked slightly put out with herself. *"Silas Marner? Give me a break.* Middlemarch *notes, okay, maybe, but homicide over* Marner? *Sheesh."*
She bounced away into the darkness, leaving Lura to grind Amanda's teeth in frustration.

Her one consoling thought was that perhaps Melisan was having an equally crummy time of it with the bimbo.

In his lonely tent, Dr. Hack was wrestling with the devil. Like Amanda, he had received two letters, but he did not

share her casual attitude towards the post. He had ripped
open and gutted his two battered envelopes as soon as he was
alone. Hindsight made him wish he had buried them unread.

The first was a cheerful, polite, jolly letter from the head of
the department of Relevant Sciences at the small college
where he taught during the year. The salary they paid was an
insult to poverty, and the fact that Deward College was a
diploma mill for every lazy, shiftless, stoned, and straight-out
stupid kid whose Daddy wanted to buy him a degree was no
comfort to Dr. Hack. He still had some pride left, some
vestige of academic integrity.

That and a nickel will buy you a cup of coffee, said the
voice.

Dr. Hack was too stunned to notice that his plaguey voice
knew nothing about inflation. Dr. Hack was being let go.

The department chairman was very jovial about it. The
letter brimmed with palsy-walsy asides and winks. You know
how kids are these days, heh-heh-heh, it said. Idealistic as all
get out and only willing to study those subjects that would let
them be best able to serve their fellowman upon graduation.
In short, the wishes of the students combined with the exigen-
cies of a new college budget had forced the department of
Relevant Sciences to conclude that archeology was no longer
Relevant.

" 'We are sure,' " Dr. Hack read aloud, tasting every
bitter word of it, " 'that a man of your qualifications should
have no trouble securing employment elsewhere. Please feel
free to ask us for references.' " He crumpled the letter and
jammed it into the sand with his boot. "My qualifications,"
he repeated ruefully. "My qualifications are one long list of
cruddy third-rate colleges, one right after the other, and the
longest I stayed anywhere was Deward, just because they
couldn't get anyone else at that salary." He smiled at the
irony of his leave-taking the past May.

"And of course when you return in the fall," the department head had said confidentially, "we'll have you sign that
new contract for a five-year appointment and promotion to
full professor. There won't be much of a raise, but we all
know that the *real* scholars rank honor, *and tenure*, above
money, don't you?"

He pronounced the word "money" as if it crawled with
maggots. Dr. Hack, eyes glittering at the prospect of eventual
tenure and his first five-year contract ever, had almost kissed

the chairman's hands. The letter implied that there was another target the old archeologist could kiss now.

The second letter should have contained a cyanide pellet. It would have been a mercy. Instead it was news from Dr. Hack's long-time colleague and friend, Henry Montgomery. There was nothing wrong with Henry's letter in itself. Henry rambled on about how his kids were growing up and how he didn't know what his wife was up to these days, caught in a bind between baking brownies for the Church sale and campaigning for the rights of women. He never wrote a word about his job. Henry was too sensitive to do anything like that to an old pal. He had received tenure at a top university somewhere in the savage heart of California at about the same time that Dr. Hack was being let go at his twelfth ivy-covered fool farm.

No, Henry's letter was innocent. It was the moldy photograph enclosed that carried poison. On the back of it, in pencil, was a dim date from the early 1950s and the question, "Remember Wadi-al-Qibir?"

Wadi-al-Qibir. Henry and Randolph working together on a major expedition. Randolph begged Henry to come along and help him write the series of earth-shaking books and monographs that were sure to be needed once Randolph led his men to a discovery that would rank with Schliemann's Troy. Randolph was positive that they would find a lost outpost of the Ottoman Empire within yards of the fly-blown dungheap that served as an Arab village. He had raised the money for the quest based on research done over a ten-year span. Randolph was an ace at research, but his writing style baffled the driest brain. That was where Henry came in. He couldn't research his own name in the phone book, but could that man write!

They dug where Randolph told them to near Wadi-al-Qibir. They dug and dug and dug. They dug until they hit a dead camel. They dug until they struck a cache of empty German petrol cans. They dug until the money ran out, and then they dug no further.

Randolph was enraged and bewildered. The outpost had to be there! Well, one of the native diggers replied, it wasn't. But it had to be! There was a manuscript in Alexandria that practically screamed DIG HERE. He would prove it to them. He would go to Alexandria and bring back a copy.

While he was gone, Henry took an evening stroll through

the pathetic village. The sun was setting in streaks of scarlet and purple on the western horizon, but the town dump blocked the view. For a few coins, Henry gained entrance to one of the better homes, one with a flat roof, from where he could drink in every breathtaking hue of the darkening sky.

As he stood there, leaning on the whitewashed parapet, he thought he saw something peculiar about the lay of the land near Wadi-al-Qibir. He could not be positive, but it looked like there had been some seismic activity in the vicinity. In a natural bowl formation beyond the western dunes he could just glimpse something resembling a recent ruin, and beyond that a dark furrow in the earth.

Henry's host was politely attentive to all his questions about the far-off bowl and furrow formation. Attentive but devilishly absent-minded. Some more coins jogged his memory. Ah, yes, such a shame what had happened there. That bowl had once been a pleasant hillock, set high and cooled by breezes funneled through the wadi. Yes, that furrow was the wadi from which the town derived its name. But when the Germans came, they took the original site of Wadi-al-Qibir for themselves and this humble village was thrown together to shelter the refugees while their beloved homes were occupied.

Ah, Allah is great. One night the earth buckled and heaved, and in the morning the surviving Germans received radioed permission to take a less jumpy site for their quarters.

Why, didn't the generous American think it was strange that this town called Wadi-al-Qibir lay so far from a real wadi and got all its water from wells?

They dug at a certain distance from the site of the ruined village and unearthed relics from the days of the Spanish Armada. They dug further and found evidence of occupation at the time of the Crusades. The hill and the wadi as they once had been had sheltered many inhabitants. They tried to contact Randolph, but he was too busy swearing out a formal complaint against an Alexandrian typist whom he felt had cheated him of five dollars in American money as the fee for copying his essential reference.

And yet, things might have been different if Henry had not found that most romantic of all relics, the celebrated Richard Jewel. It was a medallion of native design, but the reverse boasted an inscription telling the world that this trifle was a sign of brotherhood and honor from the great Salah-el-Din, or

Saladin, to his admired opponent and respected foe Richard, King of the Infidel English.

Someone—Dr. Hack knew it wasn't Henry—wired the papers and the Richard Jewel was the talk of Great Britain before Randolph agreed to drop charges, pay the five dollars, and get back to the dig. From Great Britain to America flew the news, and influential backers began to wonder why it was Henry Montgomery who had pulled their archeological chestnuts out of the fire and not Dr. Randolph Hack, the man who'd gotten their money.

The photograph had been taken on the day before Dr. Hack set out for Alexandria. His youthful face mugged at the camera, a "fun" pose showing him and Henry standing by one of the failed shafts and feigning puzzlement. Who stole the lost continent of Atlantis? Who's hiding the lost stronghold of Wadi-al-Qibir? Look in your back pocket, Henry, I know it's got to be around here somewhere.

In the letter, Henry said he sent the photo because now his oldest boy was the spitting image of the young Randolph Hack.

"Poor bastard," said Dr. Hack. Atamar, at his shoulder, wondered which poor bastard he meant.

The demon cupped his wings around the archeologist as a man cups his hands around a spark before blowing it into flame. Dr. Hack saw nothing of those wings, although it struck him that his tent was cooler and more shady than he recalled, almost as if someone had opened a huge parasol overhead to keep off the sun.

Is that better? Atamar whispered into the mortal's mind. Poor soul! You deserve any comfort you can pry from life. No job, and very few schools are eager to hire a failure.

"I'm still a good teacher," Dr. Hack thought he said to himself.

You'd have to be good at something. The dig for Wadi-al-Qibir was only the first of many excavations that you headed into bankruptcy. You came close to great discoveries, but close never counts. It was always the lot of the next dig on the self-same site that you abandoned that found the remains, the ruins, the relics. Soon your colleagues watched you carefully, because they knew that wherever you dug, the real find would be close enough to touch, but never found. Then they would step in and find it.

"Any fool with thick glasses and a strong back can do field

work," Dr. Hack offered in his defense. "No one can equal my scholarship when it comes to research."

Oh, I agree. But what good is it if you can't find what you're after except on paper? They didn't exhibit the *theory* of King Tut's tomb, but the treasures.

"Flashy stuff," sniffed Dr. Hack. "The Rosetta Stone was just a hunk of rock, and yet its value is immeasurable."

And who found it? A common French soldier without a tenth of your training or knowledge.

"He was lucky. It was a fluke."

Whom the gods love, they make lucky. How does it feel to be the despised of Heaven?

Dr. Hack took off his glasses and rubbed his eyes. They stung and smarted as if he'd been leaning too near a campfire. The tent looked darker, but now it felt warm. He almost walked out into the blazing midday sun to get some relief. The whisper stopped him.

You can't find momentous treasure-troves. You can't write well enough to become a famous armchair archeologist. You're a mediocrity in the classroom of any halfway decent college. You're getting old, and you don't have tenure. You don't even have a job. There are new men entering your field every day. Geordie Burns could be your son, and he's got a toehold at Princeton. Schools like that mean something to the people at Marmota. Who will they hire to head next year's expeditions? The unaffiliated Dr. Hack, or Princeton's pride, Geordie Burns? Better do something soon, Dr. Hack. Better make a few hard decisions. From unaffiliated to unemployed is but a piddling step.

The heat became unbearable. Sweat ran down Dr. Hack's face into his eyes, biting them with salt. He paced the tent wildly, then sat heavily on his cot and soaked his handkerchief in cool water from his canteen. He lay down and spread the soothing cloth over his eyes. Atamar touched one corner of the cloth and it began to steam.

Dr. Hack sat bolt upright and threw the cloth away from him with a little groan. There was no rest for him this siesta hour. He would study his notes on Quintus Pilaster instead, study and re-study them so there would be no possibility of failure this time. He smiled sardonically when he thought that this was to be the first dig site that Marmota had not ordered pre-tested for guaranteed finds. Marmota liked their clients to accomplish something besides shovelling and sifting untold

pounds of sand. They sent pre-test teams who later told Dr.
Hack precisely where to have the kiddies dig. You'd almost
think they knew about Hack's reputation for near misses.

They do know. You're the only one they do this for. And
they're getting damned tired of the extra expense. This is also
going to be your last year with Marmota Travelrama, poor old
Dr. Hack. Unless you show them that you can find something
on your own. Atamar's laugh filled Dr. Hack's head with the
sound of clanging brass.

"I *will* find it!" Dr. Hack snarled, nose deep in his research notes. "Quintus Pilaster established a large monastic
community in this locale. There were over forty cells! He
even mentions a big rock like the wing of a bat that cast a
fearsome shadow. There's the rock! The ruins have to be
nearby."

Nearby. Yes. But the rock lies low and casts no fearsome
shadow. The sands shift and change. Who knows in which
direction the ruins lie? And you don't have enough manpower
to dig up the entire area. There was a Russian expedition that
came here once, not long ago, with the same goal in mind.
They failed.

"I won't!" declared Dr. Hack boldly. A chill thought dimmed
his confidence. "I can't," he whispered. "There really isn't
anywhere for me to go from here. I've got to succeed this
time. I—I think that I'd—"

Yes. Yes, coaxed Atamar, beckoning from a throne of
bones and treasures. Do go on.

"I think that I'd sell my soul for it," stated Dr. Hack.

Good boy, said Atamar.

5

Give My Regards to Hades

"MURAKH!" SQUEALED LURA, vaulting high in the air as the irrepressible demon announced his presence, as always, by sneaking up behind and pinching her. She whirled around and siezed him in her arms, then held him at arm's length for a good look at his outfit. The demons of the desert went naked, but Murakh was a cosmopolitan spirit. He felt that if you dressed the way your clients dressed, they felt more sympathetic to your offers.

"I've brought you a present, Lura," he said, showing teeth a shark might covet. Murakh was one of the younger demons, spawned out of the excesses of the Middle Ages. At the time of his conception in the retort of a Burgundian devilmaster, it was all the rage to give plays with devils on stage and a gaping Hellmouth as background. Sinners and heretics were shown being cast into the fires behind the Hellmouth. It was a nice bit of business, a *shtick* that the magician could not forget. So he gave Murakh a Hellmouth, wide and toothy, making the poor demon look like a Cheshire Cat gone bad.

Lura stared at Murakh, not even asking about the present, which was unnatural. "What happened to your mouth?" she demanded. The teeth were there, but the opening itself appeared to have shrunk to normal size.

"I am once more the victim of mortal limitations," sighed Murakh. "What can a demon do? We are all born out of unformed evil, but our looks are not our own. Men give us the faces they like to imagine we wear. Only the highest keep their original forms, like Atamar. But you and I can be taken and reborn by any mortal with a brazier, a pinch of sulfur, and a wand. Do you remember what I used to look like before that Burgundian fool got hold of me and thought he'd created my very essence?"

Lura tried to remember. She thought back to Murakh's first visit, full of condolences for the loss of Quintus and the awful verdict of exile. He had looked a lot like Atamar in those days.

"Yes, I did, because that was how the Romans liked to imagine us, bad but beautiful. But those medieval sots made us repugnant, grotesque. The only consolation I had was knowing that each change of form meant I would enjoy new youth. Ah, Lura, once you're freed from this sandy prison, you must let yourself be summoned and transformed by a mortal! You have no idea of how wonderful it is to be able to relive one's youth."

Lura moped. "I wonder if I'll ever get that chance. We're all after souls, busy as beavers, but that doesn't mean we'll land one. There goes my target now." She pointed with her tail as Faith Schleppey went about the distasteful but necessary job of khazi detail.

"Hmm," said Murakh, examining the girl. "Looks smart, but she could stand a little transformation herself. Now *there* goes a more likely prospect." He indicated Amanda Rhodes, who was edging her way towards Geordie's tent. She was about to enter when the flap lifted and Geordie emerged, brimming with good health and perfectly balanced blood-sugar. They chatted briefly and strolled around the camp together. Faith gave them a baleful look from the khazi.

"Jealous," remarked Murakh. "Not a bad starting point for damnation."

"I wish I could agree with you," said Lura. "But it's an uphill battle, and we don't have too much time. Atamar just told us that he's been riffling through the papers in the main tent and it seems that this expedition is only supposed to be here for two weeks. They're just kids, except for the leader, doing a dig for a lark.'' She sank down on the black rock and cradled her head in her hands. "Two lousy weeks!"

"Darling," comforted Murakh, "I know you can turn jealousy to homicide in under two weeks."

"Not with that one," grumbled Lura. "She's *rational*. I give her pleasant dreams of strangling the other female and even as I'm leading in that gorgeous male to complete the fantasy, she wakes up, does ten sit-ups, and I have to start from scratch."

"Poor lamb," said Murakh. "Well, don't you worry. Even if you don't get her soul, one of your colleagues will bring home the spiritual bacon and you'll be home before you know it."

Lura's brows came together in a scowl. "You don't think I can do it!" she exclaimed.

"I never—" Murakh tried disclaiming.

"Yes, you did! I could tell! Well, I'm going to get her soul—or any soul I want!"

"You know, sweetie, you might have better luck if you used your regular methods," suggested Murakh. He nodded meaningly to where Geordie was delicately brushing grains of sand from more grains of sand in a shallow tray.

Lura's mouth watered, an unfortunate habit. Memories of the camel driver teased and tantalized her. There was no law that said she couldn't slip a sip from Geordie's appetizing veins, then tempt him into her power by more pleasant means. And the pact she'd made with Melisan? Unconsciously she practiced a guileless expression. Pact? What pact? Oh, *that* pact? Why, she thought it was only in effect for that day.

In gratitude she treated Murakh to the Embrace of a Thousand Serpents before gliding hellbent for Geordie. Murakh smiled and tidied up his rumpled clothes. Now there went a lady with a purpose!

"Up to your old tricks, Murakh?" Atamar's voice was sere and cold as the night wind.

The transformed demon brushed invisible dust from the soft collar of his sports shirt and lowered his eyes. "I don't know what you mean," he replied calmly.

"The others don't know you as well as I do," said Atamar, his mouth a grim line. "They think you're wonderful, the only demon out of legions who ever thinks to visit us, to bring us news, to bring us gifts. But I know what you really are, Murakh, and as soon as I've accomplished my task here on earth, all of Hell will know you for what you are as well. Not even Satan likes traitors."

Murakh blanched, but fought to keep up a good front. He showed every tooth in his head and said, "I can understand your bitterness, Atamar. Failure must be terrible, and you've got to live with it. But don't blame me for it. I didn't kill Quintus."

Atamar held Murakh with his eyes. The great wings beat the air with a slow, menacing tempo. "Didn't you?"

Murakh blinked and pulled away. "I don't have to listen to this," he shouted. "No one's forcing me to stay here and be falsely accused. Here!" He tossed a small black box to Atamar. "It's a present for Lura. Give it to her for me, if you're the only honest demon in creation!" He vanished like a flower shrinking back into its seed.

"Someday, traitor," said Atamar, sending his voice plummeting after Murakh into the caverns of darkness. "Someday I will stand before the lords of Hell and tell them all I know about you. And on that day, you'll beg for exile, but I'll see that they sentence you to obliteration!"

Lura came skipping up the dune to the black rock with a beatific smile. "Where's Murakh?" she asked.

"Gone," barked Atamar. He turned to go, then said as an afterthought, "He left this for you." He flicked her the box.

Lura paid no attention to Atamar's angry tone. She couldn't get the box open fast enough. Inside, on a velvet cushion, was a pentacle carved from a single diamond. Lura gasped. The slip of paper tucked behind the cushion was nearly overlooked, so bedazzled was the little succubus by Murakh's gift.

Years of thinking over past mistakes had matured Lura. Never overlook anything. Details can make or break you. She plucked out the sliver of rice paper and read Murakh's kindly words to the wise:

Lovely one, Hell has been impoverished too long by your absence. Only the thought of spending further centuries without you forces me to speak. You know how I feel about treachery. Have you been having more than unusual trouble with your mortal prey?

"Have I ever!" Lura said aloud, recalling her many attempts to tweak Faith's dislike of Amanda into something Cain could be proud of. She had even descended to concocting

visions of Geordie teaching Conversational Hittite in the
buff. Faith grunted, woke, and did fifty sit-ups. Lura read on:

*Not everyone is having such trouble. One soul alone in this
miserable assortment will yield to temptation—one; and if
you are not the one to bring it down, in exile you remain. The
Council has spoken: One demon, one soul. These are the
terms of your repatriation. Did you know that? No? Ask
yourself why not. And also ask yourself why the one demon
among you who does know the Council's terms hasn't deigned
to share this knowledge with you. Ask yourself why he has
arranged it so that the ripe soul of which I spoke is the one he
pursues. Ask yourself. Ask the others. But as you know his
temper, I wouldn't advise you to ask Atamar.*

"Ah," said Lura. "I wouldn't have thought that of him.
Well, but why would Murakh lie about it?" She crammed the
paper into her mouth and chewed, then swallowed. There was
no harm in being careful.

Across the camp, near the khazi, Melisan was contemplating a flawless ruby toe-ring and a similar scrap of paper. Her
thoughts were Lura's, and her procedure for disposing of the
note, once read, was the same.

In a cool corner of the gentlemen's tent, Gerial and Horgist
split a bottle of fine spirits, courtesy of Murakh, and silently
asked each other if what their wandering friend said was true.
You wouldn't think such things. You didn't like to believe ill
of someone you'd spent so much of your life with, but still
. . . They poured out the last of the brew and kept private
counsel.

Gerial's offer to show Horgist the new tapes of his video
heart-throb was drowsily refused. Not even Gerial's enthusiastic
description of how the lady slipped a live frog into her mouth
during the instrumental part of the number got his attention,
and Horgist had always liked animal acts.

"Why not show it to your mark?" Horgist suggested,
yawning. "From what Murakh says, these rock videos are
called tools of Satan in the world outside. A good worker
uses his tools."

The thought of further contact quashed Gerial completely.
He knew he would have to go back, to try again. This,
together with what he'd just learned about his revered lord,
gave Gerial an appropriately color-coordinated case of the
blues.

• • • •

Sunset touched the desert, and an icy wind blew out of the north early that evening. The diggers gathered around a campfire to trade reports of how they had spent their day. Cold as that night was, each mortal kept his distance from his neighbor. Amanda, forced by circumstance to sit between Faith and Don, held herself rigid as a statue. Lately she felt—how to explain it?—uncomfortable in her mind about Faith. The girl was no challenge when it came to looks, yet something buzzed in Amanda's ear and said with frightening assurance, "Looks are not everything." A parade of handsome, famous men marched before Amanda's inner eye, each one accompanied by the smart-but-plain love of his life.

You know, said Melisan confidentially to Amanda, you're on khazi detail today. You've got time to do a lot of deep thinking in the khazi. Think, Amanda. I know it's a strain, but try to think. Just once won't hurt. How long have you been dogging Geordie, my pet? And what has happened? Nothing. You're his *pal*. The man isn't blind, Amanda. He can see how beautiful you are. Then why hasn't he reached out and taken the gift you've been practically forcing on him? Someone else has a hand in this, Amanda. Someone not very pretty, but oh-so-very bright. What has she been saying to him about you, Amanda? How much is truth and how much is a plausible lie to turn him from you . . . to herself?

"That little pug-nosed bitch," murmured Amanda. She knew what Faith was telling Geordie. Hadn't she once done the same dirty trick to Frank Cabot's old love? Miss Regina Lacey Winston and the *entire* Yale squash team? Who would believe it? Frank Cabot, for one.

Well, smirked Melisan, studying her nails, we know how to put a stop to little pug-nosed bitches, don't we?

"I could kill her," said Amanda, who didn't mean it.

You could, purred Melisan, who did.

"But why bother?" Amanda went on. She enjoyed arguing with herself, especially if she could talk her way out of doing something she felt was basically unworthy of a Rhodes. Homicide was for the lower classes and the New Money, or so Mummy said. "In less than a week we'll be out of here, and Geordie won't see her for dust. There's no reason why I couldn't engineer a teensy little mid-semester transfer to Princeton. My grades are good enough, and God knows it's about time we got some good out of Gumpa's endless monologues about dear old Nassau!"

It wasn't that Amanda disliked her grandfather. He was a
dear man, and she would have adored him without reserve if
only he'd stop looking at her, mutter something about
Princeton, and turn on Mummy, accusing her of deliberately
bearing a lone female child.

"Gumpa," sighed Amanda, "there are women at Princeton
now."

"Then why aren't you there?" The silver-haired old patri-
cian scowled.

Truth to tell, Amanda's reasons for not going to Princeton
were simply that she found it more congenial attending a
lesser college where top grades were earned with little effort.
Ah, but now Princeton had something to offer her, and a little
hard work might make Geordie realize that she was more than
just another sex-starved pretty face.

She might go to Princeton, too, Melisan mentioned. But if
you were to kill her, way out here in the desert where it could
look accidental . . .

"Oh, dear, must I?" moaned Amanda. "Murder is so
depressing."

Damn it! Melisan said purely to herself. Why didn't I take
the smart one? For Amanda's benefit she added, It doesn't
have to be. I could show you ways to do it and never be
caught. It could look like an accident. Lots of accidents
happen on digs.

"I know," Amanda responded to the provoking inner voice.
"I broke two nails already." She held up one hand to display
the damage.

Nails! How can you think of nails at a time like—Say,
what are those shiny things?

"Nail gems. Aren't they adorable? *Cosmo* says they're the
latest thing; drives men berserko."

Gee, I really like . . . Ooops. I mean, there are other ways
of driving men berserko, Amanda. Men like Geordie. I could
show you how. There are certain areas of the human body
which, when touched, can make the eruption of Vesuvius
look like a gerbil's burp.

"Oh, you mean like the G-spot?"

The what?

Amanda explained, occasionally quoting verbatim from "Al-
phabet of Passion," an article that had done much to enhance
last February's issue of her favorite magazine. Melisan stood
on tiptoe, wings fluttering faster and faster until her feet left

the ground and she was at full hover. Abruptly, just when she was getting to Betancourt's Quadrangle, How To Find Yours and Use It, Amanda stopped what had become a fairly one-sided inner conversation.

"Hey, if *I* know this already, why am I explaining it to myself? What's going on here?"

Uh-oh, Melisan said, and scooted out of Amanda's mind to replan and regroup. Maybe she hadn't gotten such a dumb one after all.

"My colleagues," Dr. Hack intoned as Steve finished telling an already bored audience the story of his day's work. "My colleagues, I know you're all getting a bit discouraged. And I don't blame you. After all, here we've been digging away for ten whole days and still nothing to show for it." Ten days! The things he had to say to this passel of spoiled brats who fainted over callouses and bitched about minor sunburns! What did they hope to accomplish in ten days on a *real dig?* A real one! Not the usual Marmota prechewed and regurgitated charade that passed for archeology.

My, my, mused Atamar, tickling Dr. Hack's left ear. Aren't we forgetting what will happen to us if we bring back a group of dissatisfied clients? Marmota won't like that. Another brilliant failure, courtesy of Dr. Randolph Hack.

Not this time, Dr. Hack answered fiercely. It's not a failure if it looks like a success!

What? blinked Atamar.

"And so," Dr. Hack went on, "I have a reward in store for all of you. You've worked hard, like real professionals, and we're going to break up camp now faster than the best dig team in the business and bundle into our jeeps and high-tail it over the dunes to our new dig site, where we've been called upon by a fellow scientist to aid in the excavation of the crusader stronghold of Wadi-al-Qibir!"

Geordie whistled with admiration. Where did this frail, pale, speckled and spectacled man get breath enough to spew forth a sentence that long? He had to admit it, Dr. Hack was a man of surprises. Geordie remembered the rage suffusing the scrawny archeologist's face when he, Geordie, had dared suggest that they were digging in the wrong place. He, Geordie, knew that Marmota wanted the kids to have a good time. He, Geordie, did not want to be tarred with the same brush of failure that had liberally bespattered Dr. Hack's excuse for a career. But when he (Geordie) asked to see the documents upon which Dr. Hack based the decision to dig, he (Hack) had refused.

"He's mine!" shouted Dr. Hack, clutching the sheaf of papers to his birdlike bosom.

He? Oh, Quintus. Fine, thought Geordie. Let Hack keep him, if he could ever find him. But if he didn't find him soon, there would be some angry letters written to Marmota.

And now this about-face, abandoning the fruitless site with the excuse of helping fellow archeologists in trouble. Very neat. Maybe there really was trouble at Wadi-al-Qibir. It was a textbook example, that dig site, and Geordie treasured Montgomery's treatise on the Richard Jewel. There was plenty of stuff yet to be unearthed there. No, not a bad trick at all. Geordie had to admire Dr. Hack, and where Geordie once gave his admiration, there it remained. Unknown to Dr. Hack, he had just acquired as lifelong disciple the one soul he hated above all others.

"Wadi-al-What?" asked Faith.

"Qibir," provided Steve. "This is great! I always wanted to see—"

NO!

Wings the color of grief shot out in furls of lightning and split the night sky, sending the stars screaming into blackness. The moon watered and ran down in tears, struck from her orbit by a gigantic hand. Atamar's shoulders brushed the clouds, turned livid by his raging, and the force of his silent scream sent cracks rippling across the face of the desert.

Dr. Hack pitched from his camp stool and would have sprawled face-first into the fire, but the sands gulped it down flame by flame. No moon, no stars, no fire, the hopeless darkness of an endless search that had no goal. Amanda grabbed Faith and whimpered as the earth shifted beneath them. Don yowled like a cat. Geordie was flung flat to the arching, undulating sands where he lay spread-eagled, clinging to the fragile crust of a treacherous world. Steve rolled and pitched with every movement of the desert, an old sailor riding the crest of familiar waves. He smiled, and the stars gained courage to answer him with faint twinklings. The earth sighed, shuddered, and subsided.

"I want to go *home*!" wailed Amanda when the last rumble faded back into the cool night.

"It was only a tremor," said Geordie. A thin wash of

moonlight silvered her face. Yes, he told himself. I was right. There's never been any woman as lovely as this one.

And since no demon had yet to pierce the dreams of Geordie Burns, none could know just how much the idea of matchless beauty meant to him. He put his arm around Amanda and no one saw it as anything more than a gesture of comfort. Brotherly.

"Yes, a tremor," panted Dr. Hack, fumbling in the dark for his glasses. Already he cursed his luck, suspecting that they had vanished down a fissure, one of the countless small cracks that opened and closed like bear traps during quakes.

"I don't care if it was a hiccup!" raved Amanda. "I want to go *home*! And the minute Abdul—or whatever that Arab's name is—shows up with the water tomorrow, I'm going to get back to Cairo and then straight back to the States!"

"Now, Amanda," faltered Dr. Hack, still feeling around blindly. "A tremor is nothing to get upset over. Why, they've had worse quakes in the States, and you know it. What about California?"

"Which is just why I will not go to California," countered Amanda. "And which is also why I won't stay here, either!"

"Now, Amanda," Dr. Hack repeated, struggling for a good, authoritative argument to keep that puling nitwit from blaming the tremor on him and demanding a refund from Marmota. He felt he would be able to think better if he could locate his glasses first. "Now, Amanda . . ."

"I brought a lantern," announced Faith, bobbing along behind the flashing beacon of light. It swept around a circle of pale faces until it picked out Dr. Hack, on hands and knees. "The tents are all down, but not much harm done. Where do you want me to aim the light for you?"

"Well, bless you, Faith," Dr. Hack exclaimed while Lura winced. "Just give it to me and I'll aim it myself. I've lost my glasses and—"

"I know. Look for the sparkle," said Faith.

The beam of light wavered and rolled in a random pattern over the recently disturbed dunes. Only Faith and Steve searched for the glitter of glass. Don was too distraught after his late ordeal, and Amanda was so agitated that she unthinkingly shrugged away from Geordie's embrace to huddle in a small lump of self-pity on the sand.

"Stop!" yelled Faith. The beam froze. "Back a little. To the right. I don't have very good night vision, but I thought I saw something shining off that way. Kind of far for your glasses to fly, but—''

"I have my glasses," said Dr. Hack, who had just laid hands on them by chance while bending over to tie a loosened shoelace. They had been less than a foot away from him the whole time.

"But I see something shining," persisted Faith.

"So do I," agreed Steve.

"Now, kids—" Dr. Hack, glasses restored, was all for replacing the tents and getting some sleep, but the gleam of phantom whiteness shone for his eyes also. He aimed the beam more carefully and stared.

The sarcophagus was carved of the finest marble. Pitted by the sands of centuries, it still gleamed and shimmered as if it were a newly fallen moon. The archeologist's light reflected a sheet of brilliance from the featureless lid, except in the one small spot where a loving though unstable hand had inscribed in faulty Latin, HIC IACET MAGISTER MEA QUINTUS.

PART II

1

Dem Bones

THE MOST IMPORTANT thing, the indispensable, the vital requirement, the matter of life-or-death, is subjective, thought Gerial, biting his claws. For one mortal it's a new car, for another it's a divorce. The main thing is for them to reach an agreement or a compromise soon, or they won't get either one. Just listen to them fighting about it! And there sits the Arab fellow who'll ignore all of their orders and bring back whatever he damned well feels like. Or more likely, whatever gives him less work to bring. But still they argue.

"Extra khazi materials!" shouted Dr. Hack, experience making him wise.

"A telephone line!" squealed Amanda.

"A backup short-wave set!" was what Faith was pushing for.

"Fresh clothes!" maintained Don.

Steve and Geordie were scurrying around and around the sarcophagus like a pair of demented squirrels, so any contributions they might have made were lost. Directly against Dr. Hack's orders, they were "doing things" to the big stone box. Dr. Hack had forbidden them specifically to "do anything" to Quintus' eternal home until the proper people had had time to arrive on the scene.

The Arab lounged in the jeep and suggested that one of the four combatants come back to town with him and make sure that he brought back the right things. It was his own humble way of guaranteeing an extra pair of hands to help him with the cargo.

"In this way," he explained, "we shall be assured of the proper material being present at the site for the reception of the gentlemen of the media. Truly it would be a disgrace to us all were they to encounter us lacking in the proper facilities upon their arrival."

Dr. Hack translated the flowery monologue into English, then into American.

"What he's saying," said Faith, "is we absolutely have got to have a backup short-wave."

"Telephone line," corrected Amanda.

"Additional khazis," prompted Dr. Hack.

"Oh, right. Sure," commented Don with some sarcasm. "Then they can take our pictures for the *international* papers in these filthy, crumpled old rags. Just what we always wanted! Noted slobs discover remains of saint."

The Arab shrugged and waited. He knew that if he waited long enough, the esteemed gentlemen of the media would case the situation and bring their own phones, short-wave sets, and khazis. Sometime in the remote past, his ancestors had dragged their feet and as a result were too late to get in on the labor gangs who raised the pyramids. It never pays to rush.

"Saint? Who said saint?" demanded Faith.

"Dr. Hack, that's who," Don shot back.

Dr. Hack raised one freckled hand in modest disclaimer. "Don, I'm afraid you misquoted me," he smiled. In fact it was Don's unerring talent for exaggeration and grandiose detail that Dr. Hack counted on when the press finally arrived. Not for nothing had he insisted that Don author the telegram of their discovery to Marmota.

His judgment was good. TOUR 307 FOUND RELICS OF SAINT QUINTUS (STOP) MIRACULOUS DISCOVERY (STOP) ADVISE (FULL STOP) Dr. Hack's copy of Don's feverish prose lay folded next to his heart, where the plain piece of paper seemed to radiate a comforting warmth. Dr. Hack had good reason to smile.

The Arab's daily jeep brought ten answering wires from Marmota, including the offices in Jerusalem, Rome, London, and home base in New York. The media had been contacted and were en route. The parents and guardians of the diggers were notified of this momentous discovery. The archeological old-boys network was abuzz with rumors. Ms. Louise Ferrabosco, founder, directrix, and guiding angel of Marmota Travelrama, Inc., would herself fly on wings of love to the site. More wires to follow.

"Now, kids," said Dr. Hack, shaking his head gently, "I'm sure you know that no one's considered a saint until confirmed as such. But I'd say that with the discovery of Quintus Pilaster's sarcophagus, we might be well on our way to assuring his canonization. After all, miracles at the tomb of other saints are a well-known phenomenon. Poor Quintus has never had that opportunity, being buried all this way out in the desert. It will only be a matter of time before—"

"You told me he'd already performed miracles!" Don exclaimed, indignant at being cheated of his role as talent scout for sainthood.

"Well, yes, there is the testimony of several sources, including the manuscript of Fabius Infarctus, but scholars have expressed a few doubts about Fabius' honesty."

"Oh, yeah? What makes them so sure he was lying?" demanded Don, on the defensive. "I guess they never told a lie in their lives!"

"Fabius Infarctus, as his autobiography—entitled simply *Gestae*—states, was born a slave. He claims he felt the stirrings of conscience and was drawn to the new religion preached by the saintly Quintus, so he begged for conversion and joined the holy man in his self-imposed desert exile. There, he says, he remained until Quintus' untimely death, then returned to Alexandria and became a self-made rich man, one of the city's most famous wine merchants."

"So where does it say he's lying?" Don sneered.

"For God's sake, think!" said Amanda, echoing what Melisan had been saying to her almost constantly. "He was a slave! He'd use any excuse to get loose, so he claimed he got religion and made a run for it! After Quintus died, maybe he figured it was safe to—"

The sky began to thrum with the rapid beating sound of helicopter blades. Three winged bubbles skimmed through the crystal blue of the desert sky, then hovered in formation over a nearby stretch of flat sand before drifting down to land. Dr. Hack's eyes had grown better and better since discovering the sarcophagus. He picked out the Marmota emblem on the lead copter and barked orders for the Arab to drop everything and drive straightaway for the makeshift landing strip to pick up the newly arrived guests.

"Damn it!" he said in an undertone, running long fingers through his hair. "And here I am, a mess!"

"I told you to get us fresh clothes," Don complained.

The sound of the dull crash stopped Dr. Hack from telling Don not to pule. Rule One for Marmota clients who hoped to dig with the famous Dr. Randolph Hack: No Puling.

Small and stony, Gerial remained glued to the side of the sarcophagus, impersonating a grotesque. In the excitement of the hour, no one thought to notice or question such an anachronistic decoration. He had been steeling himself for another assault on Steve, but he was not up to venturing into the boy's subconscious again. He decided to try his wiles on the waking mind. It just had to be better!

Pushing off from his moorings with his tail, Gerial jettisoned himself into Steve's spinal column when the boy had his back turned to the sarcophagus.

Hand over hand the blue demon shinnied up the spine until he could get a good grip on the brain stem and pull himself into the gray matter. So far everything looked normal. It was dark and warm, but that was to be expected. The blue demon conjured up a palmful of orange glow with which to light his way. He entered the forebrain.

A smile made Gerial's tusks curve up and nearly stab his cheeks. The orange light in his palm shot sparks of bliss. he was an explorer stumbling into a dragon's trove, and the worm dead of old age. Here was treasure unlooked-for, and free for the taking. He praised himself for having persevered.

There in the shadows of thought knelt Dr. Hack, hands around the throat of Geordie Burns. The younger man's complexion was a deeper cyan than Gerial's, his tongue protruding prettily. And there in a neighboring thought was Don, jumping up and down on Geordie Burns' helpless body. The sound of snapping, crackling, popping ribs reminded Gerial of an outspoken dry cereal Murakh had brought him once.

The blue demon heard shrieks behind him. He turned and saw a third Geordie Burns spread-eagled between two teams of wild Arab horses, each being whipped to a frenzy by Faith Schleppey and Amanda Rhodes, each lady screaming, *"He's mine!"*

In the middle of it all stood Steve. His eyes roamed from one group to the next, dispassionately, the ultimate voyeur. Gerial thought his heart would burst for joy. He approached the indifferent observer.

"You . . . like to watch things like this?"

"All I can do is watch. It's not my place to interfere." Steve sighed. "Direct intervention is not permissable, no matter how much I'd like to do it."

"Heyyyyy, don't let it eat you, my man. You get off on this stuff, I can help. The rules change when you're not mortal."

Steve managed a small smile. "Do tell."

"I can let you see all this stuff happening for real, you know? I can turn them all against each other, drag it out, keep it going. You can see it all! All the hurt, all the pain, all the suffering you want!"

"Can I?" The tease of a smile was still there. "With you beside me, watching, too?"

"Sure, with me . . . watching?"

"Don't you like to watch things like this?" Steve's hand swept the compass of mayhem.

Gerial scratched his underarms nervously. "I don't mind it," he mumbled. "I love violence. I'm a demon."

"So you are. With a demon's hard heart and thick skin. Nothing frightens you. You could watch mortals destroy themselves by the eon. Why don't you and I talk business, Gerial? That's why you're here, isn't it? To strike a bargain? I haven't been bound to one spot, like you. I have seen much, and I long to share it. Let's deal, and let our deal please us both. Let me guide you as you would guide me. Come with me and I'll show you all the atrocities mortals have done since the time of your exile. Will you like that? Will it make you feel better, comparing your crime with all of theirs? Will you be justified in your own eyes for the one act that made you a demon?"

Gerial found himself again backing away from Steve's outstretched hand. "How do you know?" His voice cracked. "How could you know?"

"Come," Steve said. "Come."

Gerial felt the brain beneath him give way. He sank

deliberately, but Steve followed, murmuring vile promises of human-made horrors to be seen beside which Gerial's ancient sin was nothing. The hellhound fled down the brain cells' pathway; the alien boy followed, until Gerial's retreat ended with his back to a glassy wall.

"Why do you run away? Can't I tempt you, Gerial?" Steve asked. "Famine. War. The slaughter of innocents. Life, hope, and promise wasted. Sights to delight a true demon."

Gerial clapped his paws to his eyes. "No! I don't want to see! You can't make me! I—" He tried to take another step away, but the smoothness behind him was firm.

"Don't go any further," Steve said lightly. "You'll give me one of those right-in-the-eye headaches."

"Wha—?" Gerial stole a look over one shoulder and saw an upside-down world. For a moment the disorienting sensation of seeing things through a mortal's eye made him forget his fear. He pressed his nostrils to the lens and gawked. Quintus' sealed sarcophagus hung from a sandy sky where Geordie Burns too clung bat-like. Gerail did a headstand to see things right-side up. As he balanced on his paws a wiggle of black lightning crept into the field of vision.

The serpent looked up at Steve, recoiled, and showed fangs.

"Hot popping simoniacs! A snake!" Gerial flipped back onto his feet and made a break for it. A blue blur bloomed from the crown of Steve's head and did a half-gainer into daylight.

He was aiming for his old place on the sarcophagus' side, but in his panic he misjudged the distance and smacked flat onto the heavy lid. Before he could gather his wits or his limbs and get back to the safety of the black rock, Gerial felt the stone beneath him move. He closed his eyes tightly—he'd always had an unnatural fear of earthquakes—and dug in with every digit he had. It was no use. The stone grated, warmed, and began to glow with fiery light. It rose up like a dowager quitting the dinner table, and then, when it had achieved sufficient altitude, it turned long-edge-down and drove into the sand. Impact was too strong for the blue demon, who lost his toeholds and slammed right on his back. Getting his breath again, Gerial put distance between himself, Steve, and the frisky sarcophagus.

●   ●   ●

"Oh, look!" Amanda clapped her hands delightedly. "Geordie got the lid off!"

"Oh, *no!*" Dr. Hack puled. Totally ignoring the approaching jeep in which two khaki-clad women bounced and squabbled, he sprinted to the rescue of the sarcophagus.

The lid was indeed off. It lay imbedded in the sand on its long end, looking like a marble backboard for a game of handball. Steve stood inches away from it, staring down at his feet as if he had only discovered them a minute ago. Geordie stood behind him, out of reach of the sarcophagus. Unless the young man was part elastic, there was no way in which he could have moved the weighty lid. Dr. Hack took in the scene aghast, thinking of nothing but the fate of the sarcophagus' tenant. What would sudden exposure to the air do to the remains after all these centuries? What would—?

Only on second glance did he notice the crushed black body of the deadly viper, pinned and destroyed by the upended marble slab.

"I don't know where it came from," Geordie faltered. "It just came from nowhere. It was that close to Steve's bare leg, ready to strike, when all of a sudden we heard a grating noise and WHAM!" He pointed to the carved lid. "Maybe another tremor pitched it loose," he offered feebly.

"Wham," murmured Dr. Hack.

"Oh," breathed Faith, on tiptoe beside the opened sarcophagus. "Look."

His skin was brown and tight and dry, but that was to be expected after all that time spent in the desert. The edge of his robe was frayed, but it was obviously of humble cloth. In his hands he held a stout staff of olive wood. He might have been a shepherd, but there are all sorts of sheep. In the crook of his left arm there rested a tightly bound papyrus scroll. He was barefoot. He was smiling . . . What was the word for that kind of serene smile?

"Beatific," said Dr. Hack softly. "From the Latin, *beatus,* meaning blessed."

Nice touch, the snake, said Gerial.

Thank you, said Atamar.

2

Miserere

THE AMERICAN PRIEST and the British priest were the best of friends. That is to say, they could fight about any subject, savagely, for hours on end, and never have to couch their arguments in polite terms. On one occasion Father William Stanhope had called Father Lewis Freeman a walleyed mud turtle for his viewpoint on birth control. To this Father Lewis replied that it might have been a blessing had the Church allowed birth control earlier, as it might have prevented the unfortunate accident of a world blighted by Father William's presence. Then both of them laughed and sidetabled the discussion. They had sense enough to know when a topic became too heated for even their well-grounded friendship.

Now the two of them were deep in the preliminaries of a debate on the amazing news from Egypt, the finding of the remains of a man who might possibly be a new saint. Rome baked in the August sun, the superheated air of the streets made noxious by the fumes from a hundred choked avenues, all overrun with zippety sports cars, stalled tourist buses, and skooting motor bikes.

"Perfectly preserved, they say," remarked Father Lewis,

lacing his fingers around the stem of his goblet of mineral water. "A trifle dry, but otherwise looking well for his age."

Father William deplored his cohort's flippancy. He was approximately fifteen years older than the British priest, and although he prided himself on his liberal opinions, he could never resign himself to Father Lewis' total lack of dignity.

"My dear Lewis," said Father William, smoothing down an unruly lock of snowy hair, "we are speaking of a potential saint. No one is more skeptical than I about the authenticity of this find, but just in case I should happen to be wrong and we do indeed have a *Saint* Quintus Pilaster, I do wish you'd stop speaking of him as if he were your—your old schoolchum!"

"Come now, William," chortled Father Lewis. "Let me have my fun with the old boy now, can't you? Once he's canonized, I'll address him by the book. You know I will. I'm remarkably stodgy for my age."

Father Lewis looked anything but stodgy. He might cling to the sober, conventional habit, but he still looked more like a beef-cheeked chap who preached socialism, drank his daily pint of bitter, played darts, and roared damnation at rival football clubs on the weekend. To quote Melisan, looks are not everything. Father Lewis was a born reactionary, while the sedate front of Father William concealed a brightly burning brand of reform.

Their friendship, as well as their basic differences, gave their superiors good cause to see in them the perfect team to fly to Egypt and investigate the finding of Quintus (or St. Quintus) on the site.

A sallow, flat-chested, glum American teenager slumped past the sidewalk café table where the two priests sat. Her mother and father marched ahead, dutifully soaking up every drop of Roman atmosphere they could, and quickly, at these prices. Two happy Roman youths on a motorbike zoomed up behind the sour-faced girl and while one yelled something improper in broken English, the other snatched her purse.

"I would not be too quick to view old Quintus as a fraud," commented Father Lewis, whose seat gave him a perfect view of that often-repeated Roman street drama. The girl was howling with shock and her parents were clamoring for the *carabinieri*, who would only tell them to fill out the regulation purse-snatching-from-motorbike form. "I should think that in these times, we can use all the saints we can get."

•   •   •

At Father Lewis' insistence, they took nonsmoking seats on the flight to Cairo. Father William would have preferred to sit among the smokers and preach against the evils of tobacco. No one ever told a priest to shut up, except Father Lewis. The limpid blue of the Mediterranean slipped away under the filmy shadow of the plane. Father Lewis leaned his forehead against the porthole and dreamed.

"According to this," Father William's business-like voice destroyed the silver towers that Father Lewis built in revery, "we've got plenty of mentions of a *man* named Quintus Pilaster, but extremely few comments on his life that would hint at sainthood."

"If you're speaking of his contemporaries—" began Father Lewis.

"Of them and of later writers. Here, for example, is a selection of the Byzantine diatribe against the worship of icons, which this writer claims was made worse by the worship of *dubious* saints." Father William adjusted his bifocals and read, " 'They are swelled up in their pride. They make them icons in defiance of the holy Commandment. They are grown so shameless that they go beyond the bounds of evil, not merely making icons of Christ, the Virgin, and the Apostles, but overmore they paint them pictures of those who are not truly recognized as saints: Arsinoë of Memphis, James of Padua, Quintus Pilaster of the desert, Harmonia Pulchra, and a host of others, each more suspect than the last.' That is a direct quote from the *Contra idolorum populi* by Basileus Coprologos," Father William finished with satisfaction.

"I beg your pardon," said the gentleman seated across the aisle, "but are you speaking of the new miracle-tomb?"

"Ho, ho, ho! And there we have it!" Father William slapped his thigh. 'Miracle-tomb already! Why wait for an examination by the Church? Let the media canonize him!"

Father Lewis ignored Father William's outburst. The older priest liked to support the media when they fought the forces of ignorance and conservatism—interchangeable terms, in Father William's book. But just let a glimmer of caution show up in print, or on the lips of some television commentator, and Father William was in the saddle and off to the hunt, riding down the wily, hidebound, petit bourgeois influence.

"To answer you, sir," Father William continued, thrusting out his lower jaw at the man across the aisle, "I am not speaking of the new miracle-tomb. There is no such thing.

What has happened so far with regard to the finding and opening of the alleged sarcophagus of Quintus Pilaster is all explainable in purely scientific terms. There has been no evidence of supernatural influence. None at all.''

"Oh," said the man, giving Father William an uncertain smile packed with teeth. "I see."

"Perhaps you don't, my good man," Father Lewis intervened, leaning across Father William's attaché case to give his side of the story. "We are going to see if the stories that have come to us about the tomb are true, first of all. Then, if true, we shall seek the explanations behind them. As of this moment, we have no proof *one way or the other*," he emphasized for Father William's benefit, "that we are not dealing with the supernatural, the miraculous, and the saintly."

"Dear me," said the man, revealing another inch of pearly smile. "I had no idea. So you're going there to investigate it all? How fascinating. I suppose it will be quite a relief to the archeological team to have members of the Church on hand to maintain order. From what I've read in the papers, things are growing rather frenetic at the site. Giuliana Caruso's interview with Dr. Randolph Hack made it sound as if they're all at each other's throats. Over the credit for the discovery, you know?"

"After one of Giuliana Caruso's interviews," said Father Lewis, "I'd run mad and bite the first person I could find. The lady is abrasive, and not above provoking quarrels that do not exist, solely to get a story."

"Giuliana Caruso," Father William contradicted, "is one of the few honest, clear, unaffected voices in the media."

"Giuliana Caruso notwithstanding," conceded Father Lewis, "we share your hope that our presence at the site will restore order."

"Thank you, Father," said the man. "I do so hate to read about petty jealousies at a time when one of the world's great archeological finds in being studied. You know what little spats can become if they get out of hand."

"Quite," said Father Lewis. It was odd, but he suddenly felt the overwhelming urge to pray for peace on earth, specifically at the dig site. Really, it was quite daft, but— The little man across the aisle excused himself and wandered back to the restroom. Father Lewis was about to mention his strange impulse to Father William, but never had the chance. The

American priest was leaning back, eyes closed, lips moving, hands folded in an attitude of supplication.

In the restroom, the man from across the aisle released his toothsome smile to its fullest and passed one hand across his face to wipe away the illusion. Peace! Peace and the good influence of those two worthy men of the cloth! Now let Atamar try his damndest. Murakh had brought in the cavalry just before the nick of time.

"You should thank me, Atamar," Murakh told the mirror. "You won't, but you should. You're as much a stranger to gratitude as to yourself. I'd tell you the real reason why you failed with Quintus and the Russians if you'd listen. Why try? You'd never believe me. So I shall continue to pull the strings, and if you're lucky, you'll never see them. If you do . . . well, I'll have one string left to pull that will remove all question of your exile's end forever."

"I don't know who could possibly be in there," said the stewardess when the plane had landed and unloaded her passengers. "The door is locked and no one answers when I knock."

"Let's hope no one's sick," said her co-worker, using the emergency keys. Together they swung the restroom door open.

A gust of hot air puffed into their faces and rolled down the aisle in a tumble of maniacal laughter before streaming up into a column of dingy yellow smoke and fleeing the plane.

"So that was it," the stewardess said flatly. Then she fainted.

3

Man's Best Friend

"WHERE DID THAT dog come from?" asked Amanda. She perched on top of an empty crate and swung her long legs back and forth like a schoolgirl. It was good to get away from the center of camp these days. Lately she'd been prey to the impossible feeling that the desert was closing in on her. Amanda hated crowds, but more than that, she disliked mysteries. All of a sudden here was that squint-eyed moop, Don Swann, in the company of a beautiful dog, a dog with blueblack fur and fat, hairy paws.

"I dunno," shrugged Don. He was looking at Amanda with a worshipful, moist, imploring gaze. It struck her that the wrong fellow was wearing the leash in this relationship. "I guess he wandered here from the Arab village or something."

That's a Newfoundland if he's any kind of dog at all, thought Amanda. I've seen the village dogs, and they're all starveling mutts. Any family with a dog like this would have named him Khus-Khus and served him for Thanksgiving dinner ages ago. There's too much fur on him for the dog to breathe and too much meat on him for the dog to survive.

"No, seriously, where'd he come from?" she asked, her heels drumming out the beat for *Bolero* on the empty crate.

"I told you, I dunno," repeated Don. "I was asleep after my turn on guard by the sarc, and when I woke up, I thought I was maybe dying from a heart attack, you know? I'd been having this dream—" Don dared not finish. The dream had been the most recent in a series of more and more graphically choreographed erotic ballets featuring Miss Amanda Rhodes in a variety of roles. That wasn't so bad, but Don noticed he woke up tired, and it was starting to tell on his looks. Sex, supposedly the cure-all for blotchy skin, had instead given Don a complexion that was—well, he looked as if he'd needlessly provoked a swarm of bees. It had gotten so that Don yearned for dreamless sleep and was considering asking Dr. Hack to get him some pills.

"And you dreamed up the dog?" asked Amanda.

"Gee," Don grinned sheepishly. "I dunno. I guess I did, because like I said, when I woke up I had this heavy feeling on my chest and there was this dog, squatting on me."

"Maybe he belongs to one of the newspeople," suggested Amanda.

"Or maybe he's a spirit-guide," said Don.

Amanda's tattoo on the crate stopped. "A spirit-guide," she said. "Sure. What's a spirit-guide?" She need never have asked. Already Don had plucked a well-read paperback book from his rear pocket and proffered it for her inspection. On the cracked and torn cover a naked woman writhed while a man in an ancient Egyptian costume lifted whole from *The Ten Commandments* tickled her belly with a serpent-hilted dagger. *Witchcraft of the Ancient World*, by Francis Gutthorp, Ph.D.

"Bet you didn't know I was a scholar, huh?" said Don.

"My dear Dr. Hack, you must act as if this were an ordinary Marmota Travelrama, Inc., tour, and think of me as no more than a great big friendly watchdog," said Ms. Ferrabosco with a silvery laugh. She was proud of that laugh. Few woman of her age or Junoesque build could carry off a nymph-like laugh without sounding foolish. Ms. Louise Ferrabosco had not gotten where she was by playing the fool.

"Ms. Ferrasbosco," Dr. Hack leaned forward earnestly, passing her a fresh drink, "how is that possible? Believe me, we couldn't ask for a nicer watchdog, but the site is

overrun with non-Marmota personnel. I have had to insist that
one of my group be on guard at the sarcophagus at all times,
to prevent vandalism. And as for Giuliana Caruso and that
trained photographer of hers, they seem to spring up out of the
sand at the worst moments.''

"You don't have to tell me about Caruso," said Ms.
Ferrabosco stiffly. "No sooner did word of your wonderful
discovery get out than she was plunked down in the Rome
office of Marmota, threatening to publish all manner of lies
about our program if we didn't fly her to the site and let her
interview her knobby little head off! You can imagine my
feelings, flying all the way out from New York and finding
that repulsive creature here, at Marmota's expense, no less!
And you do know how much Marmota Travelrama, Inc.,
shuns cheap publicity. It detracts from our sophisticated image.''

"Oh, but of course," solemnly agreed Dr. Hack. "As a
serious scientist, I can tell you that Marmota can't shun cheap
publicity more than I do myself.''

"Well, we all appreciate the effort you've been making,
putting up with all of these tiresome reporters. You've been a
credit to Marmota," Ms. Ferrabosco decreed, patting Dr.
Hack's knee. "But now your worries are over. You can
devote yourself completely to the study of Quintus and any
further excavations you might want to do in the area. Marmota
has received consent from the parents of all your dear little
diggers for them to remain at the site until September—back
to school then, you know!—and at only a fraction of the
regular Marmota tuition.''

"Why, that's very kind of—"

"And as I said, I'll play the watchdog. I'll see to it that
you're undisturbed in your studies. If those terrible newsmen
keep after you, I'll fend them off myself. If need be, I'll
borrow that charming assistant of yours to feed them a few
tidbits now and then. That Caruso woman has expressed
interest in interviewing him, but you can just imagine what's
going through her smutty little mind. So don't you worry, Dr.
Hack; Geordie and I will keep the buzzards at bay.''

Again the Amazonian Ms. Ferrabosco released a cascade of
silvery laughter. In the burning privacy of his own mind, Dr.
Randolph Hack fantasized fetching a ladder, scuttling up it,
and strangling the mirthful lady.

Hack withdrew into his tent to brood. He stretched out on
the cot and threw one arm across his eyes.

I could steady that ladder for you, Atamar offered.

"You again?" Hack grumbled. "I can take care of my own murders, thank you very much."

Will you, though? Or will this be yet another instance of the famous Hack Lack of Follow-through?

"What would you know about it?"

More than you think. Don't be afraid of me.

"Of my own insanity? Never."

Don't think of me like that. There are powers that guide men, call them what you will. Instinct? Luck? A hunch? They speak, for those willing to heed. Your friend did, and he was the one to find the Richard Jewel.

"So speak. I'm heeding my head off."

Tsk. Touchy. I am serious, Hack. I can help you. Do you want Geordie out of the way? Do you want the media people to pay attention to you and you alone? We can see to it, between the two of us.

"Tempting thought." Dr. Hack's voice grew fainter.

And so easy to make real. All you have to do is—

A soft snore dismissed further negotiations. The demon lord turned visible inside the tent.

"Have your rest while you can, my friend. You're coming along just fine." He blew away through the tent flap.

Have you seen Atamar around here anywhere?" Lura asked Melisan *sotto voce.*

"Atamar?" Melisan feigned ignorance. "Oh, him? Why, I couldn't say." She looked complacently at the sparkling ruby that graced her slender foot. "Why? Are you ready to turn in a soul?"

Lura did not respond. Melisan lost all pretense of calm. "Answer me!" she snapped. "I asked you if you'd landed a soul!"

Lura's backhand caught Melisan across the mouth. "Lower your voice," she ordered. "I'm not asking about Atamar's whereabouts for nothing. Now tell me, where is he?"

"You hit me," gasped Melisan. Lura liked a healthy hair-pulling, scratching, cursing, wrestling tussle when her temper was up, but the cuddlesome succubus had never slapped, punched, or struck another demon in her life. It wasn't her nature.

"I'll smack you good and proper if you don't give me a straight answer. I want to talk to you, but I want to do it

privately. Gerial's busy and I know where Horgist is, but I'm
not saying another word until I know that Atamar's ears are
way the hell and gone.''

"He's right there," mumbled Melisan, rubbing her cheek.
She showed Lura the fresh, prim outlines of Ms. Ferrabosco's
pavilion. A jagged shadow hovered nearby. "He can't hear
you.''

"Well, keep an eye on him and sing out if he comes this
way," said Lura. Her soft face had gone from tender, smiling
curves to sober, forbidding angles. She looked dead serious.
Even her tail was curled sedately around one arm.

"Melisan," said Lura, "we haven't a dead dog's chance of
getting a soul.''

Melisan opened her mouth, but nothing came out. She wanted
to say, "Ridiculous!" She wanted to say, "Are you mad?"
She wanted to say, "With all these extra mortals flapping
around, we're as good as hellbound right now!" Something
in Lura's manner gave her pause. "Wh—wh—wh—?" was
all she could manage.

"Look, Melisan, we're both succubi," said Lura. "We're
not the best of friends, but being cooped up in this hole for
centuries would destroy friendship, passion, and lust in one
neat bundle. But if we don't make up our differences and use
every brain we've got between us, we'll be stuck here for
eternity!" Melisan made a sick gurgling sound. "I don't want
to do this," Lura proceeded, "but I'm going to have to be
honest with you. Do you see this diamond pentacle?''

Melisan saw it and duly admired it. It was almost as fine as
her ruby toe-ring. It was also new.

"Murakh gave it to me," said Lura, confirming what
Melisan suspected. "And he also gave me something better:
advice. It came in a little note in the box with the pentacle. I
didn't want to believe it, but I've been working and working
on my mortal, with no success, and I just have to believe
what he said now. He said—''

"Hell hates a failure," recited Melisan, recalling the slip
of rice paper that came with her ruby. "The Council decrees
that only those of us who bring down souls shall return. There
are never enough souls to go around. Atamar divides our
powers so that we will be incapable of snaring souls while he
takes the most susceptible one for himself. He means to leave
us behind.''

Lura took a long, deep breath and let it out slowly. "Just

what he suggested to me. And I'd be willing to wager that he gave a word of good will to Gerial and Horgist, too. Murakh said he never could abide injustice. There's something in his words, Melisan. Remember the good old days? It took all five of us together to tempt Quintus.''

"Ah!" sighed Melisan dreamily, shutting her eyes. "That was wonderful, wasn't it? Yes, together. We worked together. But split up, our powers might not be enough. And Atamar's hand was behind our agreement to go after the females, too!''

Lura looked puzzled. "Was it? I thought we came to that decision on our own.''

"Remember Quintus!" declared Melisan. "We worked as a unit then, with Atamar guiding us all by the force of his thoughts. He has that power, Lura. Why shouldn't he be using it right now, influencing us to go for female souls when we're really designed for the entrapment of males?''

Dawn came, and with realization came Lura's justified anger. "Why that lousy—! And for all we know, he was the one who *forced* me to drain that darling camel driver before taking his soul! Yes, I'm positive he did! Then he blamed it on me, when all the time it was sheer envy, him thinking I'd get back to Hell before he did! I ought to wring his neck!'' The hint of her old smile softened her scowl as something occurred to her. "But why wring his neck? That would be too good for him. Instead, let's find Gerial and Horgist and make damned sure they know what our beloved leader's up to. And then—''

"We sabotage him," chimed in Melisan. "Just the way he was planning to double-cross us. All that bilge about one demon being more than a match for a mortal! Bushwah! If that were so, how come it's so easy for one puny mortal to summon up any demon he chooses?'' Melisan shuddered. "Remember Fasha? Vergilius called her up once because it was Saturday night and the old mage was bored. Did you see what she looked like when she finally came home?''

Lura trembled. Centuries ago, it was, yet who could forget the powers of Vergilius, the greatest mage of the ancient world, or the bizarre, perverted, unsavory "amusements" he took with succubi?

"We're wasting out time on Earth," Fasha declared when she recovered her ability to speak coherently. "They do a better job of sending each other to Hell than we could ever do. And I no longer believe that we'd want some of them down here!"

It was true. You never knew quite how to regard mortals. When you figured them for power-mad fools, they showed intelligence. When you thought of them as sheep, they out-ravaged wolves. When you expected them to be weak and helpless, they turned on you with a hidden word of command and locked you in a bottle or walled you up in an oak tree. Mortals! The very word made the more tender demons shiver their claws off.

"A good plan," said Lura. "We get together with Gerial and Horgist for self-protection. By the breasts of Dian, I only hope there aren't too many of them for us to handle!"

"If we're very quiet," said Melisan, stealing a tremulous look to where Giuliana Caruso came goose-stepping over the sand, "maybe they'll leave us alone."

"The poor son-of-a-bitch is as good as mine," said Atamar to the shaving mirror that hung in Dr. Hack's tent. He breathed on it, and the silver behind the glass writhed in a reflection of Dr. Hack's mind. The spectacle was grotesque, disgusting, filled with brutality that evoked Murakh's descriptions of the Inquisition. The victim was plain, and the crime in the making was to be murder, a certain passport to Hell. Now it was only a question of that one white stain, lurking in a corner of the glass and shimmering with its own gentle, peaceful light, ruining the effects of torture, jealousy, ambition, and madness.

"A scruple," hissed Atamar. "A small one, but still . . . Well, I can deal with it. We're as good as home on this man's ticket now. A day or so more, the opportunity and it will be done. Only a few details to arrange."

Details, like paperwork, were the plague of a creative administrator, or so Atamar felt. Not that he would have to resort to real paperwork, like the blood-signed contract. He'd meant it when he'd told Lura it was just a formality. Sin unrepented was the one way to snag a soul, that much was clear and simple, but details ate you alive. Minor things such as when to let Dr. Hack kill Geordie, how to have him do it, whether to let him get away with the crime and suffer re-morse, whether to send an unlucky witness to the scene and require a second murder, when to arrange Hack's own death to prevent his repentance, all had to be settled.

"An accident," Atamar decided, with a final frown at the soft white glow of Hack's last scruple. "We'll make it look like an accident, but let Hack know he caused it. He'll rationalize his guilt whenever remorse grows too strong, and they *never* repent when they rationalize! Atamar, you've still got it!"

He felt smug for the first time in ages. Soon he would be home, and while Hell was a constant, bitter reminder of that first home that he had lost, the handsome demon had to admit that it was a damned sight better than Earth. You could depend on Hell.

"I should have thought of this long ago," he said. "I never had a better idea than splitting us up. It's impossible for me to think with Lura and Melisan chattering away, and Gerial acting disgusting, and Horgist snoring. If we'd have spent half the time catching souls that we spent arguing in committee, we'd have landed one of those Russians. But when I'm with the others, I sink to their level. Bah! It's a good thing the Council sent me after Quintus with those four misbegotten imps in the first place. Didn't I design the temptation tableau that nearly got him? If only he hadn't died! Ah, but Hell doesn't care for excuses."

"Or failures," murmured Melisan, casting an arc of green light that burst into choking, blinding smoke just over Atamar.

Atamar's world tilted and collapsed. Balls of flame exploded behind his eyes and his own pungent stench was whirled into oblivion by a gagging reek of violets, Lura's chosen musk. Rubbery yellow paws touched his head, black-rimmed blue claws seized his feet, and pushed against each other until he felt his essence dwindling into a despairing handful of fury. The yellow paws squeezed harder, and he was nothing but thick smoke, the color of blood, poured down an endless tube that throbbed with marbled purple light. He landed hard in a place where the walls curved endlessly and his world was all an amethyst splendor webbed by a network of darker veins.

"There," said Horgist, ramming the stopper into the neck of Lura's old Phoenician bottle. "That should hold him."

"It was so easy," mused Lura. She did not sound as happy as befitted such a well-executed ambush. She could not take her eyes off the bottle.

"Because we worked fast, and we worked together," said Horgist. "Murakh was right. I sense that Atamar was very close to success. Look there in the mirror. It's fading, but it still bears the impression of his intent."

Gerial looked. A familiar face looked back. The stain of white that Atamar had seen wavered into the ghost of Steve Ritter, hand perpetually outstretched to the blue demon.

Go away and leave me alone! Gerial thought fiercely. I don't want to play your watching games. I don't want to know how unspeakable mortals can be!

Nor do I, Gerial, but I have no choice. I must know. See where I have been sent, the ugliness with which I must dwell. He gestured at the whirling miasma of Dr. Hack's reflected thoughts.

Your kind of place, kid. The blue demon's lip curled.

But not yours. It doesn't have to be yours. Take my hand, Gerial. Let me—

Gerial struck the mirror from its hook impatiently. It smashed to fragments against the corner of Dr. Hack's footlocker. "I don't want to know what he was doing," the blue demon growled. He too sounded less than proud of what they had all done together. He looked sharply at Horgist and demanded, "Now that we've got him, what are we going to do with him?"

"Simple," Horgist yawned. He made as if to stretch his weary, boneless body, then abruptly hurled the purple bottle end over end through the tent flap.

Lura gave a little cry and ran outside, searching the earth and air anxiously for the flask. The sun was strong, but not strong enough to point out even a fleck of purple glass in all the golden expanse of sand or all the jumble of the camp. "Where is he?" she shrilled, dashing back into the tent. "Where did you throw him?"

"Calm down, Lura," said Horgist in his dull, bubbling voice. "What do you care? If he was telling the truth about what we've got to do to get home again, he'll be transported to Hell along with all of us when we land our soul. We can apologize to him then, say it was a little prank, no harm done. And if Murakh was right, and only those demons who have an active hand in bringing down the soul will be released from exile—why then, he deserves eternity in a jug for trying to betray us!"

"I—I thought we were going to keep him in the flask for just a bit, then let him out and question him," mumbled Lura.

"Let him out? When he's alert, his powers are more than a match for us all. Have you forgotten what he once was? We're sucklings compared to him, infants!" shouted Melisan. "Let him out, and if Murakh's right, it'd be us crammed into that bottle next!"

"Oh," said Lura tonelessly, and ran away to hide the first cold tears.

Gerial stood at the tent flap and let his eyes wander, also looking for a glint of purple against the sand. He saw none. The others were calling him to join a conference about which soul to go for as a team. "Poor son-of-a-bitch," said Gerial, and went to meet with them.

4

Ladies and Gentlemen of the Press

THE EXCAVATION WAS progressing nicely, to the satisfaction of everyone except the media, Dr. Hack, Amanda, Don, and Father William. To be honest, Amanda's dissatisfaction had little to do with the dig. No more did Don's. With his monstrous, shaggy, coal-black dog trotting at his heels, he followed Amanda like a bad reputation, and his vexation waxed daily as he saw that her footsteps took her near, past, and into Geordie Burns' tent more than absolutely necessary.

Amanda, for her part, was slowly losing her grip on reality. A word to the wise was supposed to be sufficient, and Princeton didn't s'posed to hire no fools, but as the days wore on, Miss Rhodes came to believe that perhaps they'd made a mistake in Geordie's case. The man could not take a hint. She had done everything possible to insinuate her admiration, her passion, and her availability, short of ripping off her clothes and his and grunting "We go bed, Barbarian." At times she was tempted to do precisely that. Geordie had a body that reminded her of the late Robert E. Howard's indestructible Conan at his most muscular and luscious stages. How did a girl get Conan to notice her and still be a lady?

The result of these two young hearts so constantly thwarted was that they came to hate the sight of each other. Horgist, sweltering under the heavy blue-black pelt that disguised him, forced his somnolent brain to remain alert. Properly nurtured, Amanda might slaughter Mr. Swann or Mr. Swann might try to teach the ungrateful wench a lesson by taking her by force. Frankly, Horgist was betting on Amanda.

"Why do Amanda and Don fight all the time?" Steve asked Faith casually. He was on guard at the sepulchre and she had brought him a glass of cold tea.

"One of two reasons," said Faith. "Love or hate."

"That about covers it," Steve laughed. "Which do you think it is?" Above the clatter of camp noises you could still hear Amanda calling Don a hopeless moron. It was anybody's guess what he'd done this time.

"I don't much care, Steve," said Faith. "And if you want my opinion—"

SNAP!

It was Giuliana's pet photographer. His name was either Mario or Chuck. He didn't mind lying about it. He had the stealth of a brick-shy alley cat and an endless supply of film. He also had the genius needed to snap each and every one of his subjects at the exact moment when hair was awry, mouth gaped stupidly, or finger was up nose. You would hear his SNAP, his muttered Italian glee, and the scritchy sound of his retreating scuttle.

"I'm going to make him eat his telephoto lens before we pack up and leave," said Faith calmly. "I've promised it to myself as a special treat. That lens will wind up inside that shutter-happy creep, one way or the other."

"You've never said the newsmen bothered you before," said Steve with sincere concern. "If you like, I can do my part to fend them off you. It's not a very strong right arm, but I'm always happy to help a maiden in distress."

Faith tilted her head to one side and considered Steve's bland, willing face. How strange, she thought. There was no way on earth it could be, and yet it was impossible to dislike the boy. He was all smooth-edges, all comfort and caring, but with not a hint of an underlying self-interest. He really wanted to help her, and he didn't give a damn if there was anything in it for him.

"Maiden in distress, huh?" she half-smiled. "Where did you pick that up? It's adorable, but just a tad dated."

"So am I," said Steve. "I think I took a wrong turn at the seventeenth century, but I'm happy to be here."

"You're a riot. I'll be back in twenty minutes to relieve you," said Faith, squeezing his hand.

Alone under the awning with Quintus, Steve paced the thin line where shade met sunlight. At Dr. Hack's command, a tent with open sides had been erected over the sarcophagus and a series of canvas draperies thrown over Quintus, to be removed only at the word of Dr. Hack himself. Father William and Father Lewis were the exceptions to the HANDS OFF policy, and Steve relaxed when he saw the two priests approaching. Father Lewis resembled a black beetle, still in full cassock in spite of the sun. Father William clung to his clerical collar, but the shorts and sandals he wore were not regulation turn-out for his calling.

"Anything new?" Father Lewis asked affably, with a sidelong glance to where Quintus lay hidden from view.

"Nothing much," returned Steve, just as pleasantly.

"Aren't you Ritter?" asked Father William sharply. Steve allowed that he was. "The one with the snake?" Steve nodded. He had been interviewed about that snake so often that he felt he should have paid restitution to the reptile's family.

"What did they do with the snake?" asked Father Lewis.

Before Steve could answer, Father William exclaimed, "What did you expect them to do with it, for Heaven's sake? They buried it! Were you expecting it to be enshrined? This man," Father William confided in Steve, "would've grabbed that dead snake and submitted it as evidence of miracle. And if I don't keep an eye on him, he might catch a live snake and try for an instant replay of the trick with the coffin lid."

"I am merely trying to take all things into consideration," said Father Lewis. "I'll admit that it would be nice to have another saint recognized, particularly one that has been neglected for so long. Moreover, in a skeptical time when even men of the cloth won't believe in a miracle unless it is first verified by *Time* magazine, we must keep our faith in wonders."

"It will be a real miracle if we stop wasting time digging up a bunch of saints when we have more than enough already," said Father William. "Then maybe the Church can get around to tidying up the earth. Never mind. We're here for the scroll."

"Poor old Father William," Lewis whispered in Steve's ear as the boy slowly pulled back the canvas covering: "Hasn't been the same since he saw Anthony Quinn in *The Shoes of the Fisherman*."

A sound of sneakery directly behind them informed Steve that Mario/Chuck was still lurking, getting ready for another award-winning shot. "Smile, Quintus," said Steve aloud.

"Good Lord!" cried Father William.

"Santa Maria Maggiore!" yelped Mario. No one named Chuck would use such an exclamation. He was too shocked even to raise his camera.

Father Lewis said nothing, fingers crammed into his mouth just as he'd done when a child in Sussex and frightened by thunder. Steve was silent, too, but his face betrayed nothing.

And Quintus, found smiling, continued to smile. But the scroll that had lain cradled in his arms, the scroll that Dr. Hack said the priests might examine, the tightly rolled parchment scroll was not rolled or cradled any longer. It floated up, drawing with it the dead man's hands, then his arms. Father Lewis thought he heard a humming sound. He knew he saw a twirl of irridescent colors drench the parchment as it rose. First one of Quintus' hands, then the other let go their death-grip. The English priest actually saw the fingers straighten one by one, the hands gently cross themselves on Quintus' bosom after they released the scroll. The wooden core turned, leaving a tongue of closely written text behind as it glided over the body, propelled by invisible hands. On and on the scroll unrolled, from under Quintus' brown chin, down over his body, to his feet, up the stone wall of the sarcophagus, over the top, down the other side, and away.

"Stop it!" choked Father Lewis, coming to.

"Catch it!" Father William tried to shout. It came out as a hoarse whisper. Mario remained motionless, alternately praying and swearing in Italian. Steve lunged for the end of the scroll still in the sarcophagus and held on. He rightly reasoned that when there was no more parchment to unroll, the scroll would stop and he could reel it in on this end.

Father William was too overwrought to be reasonable. He took off in pursuit of the far end of the runaway scroll. The roll of writing was getting thinner and thinner the farther the scroll unravelled. It was heading for the media enclave.

The ladies and gentlemen of the press, the airwaves, and

the little screen were bored. At first, when news of the find had burned up the wires, editors everywhere saw a case of a new King Tut's tomb story in the making. Then, once they stopped jumping up and down long enough to be told that this was no treasure-packed Egyptian royal grave, they dispatched their teams anyway. A saint, you say? Oh, a *potential* saint! Well, that's O.K. The religious angle's good, and we can always work in something about the supernatural. People go ape-shit for the supernatural.

But there wasn't anything supernatural by the time they got there. There was some cock-and-bull story about how the lid of the tomb smashed this deadly serpent to applesauce, but those stupid bastards had tossed the corpus delicti. Not even a prayer of getting a nice gory picture of a ruined snake.

Instead, the reporters and cameramen fell back on the time-honored glory of the media. If there is no spectacular news, make some. They dusted off their mikes and notepads and tape recorders and waded into the fray.

"Oh, my God, I need a drink!" wailed a sweet young thing from NBC. The enticing contours of her moon-shaped face were already going slightly yellow, a protest from her much-abused liver. She lived exclusively on a diet of Johnny Walker Black and anchormen.

"Cheer up, sweetie," said a colleague from a rival network. "We just got word to wrap it up here. Even with the auxiliary team that Marmota flew in to help get the digging done faster, all they're turning up is a bunch of adobe huts. Big deal. The doc said there was a monastic community here, he found it, that's that."

"What about the body? You know, the saint?" asked a rabbity sound man.

"Old news," said the girl, accepting a hooker of Scotch from her latest flame. Under the desert sun, his smile was blinding, and a credit to his dentist. "I interviewed the two priests—"

"Who didn't?" her colleague broke in. "I've got a complete set of in-depth interviews with everyone here, including that Arab kid who drives a jeep like it was a weapon. Hey, I'll trade one childhood story about Don Swann for one smutty innuendo about Amanda Rhodes!" Everybody laughed.

"I interviewed the priests," the girl went on between sips, "and the American one told me not to hold my breath waiting for an on-the-spot canonization. He's not even sure that the bit with the snake was an honest-to-God miracle. Could've been caused by an aftershock from the bigger quake that heaved up the coffin in the first place."

"Sarcophagus," corrected a prim, immaculately tailored voice at her elbow. Reclining in a beige director's chair with chambray slings, exquisitely turned out in full desert gear, complete with pith helmet, Kent Cardiff chewed his pipe and drew breath for a lecture.

"Sarcophagus," he commenced, "would seem to be an inappropriate term in the case of the stone container found in this instance. The true sarcophagus derived its name—meaning an eater of flesh—from the fact that the stone used for such funerary devices would accelerate the process of decay, thus freeing the soul for its trip to the next world. Like the Egyptians, many peoples of the Ancient World believed that the soul must remain with the body until the body is totally disintegrated. The process of cremation was favored for speeding up the separation of body and soul. The Egyptians, however, insisted on preserving the body for eternity, if possible, to give the soul somewhere familiar to dwell. Destroy the body and you destroy the soul, or so they thought. Therefore, since the body of the alleged Quintus Pilaster is still intact, I would say that we do not have a genuine flesh-eating sarcophagus, but merely an individual sepulchre, or stone casket if you prefer." He took another drag at his pipe.

"That's the last dollar I give to PBS," snarled the well-Scotched young lady.

"I say," said Kent Cardiff, sitting up straight in his frightfully tasteful chair. "What's come over that priest?"

Everyone turned to look. It was a strange spectacle, so strange that the ladies and gentlemen of the press watched it as if they were no more than ordinary gawping mortals. Here came Father William, bare knees pumping mightily, and behind him sprinted young Steve Ritter and ahead of him rolled what looked like a berserk pack of paper towels making a break for freedom.

Steve was not fool enough to be chasing the runaway scrool. He'd thrust his end of it into Father Lewis' willing hands with instructions to hold on and rewind when he gave the signal. Rather than the scroll, Steve was after Father William, now a delicate shade of scarlet. The older priest was wheezing and puffing like a chain-smoking walrus, and if disaster struck, Steve knew CPR.

The scroll lost momentum and stopped. Kent Cardiff bestirred himself, as did the young woman from NBC and representatives from the other major networks. The wooden core lolled innocently, out of paper, while it drew a crowd.

A babble of reportage filled the air as Father William tried to catch his breath and answer questions at once. Cameras clicked and whirred, microphones were shoved inches from the older priest's teeth, and well-meaning, strong-armed techies gently restrained Steve from rerolling the wayward scroll until the film crews could get a nice shot of it lying there, all undone.

"Are you sure you felt no earth tremors?"

"Could it have slipped out of your hands?"

"Do you think there are supernatural forces at work here?"

"What did you say immediately prior to the scroll incident?"

"Did you notice anything odd about the position of the—ah—remains?"

"Could someone have tampered with the sarcophagus?"

"Is that scroll parchment or papyrus?" This last question from Kent Cardiff.

Father William was doing his best to satisfy everyone without making it sound like a genuine miracle had taken place. First the lid, weighing tons, slips off the sarcophagus, and now a parchment—yes, it was parchment, Mr. Cardiff—scroll gets an attack of *wanderlust*. Amazing, but miraculous? Did levitation count as saintly work? Then what about similar episodes when the only supernatural forces involved were—

No. He absolutely, categorically refused to say it. He would rather have them start work on the basilica of St. Quintus Pilaster right now than say it. Well, perhaps he wouldn't mention it to the reporters, but he had to say it to himself.

What about the Devil?

Father William prided himself on his mind. It was neat and orderly, a little skeptical, but rational. There was no room in it for fantasy. He would accept belief in saints as the personification of goodness. It was a relief to regard their serene faces in the margins of old manuscripts and remember that goodness was still possible in this world. But as for the presence of evil, there was altogether too much ready evidence of that handy. He believed in a central spirit of evil, a

Devil, and he had read many proofs of the Evil One's powers, which included levitation. He'd never been eyewitness to any such doings, but a friend of a friend once said . . .

Until now. And he knew, as surely as he knew there was evil in the world, that if he mentioned his thoughts to the media, they'd turn Satan into a sideshow. They would interview self-styled witches, to add "color" to the story—batty old women and frustrated young misfits, all—and they would end by trivializing everything. It was wrong to trivialize evil. It was like saturating people with the violence and brutality of the darkest crimes, until they no longer felt the chill, the horror, the shame. They felt nothing. They switched the channel or turned to the comics page.

And that's the way it is . . .

"Gentlemen . . . and ladies," Father William nodded at the moon-faced miss, "please give us a chance. We've only caught up with this getaway scroll now. If you'll allow us to examine it where it lies, I think we'll be able to tell if something out-of-the-ordinary has happened here, or if we've just been over-imaginative."

The collective face of the press fell. No chance of a hot story with this cool article in charge. What they needed was a hysterical housewife-type from Astoria, not a reasoning machine. Only Kent Cardiff seemed pleased with Father William's plea for sanity. The others grumbled amongst themselves like disgruntled natives in a B-picture.

"That does it," said the lady from NBC. "He'll make out like it was the pull of the tides that shot the scroll this way. And did you see how fast it was going?"

No one had. Not one of the cameramen had exhibited the presence of mind to photograph the scroll in action. However, that didn't stop them from swearing they'd seen it zoom past like a jackrabbit, a jaguar, a jet. By the third retelling, they'd have it breaking the sound barrier.

"Well, I think we might as well get set to pack it in," said a wire-service man. "We can pick up on this story again when the dig's over and the Vatican reps have come to a conclusion. It's just spadework from here on in."

There was a loud murmur of agreement as singly and in groups the press corps resolved to contact home base and head for more sensationally green pastures. The resulting rhubarb nearly drowned out Steve's thin, frantic voice shouting, "Hey! Scat! Get away from that, you!"

Kent Cardiff, launched onto a disquisition on the difference between parchment and papyrus, turned idly to see what was upsetting the lad. His keen grey eye saw that magnificent black dog that had been hanging around the camp for several days. Apparently the beast had wandered off from its adopted master, the Swann chap, and was sniffing curiously at the wooden end-piece of the unfurled scroll.

"Get off! Shoo!" commanded Steve. The dog ignored him.

"I say, you've got to let him know who's master," Cardiff cheerfully volunteered. Brandishing his pipe he bellowed at the animal, "Begone, sirrah! Go, sir! Go, I say! Be—"

The dog seemed to compress itself into a tight ball of darkness, broken only by the jagged outline of sickle-shaped fangs in a scarlet mouth and two blazing yellow eyes. A growl welled up in the mighty black throat. Flecks of amber foam dribbled from the lolling crimson tongue.

"Mad, by my word!" gasped Cardiff, backing off.

"A dog doesn't just go mad like that," said Steve. He stared fixedly into the great yellow eyes and felt a familiar sensation of bottomless dread engulfing his heart. "You . . ."

Cameras sprang to life from every angle, and from a safe distance. Giuliana Caruso did a war dance on top of a crate and hurled curses on Mario, who was nowhere to be found. Was she to be the only reporter there for this wonderful drama who would have no photos to illustrate it? *Che va*! A boy, a man, a mad dog, and an American priest! This was the stuff of which great literature could be made! Why, the inferences alone would be priceless. And if the dog went for the priest—or even for the boy—She hoped it would not attack the Englishman. It would be hard to draw symbolic meaning from that.

"If he's not mad . . ." Father William started to say. The dog made a feint, then retreated. He did this several times, each sortie accompanied by menacing growls and yaps. The three men found themselves being herded like sheep away from the scroll.

"Good Lord," said Kent Cardiff, snapping his pipe in two with one hand. "He—he wants us away from it. It's like my old uncle's corgi in Wales. Well, I'll be—That's what he's doing to us! We're sheep!"

"Somebody go get Dr. Hack!" yelled Steve while the

cameras purred happily and microphones hovered near like bats at twilight. "Tell him to bring the gun! Quick!"

At that moment, Geordie Burns and Ms. Louise Ferrabosco came strolling through the media quarter of camp, enjoying a fascinating chat on the subject of archeology and career opportunities with Marmota. Ms. Ferrabosco was more than pleased with her self-appointed job as watchdog. She had found it possible to sidetrack any newsperson with the proper hints of lost monastic treasures, solid gold crosses, bejewelled reliquaries, and so on. Or so she had until Geordie—dear Geordie! Such an innocent when it came to the real world! —gently stated that Quintus' time slot and life-style was ages before the monasteries became wealthy. Now the press was losing interest in the dig, and that was unfortunate. She might have to come up with an excuse for postponing further excavation if no one was mentioning Marmota on the air. And postponement could become cancellation so easily!

"What's going on down there?" she asked from the rise they had just climbed. But Geordie had a younger, sharper set of ears. He heard Steve's cry for help. He saw the big, black dog's fantastic dance. Without a word, he raced forward to rescue the scroll and the beleaguered men, perhaps not in that order. Or perhaps so.

Portable cameras drank in the heady sight of Geordie Burns' incredible body, poetically glistening with sweat, as the bold young archeologist cut a swath through the crowd of media people and hastened to the aid of his comrades.

"Just a few words, Mr. Burns!" panted the young woman from NBC. Geordie glared at her and did what he had never done before—what no true gentleman would ever do—he swatted down her microphone in anger.

The dog spun around at his shout. Geordie snatched the microphone from the newswoman, and now he pitched it hard at the beast. It thudded into one furry flank, but the dog made no move away from the scroll. It uttered a warning snarl, that was all.

"Be careful, son! He might be mad!" called Cardiff.

"I'll be careful," Geordie said, closing with the animal. The plumy black tail flicked wickedly, the red lips curled away to show how long those pearly teeth were, and how cutting.

"Good dog," said Geordie. It was ridiculous, of course, but what else could he say to the slobbering cur? "Good dog, go home." With his hand he made a blunt sign for the other three to make their getaway while he distracted the dog. "Good boy. Nice dog."

They ran. They went so fast that Father William nearly toppled Father Lewis, who was drawing nigh with the other end of the disputed scroll in his hands. He was gently rewinding it as he went, using a discarded tent-peg as a core.

"Don't go any closer!" rasped Father William, clinging to his friend's collar. "There's a mad dog after the scroll, and young Burns is trying to hold him at bay until someone fetches a gun!"

"A mad dog after the scroll?" Father Lewis' voice went up an octave. "What in the world would a mad dog want with the scroll?"

"Maybe he reads Latin," grated Father William.

"Well, mad or not, we can't let the scroll be ruined," announced Father Lewis, patting what he'd rewound so far. "I've been skimming it as I go, and this document is an indispensable part of our investigation. It's more than that, it's testimony such as the world has never seen before!" He walked on, rewinding, until he was within range of the dog.

The dog saw him and lunged, aiming for the priest's throat. Automatically Father Lewis held up the rewound scroll in self-defense, as if it were a quarterstaff. The viewers held their breath as Geordie leapt forward in perfect synchronization with the black dog's spring, his hands closing around the beast's windpipe.

The priest's reflex brought the scroll crashing down to deflect the black dog's fangs. Touch. Pause. Explosion. Reality explosion, shards of glass, black glass boiling white in the throats of volcanoes, melded into dog-shape, now shattering in Geordie's hands where fur should be. A billion tiny shards of black volcanic glass as the dog crackled outwards, glittering.

Geordie continued to move forward, empty hands bleeding, forward through a rain of razors, blacker than old magic. The priest stood frozen, the scroll shining with clear yellow light in his hands, a slash of brilliance through the black rain that buzzed and fell and swirled and grew wings.

The blanket of flies swarmed around Geordie, darting for his eyes, smothering him with the foulness that dropped from their trembling blue-black wings, hitting his exposed skin like pellets of hail that seared where they fell. Time and distance were gone, and motion was a joke. There was no direction to be found, no strength to move arm or leg through that humming cloud of malevolent black bodies, countless yellow eyes aglow.

Geordie shook them off and used sheer force of will to split the thickened spaces of air between himself and Father Lewis. The scroll gleamed and called to him, sang a song of sweetness and rest. Suddenly the priest's danger meant nothing, the whirring cameras and the clicking shutters meant nothing, the desert and the sky were shorn of all meaning and dwindled to afterthoughts of fallen gods. All that mattered was to reach the scroll.

The flies swarmed up, a column of blackness mounting the blue curve of heaven, and plummeted down in a burst of obliteration that took dull yellow form and taunted Geordie out of a single, yellow, saucer-shaped eye. The man's eyes focussed on the demon for an instant, and Geordie's heart lurched in protest at the unbearable repugnance of that impossible creature. His brain refused to believe it, and his reason wailed pitifully inside his blazing skull, battering itself against walls of shadow in desperation to escape.

The sun saw Geordie stagger, topple, fall. It saw the unthinkable thing open a foaming dog's mouth in awful laughter, then melt into a thick miasma that spread unchecked over Geordie, over the newsmen, over the camp, over an always widening area of desert until all that was visible was a bewildered Father Lewis holding aloft a glorious golden light and moving his lips in rapid prayer. The light solidified into the figure of a man with a hermit's ascetic face and a glory in his smile that was all blessing. The image lingered only a moment, then melded with the fog.

The mist lifted. Bloodless faces looked from friend to friend. Did you see it, too? each asked each. Did you see it, too, or am I going mad alone? Or are we all going mad together?

They pinched each other and spoke in whispers. The cameramen stroked their instruments for comfort and felt the metal go cold and wet, as if the cameras themselves were sweating ice-water. A thin film of green slime clung to the shiny metal and blurred the lenses.

"Well, said one, trying to find a toehold back to sanity, "we—uh—maybe we should see what we got. On film. You know?" There came agreement and a general move towards the portable darkrooms.

"None of that's going to come out on film, you realize,"
said the woman from NBC. "There's no way that we'll be
able to prove what we saw. I mean, I know I saw it. The dog,
it just—" She hesitated, afraid that she was about to describe a
vision that no one else had shared.

"It looked like it blew up," said her lover. "That dog
looked like it blew up. How about that?" He began to giggle.
"Boom. No more dog. Blew up *real* good. How about that?"
He could not stop giggling until he was crying instead.

Trying to lighten things up, one of the junior-grade cameramen asked, "Hey, anybody here remember *Ghostbusters*?"
He was coldly ignored.

Father Lewis lowered the scroll but could not let go of it.
Geordie Burns lay unconscious and untouched not three feet
away from him, yet the British priest had lost the will to
move and the courage to be parted from the scroll. Steve
Ritter was the first to go to Geordie's aid, with Faith close
behind. Father Lewis stood and stared as they worked on the
fallen man.

"I was safe, you know," mumbled Father Lewis. "He
couldn't touch me. I was safe while I held the scroll. He was
afraid of it. I was altogether safe. He didn't have to try to
save me. There wasn't any need to save me while I have the
scroll."

"Oh, shut up about the scroll and do something!" Faith
lashed out. She had been far from the center of things when
the entire scene unfolded. So far as she and the others knew,
a bizarre yellow fog had blotted out the camp for a brief time,
then lifted as inexplicably as it had fallen. That was all she
knew until Steve came barrelling into Dr. Hack's presence
like a madman, hollering something about Geordie and a fall.

It must have been some fall. Everyone around poor Geordie
looked bruised. But what had he fallen off of and what had he
landed on? His face was floury white and dry, except for a
patch of sticky sweat across the brows. His eyes were closed,
the pupils nearly visible through translucent lids ridged with
purple veins. The smudges beneath and the dark hollows
under his cheeks had turned an imposing young man into a
parody of old age. His strong arms hung slack, their strength
useless. His breath would barely stir a feather.

Dr. Hack came swaggering onto the scene, clamoring for
an explanation. The newspeople tried to tell him what had
happened, but for once words failed them. Father William

was speaking urgently to Father Lewis, and there was no
hope of getting anything out of either one of them until they
settled their private dispute. Father William was trying to get
the partially rewound scroll away from his friend, and Father
Lewis was holding onto it with a grip more tenacious than
death.

Ms. Louise Ferrabosco took seven deep breaths, as pre-
scribed by her therapist, and recalled the magic dictum for
living, "The worst that can happen usually won't." What
could happen at worst? She could tell her story and Dr. Hack
would think she was insane. Ah, but there were too many
fellow madmen around for him to do that, and when the
majority is crazy, the sane ones are kept in asylums. She
knew that well; she'd majored in World History.

She took one more deep breath for luck, said to herself, "If
he calls me mad, I'm still his employer, and I'll fire the twit
for that!" and with this comforting thought, she tugged at Dr.
Hack's elbow and began to explain.

5

Last Week's News

I DON'T BELIEVE it,'' Lura blinked. "They're still packing! They're still going to leave!"

Gerial scratched his rump and grunted. "Don't tell Horgist," he advised. "Let him find out for himself. After all his work, too! Ungrateful sods. First time in eons that he bestirs himself, gives a truly stellar show, his best since Quintus Pilaster himself, and they're still running out on us." He spat a glob of acid accurately down upon the media tents. Several holes sizzled open in the canvas.

"As far as I can gather," said Melisan, painting her toe-nails with a bottle of MIZ SCARLETT polish purloined from Ms. Ferrabosco, "they were quite impressed with Horgist's act. They were even more impressed when he allowed some of their film to develop successfully, even if the rules dictate that he had to fog the film a wee morsel. But I think he made a mistake there, with the films. See, now they have photos, they don't need to hang around anymore. They won't admit it, but they're scared to stay. Now if they'd seen Horgist at work but had no proof, they'd stick around to snag a shot or two, scared or not. But they've done their duty and now they

can hightail it for home without a qualm." She breathed on
her wet nails.

"I don't suppose we need them to stay," said Lura. "We
have the diggers left, even if the others go. Lots of souls."

"I don't know, I just don't know," sighed Gerial, giving
his backside a vicious scratch. "Horgist is the oldest demon
here, and therefore the smartest, but I get the feeling that all
of his plans could stand a little improvement. He doesn't
think them through."

"Horgist isn't the oldest," said Melisan. "That would
be—" Lura's dry sob caught Melisan before she could say
the name. "Well, he's not oldest," she finished lamely.

"Age has nothing to do with it," said Gerial. "Between
the three of us, we've got a combined set of age and wisdom
that can't be beat. Didn't Melisan just point out what was
wrong with Horgist's dog act? Couldn't we all, together,
come up with a flawless plan?"

"Right now?" asked Melisan. "My nails are still wet. And
anyway, shouldn't we get Horgist in on this?"

"Oh, you know Horgist. If it's not his idea under discussion, he sacks out on us. Goes right to sleep. It's not polite,"
said Gerial, picking his nose, "but we've all fallen down on
our manners out here in the boondocks."

"We could formulate a plan and then give it to Horgist as a
surprise!" brightened Melisan. "He'll stay awake for it then!
The only vital thing is that we all take part in the execution of
it."

"Agreed," said Gerial, squatting beside the winged succubus. "Lura, do you have any inspirations to lend us?"

Lura made random patterns in the sand with her tail. "Me?
Oh, not this instant. My mind's still half-asleep. I'll take a
short stroll, if you don't mind, and wake up. It was such a
strenuous night! Your forget that I was put on nightmare
watch with Geordie. See you." She ambled off.

"Don't believe that for a second," Melisan said quietly to
Gerial. "I know where she went last night, and it wasn't to
play nightmare nurse to the sick one. She's looking for . . .
him."

"Him?" Gerial looked stupid.

"You know who," said Melisan. "The bottle. I don't trust
Lura. She gets all sentimental at the worst times. If she finds
it, she'll open it, you mark my words."

"She wouldn't," said Gerial, who hoped she would. "If

she did that, he'd—he'd be so busy punishing us that we'd still be at it by the time all the mortals cleared out of here.''

"Don't I know it!" said Melisan. She still remembered some of the absent Atamar's more creative punishments. "I think we ought to tell Horgist what she's up to."

Gerial's color went from cobalt to sky-blue. "Must we?" he squeaked. "Wouldn't it cause a lot of hard feelings if your suspicions turn out to be false? We—we might need all the help we can get for the final soul-netting, and we're working short-handed as it is."

Melisan searched Gerial's face. "Do I detect someone about to ask another nameless party to share roosting place with him once we get home?" she asked slyly.

Gerial blushed purple. "Nothing of the sort," he said hotly. "I'm just playing devil's advocate. Do what you like about Lura. She's nothing to me."

"I suppose it wouldn't hurt to keep an eye on her without playing tattle-tale to Horgist," sighed Melisan. She swung a well-formed foot under Gerial's nose. "Do you think this polish is me?" she asked.

The blue demon pushed Melisan's foot aside and stood up. "I've got an idea!"

"Chalk up another miracle for Quintus," Melisan remarked dryly.

"Why should we give up on all the extra mortals around just because they're making plans to go? We ought to know how easy it is for plans to fall flat."

"If you're trying to depress me, Gerial . . ."

"I'm trying to tell you—and Horgist, when I see him—that we should *move* on the extra mortals now! Right now, while we've still got 'em. Disguise ourselves as some of their own, infiltrate, play the part of—what did Murakh call them? Dorian columnists?''

"*Fifth* columnists. And that was a long time ago."

"So what? Let's *do* it!"

Melisan raised one brow. "I thought you had enough on your plate already, what with trying to corrupt that total innocent. You know, the mush-face."

Gerial hid his discomfort with some effort. "He's—doing all right, But he's a slow learner. I prefer my victims to have a little groundwork done on them before I dig in. True sin requires a firm foundation."

"It might be fun at that to try our luck with different

targets, as long as we do have them to hand,'' Melisan mused. ''All right, I'm with you. Let's tell Horgist.''

She tried to give him the secret handshake, but only succeeded in smearing her manicure.

''Any word?'' asked Faith. Ms. Ferrabosco looked distracted, or perhaps she simply did not hear the question. The media people were leaving as noisily as they had arrived. Faith could still remember that day, shortly after Ms. Ferrabosco herself showed up, when the horizon bubbled with land vehicles of all shapes and sizes and a second camp sprang up at a distance from the first.

''Any word?'' Faith asked a second time. Ms. Ferrabosco's bright, birdlike eyes looked dull and sad. She shook her head.

''I really think we'll have to fly him out of here,'' she said, looking over her shoulder to where Geordie's silent tent brooded. She had just left him in Steve's care, with Father Lewis sleeping fitfully on a cot. He could not be persuaded to leave the tent.

''Yes,'' Faith concurred. ''Maybe that would be best. Can we get a helicopter with stretchers?''

Ms. Ferrabosco drew a ravaged sigh. ''What a pity,'' she said. ''This will break Randolph's heart, you know. We'll seem to be running out on him, and this dig does mean so much to him!''

''Do you mean Dr. Hack?'' asked Faith, knowing the answer but wanting to hear a first-hand confession. Since Geordie's fall, Ms. Ferrabosco had been spending much time being consoled by the good professor. Together they had shared many a vigil by Geordie's bed side. The press had made minor hay of the human interest angle, but there was only so much to be extracted from a pair of middle-aged angels of mercy like Hack and Ferrabosco. Giuliana Caruso said some nice things about the symbolism of the old feasting on the ruined bodies of the young, but no one took her seriously anymore since Mario's total breakdown. She had no photos to back up any of her columns, which was tantamount to writing on water.

''Yes, Dr. Hack, of course,'' said Ms. Ferrabosco rather stiffly. She did not like this Faith thing. She made the older woman nervous. Under that curly head, behind those too-shining eyes, there were an awful lot of secrets and a powerful backlog of mindless energy. Run an extension cord up to

her, and you could light Detroit on Faith's private dynamo.
"He has been a great inspiration to us all, wouldn't you
say?"

"Oh, I thought Dr. Hack was great even before we found
Quintus," said Faith. "He's just had hard breaks. It's all
luck, being in this world, and he never got his fair share of it.
Now Geordie, I thought there was a man who'd gotten his
helping of good karma and the next guy's as well. You don't
get looks like that by accident, and a brain, and on top of it
all, he's a nice person."

"I wouldn't say he's been entirely lucky after what happened to him," Ms. Ferrabosco's voice was wintry. She
definitely did not like this girl. Only the fact that Faith
Schleppey was a paying client kept her from administering a
formal dressing-down, plus a lecture on respect for elders.
Why, the snip was speaking to Ms. Ferrabosco as to an equal!
Did you ever hear the like? By God, even if it meant admit-
ting her age, Ms. Ferrabosco would have to assert her superior years if this chit got any further out of hand.

"I didn't see what happened to him," said Faith, "and if
you ask me, I think it was a combination of strong sun and
mass hypnosis. There've been other cases like this, mass
hypnosis coupled with mass hysteria. Like the old witch
hunts. They saw demons in every chamber pot."

"We are living," said Ms Ferrabosco, fighting homicidal
urges, "in the twentieth century, child."

"The same century that's dished out more horrors than any
devil could ever dream of. I don't know what all the fuss was
about. A big yellow demon with one eye, big deal! It's not
the demons I can see that worry me," she ended with a grin.

"I prefer to keep an open mind," Ms. Ferrabosco became
haughty.

"Well, so do I, but there's a point past which a liberal
thinker becomes a gullible sucker. For instance, take Don
Swann. All this gabble about demons has got him nose deep
in a bargain-counter Satanism manual. He wasn't even there
when the alleged demon appeared, but he's all set to stage a
Black Mass and call it back again to cure Geordie. A nice
fellow, but he'll believe anything when it comes to the supernatural. He also does Tarot."

Ms. Ferrabosco said nothing. She was thinking of Olga
Hansen back in New York, Ms. Ferrabosco's personal astrol-
oger. Olga had warned her about the words of skeptics. Her

cusp could shatter if she listened to a nonbeliever for more than twenty minutes. Astrology wasn't serious, just fun, but you never knew and you couldn't be too safe, could you?

"Do excuse me, Faith," said Ms. Ferrabosco, patting the girl's cheek. "You've been delightful, taking my mind off poor Geordie's illness with that darling tale of what Don's up to, but I must go. Perhaps I'll see if he needs help calling up the Devil? Such imagination, you kids have! Ta." A hasty look at her watch showed her safely away from Faith with ninety seconds to spare. Her cusp was secure.

Geordie was pale. The lack of blood beneath his heavy tan turned his skin tone from hearty brown to weak yellow. Sweat trickled down his face, soaking the bedclothes, foiling Steve's attempts to blot it all up and keep his friend comfortable.

Father William looked up from his breviary. "Any change?" he asked.

Steve shook his head. "This is something they didn't mention in any of my health ed classes," he said.

"It isn't anything they mentioned in any medical school either, to hear them tell it," growled Father William. He referred to the bewildered diagnoses of the two medicos who had followed the media into the Marmota wasteland. The doctors spoke of needing better facilities, of having to make further tests, of the lack of laboratory results. "All of which is Latin for saying they don't have the foggiest idea of what's wrong with him," said the priest.

"I do," said Father Lewis, waking up, still holding the scroll. "And so do you, William, but you won't admit it. You'd let him lie there suffering when the cure is a stone's throw away."

"Oh, for—!" Father William gritted his teeth, exasperated with a scene he had played out many times before with his colleague. "Do you still believe that—? Fine! Great! Perfect! I give up! We'll do it, Lewis. Yes, we'll do it. Why not? But do let's hurry up and get started while the press is still here to record us making fools of ourselves for posterity. Can you imagine the good impression we'll make? You know what he wants us to do, don't you?" Father William turned to his sole witness, Steve. "An exorcism! Straight out of the shoddy novels and sleazy movies. Why not just send for a faith-healer or two and a couple of snake-handlers while we're at it? Give the media what they paid for!"

Father Lewis did not raise his voice. Ever since his experience with the demon he had retreated into himself, his grip on the outer world only as firm as his grip on the scroll. Outside the tent pure sunlight shone, but Father Lewis walked a narrow way, a crumbling path above the blackness of a hundred smoking chasms. He balanced his sanity on the tip of the scroll, and it was a tottering place to perch.

"I only wanted to help him," said Father Lewis softly. "I want to touch him with it, and by a single touch he'll be cured. You've seen its power. You know what it can do."

"You just hold onto it yourself," barked Father William. "They'll be flying this lad out of here to a hospital, and then we won't need to worry."

"They'd better hurry up about it," mumbled Steve, fighting his losing battle with the rivulets of sweat that drained and chilled Geordie's body.

Father Lewis said nothing, resigned to bear with the scorn of the doubtful. He held the cure, and he alone knew it for what it was. He could wait. If the boy died, it would not be a death they could blame on him.

Father William stalked out of the tent, continuing to rail at mumbo-jumbo and superstitious tripe. A strange quiet descended. Steve worked in silence, Father Lewis chose not to break it, and Geordie was out of it. From time to time the British priest would hug the scroll a bit more tightly and look as if he were about to volunteer some action, but each attempt ended with him subsiding.

At last Steve said, "You can touch him with the scroll if you want. If it'll make you feel better."

Father Lewis shook his head. "You don't think it will make *him* feel better, though. Don't humor me, lad. A miracle's a wonderfully delicate thing. If the scroll does heal your friend, it will prove nothing. Father William will be loudest in claiming that young Burns would have recovered on his own, at that selfsame moment; coincidence. And if nothing happens, it's proof that all miracles are frauds." He sighed and added, "Do you believe in miracles?"

"Yes." No further elaboration was offered.

The British priest smiled. "You would. You're young."

"This isn't helping me keep my youth," Steve sighed. "Know where I can find some dry cloths around here, Father?"

Dr. Randolph Hack cursed creatively for five minutes, then

started smashing things. The smashing took less time than the cursing. There wasn't much in his tent that he could afford to smash. A few shards of noncommittal pottery from last year's dig and a mass-produced good-luck Chinese godling given to him by a besotted coed some fifteen years ago, and that was all.

Outside his tent, he heard the babble of reporters and techies hell-bent to get packed and get out, back to their idea of civilization. Quintus Pilaster wasn't news anymore. In spite of all they had witnessed, the dig was old hat. Ms. Ferrabosco hadn't said a word to him yet, but Dr. Hack knew what was coming.

"What more do they want?" he cried. Gerial, hovering in the lee of his rage, had asked a similar question. Now the demon observed the doctor and hoped to pick up a few pointers on how to get and hold the fascination of the press.

"What more?" This time the question came as a groan. "They even got parts of it on film. Proof! Unless . . ." Gerial leaned closer, eager to hear what Dr. Hack would say. "Unless they don't believe their eyes anymore. Or their cameras. It's all a cheat. Everything's a cheat. What can you believe? The demon dog could have just been some hokey set of special effects dreamed up in a movie studio. Oh, it was good, but these things can be faked. Yes, I can hear them saying that right now! A nicely staged show, with Geordie and the priest in on it." Dr. Hack's voice was bitter, his smile dead.

"Special effects?" Gerial asked aloud.

Dr. Hack flinched. The voice was back. It had changed, but it was back. Maybe he was losing his mind. Maybe all of this, the dig, the finding of Quintus, the battle on the desert, the ever-hungry media, all were part and parcel of his madness.

"I thought you were gone," said Dr. Hack.

"Um . . . N-no," admitted Gerial, taken by surprise. "I'm right here." He wondered whether he should materialize or not. This wasn't at all usual, having one's potential victim address you as if talking to unseen voices was the order of the day. It unnerved the blue demon. Faintly he wished that Atamar were there to help him.

"Good," said Dr. Hack. "Welcome back. They can pull the dig out from under me, they can fire me, they can deny me the one big discovery of my life, but if a man's got his own madness, that's one thing they can't deprive him of. Don't you agree?''

"Oh," said Gerial, nibbling a hangnail.

"You do sound different," said Dr. Hack, suspicious and cagey. "You sound less masterful than before. What's the matter, friend? Don't tell me you've lost your nerve! That would be too much for me. What good is a man's madness if it's weak-kneed and chicken-livered? At least give me the dignity of a healthy madness!"

Nothing. Gerial was backing away. He did not like this scrawny, speckled little mortal. There was something danger-ous brooding within him, under that thatch of sandy hair. It would be child's play to slip beneath the skull and read his secrets, but Gerial hesitated. He didn't think it would be a pleasant journey. He'd had his fill of sub-cranial surprises with Steve. He decided to leave Dr. Hack untouched. It wouldn't do to poach on Atamar's preserves anyhow, whether or not they ever freed Atamar to take up where he'd left off with the good doc. Taking a deep breath, Gerial passed out of Hack's tent and donned the seeming of a cameraman, part khaki, part Coors.

"Hello? Hello. Are you there?" called Dr. Hack. He got no reply. He harked for a time, then shrugged his shoulders and resigned himself to the silence. "Well, Hack, you're not completely batty yet," he said. "But not far from it. I wonder when I'll go tilting over the edge?" With that cheer-ful thought, Dr. Hack left the tent in search of a broom. The Chinese good-luck godling had smashed into some very sharp fragments.

Horgist was enraged. He simmered beneath the surface of the sand and seeped up in a myriad of probing tentacles to explore the souls of the media folk above him. In each and every soul he found the sweet seeds of damnation, eagerly waiting to sprout and bloom, but no lack of scruples and outworn moral principles to stunt their growth.

How dare you leave! he fumed, while lust and lechery, gluttony and greed, hate and ruthlessness and wrath eddied useless in the air around him. Any one of you could fill my need for a soul, and still you go! What do you want from us? What haven't we given you? Stay! Stay with us for a little while longer, and I'll give you stories that you'd never dare to print, but that you yourselves can live out in flesh instead of paper.

His impotent thoughts bubbled up through the sand and rose in waves of heat from the desert floor. The media folk mopped their brows and remarked on the temperature and how good it would be to get back to Cairo and air conditioning and cold beer.

Horgist was still fuming when Melisan shimmied through the sand to tell him Gerial's inspired plan.

"Well, I'll be . . . what I already am. Not bad, not bad at all."

"Shall we?" Melisan offered an arm to her new chief.

Horgist's sole eye winked and underwent immediate mitosis. His yellow hide vanished under Hong Kong–tailored Egyptian cotton. Sculptured black hair and the sincerest of chin dimples materialized. He was every inch the top-pay anchorman, and more than that below the alligator belt.

"Let's."

In his tent, on his cot, while Steve turned away to get a fresh cloth, Geordie began to change.

6

Our Brothers in Science

"WE'RE ALL SET," said the bright young thing who hoped to become an anchorwoman someday. In the meantime, she was a gofer. That was her unofficial job title, her official one being full of words like administration and assistant and auxiliary and secondary. But what she was was a scurry-and-run person, in charge of tidying up details. She was always chipper. She could handle world disaster, international war, and a mammoth hangover and *still* stay chipper. Her superiors hated her guts.

"Are we," stated one such superior, a camera jockey who called his work cinematography. "Super. I'm glad to see the last of this hole. If you ask me, the only story we're going to get out of here is the old man's going crazy. He talks to himself, have you noticed? And he's mad as hell at us."

"What for?" the bright young thing wanted to know, deeply offended. "What've we done to him?"

"We're walking out on him, sweetie," said the cameraman, speaking as if to a backward child. "No more freebie PR. I got a look at him while you were stowing Linda's makeup case in the jeep, and if looks could kill—Well, maybe we'd have a story after all if he goes totally wacko and hatchets some geek from ABC. Ah, would he might slaughter someone from our network as well! I fairly drool with visions of memorials to be filmed and broadcast on the evening news. A Linda Hathaway retrospective. Martyr to television journalism succumbs to madman. Sheer poetry. Did you pack my shorts?''

"Yes, sir," said the bright young thing, raptly drinking in his every word. There was so much to learn!

"Speak of the devil," said the cameraman casually. Dr. Hack, mercifully hatchetless, was tramping up the dune towards them. "I'm afraid to ask what he wants."

The bright young thing feared nothing but dismissal. "May I help you, Dr. Hack?" she twinkled.

Dr. Hack ignored her. Anyone that pert and helpful must be the lowest of the low in the local pecking order. The cameraman looked snooty enough to be important. Dr. Hack addressed his comments to him alone.

"You might as well unpack," said the good doctor, trying to look and sound nonchalant while inside he danced a jig. "It doesn't look like you'll be leaving for a while."

"Sorry to disappoint you, Dr. Hack," said the cameraman, returning the archeologist's languid look with interest, "but we've heard otherwise. Not that we won't be back . . . someday. And of course *National Geographic* will want to drop by eventually. But for the moment we must regretfully—"

"Unpack, Sam," the command hit the cameraman like a fist to the windpipe. It came from no one less than Linda Hathaway. For a martyr to journalism, she was looking very well. "We're not through here yet."

The cameraman managed a sickly smile that fooled no one. "Something wrong with the jeep?" he asked tentatively.

"Don't be stupid," snapped Ms. Hathaway. She left it at that, going on to oversee the unloading of all her network's jeeps. It was her policy never to give away any news unless the cameras were on her.

"Why do you think—?" the bright young thing began. Her question was pointless. The camerman was as ignorant as she. Dr. Hack smirked, holding all the answers.

"Why—?" croaked the cameraman.

"Were you speaking to me?" inquired Dr. Hack. Sam nodded. "Someday came sooner than you expected, didn't it?" he gloated. How sweet it was to drag out the mystery, to make these mediacs suffer all the uncertainty they normally inflicted.

"Why," Sam asked, "the sudden change?" His dreams of cool hotel rooms crumbled.

"I'll be happy to answer your questions," said Dr. Hack, "along with those of your colleagues, at the press conference which I will be hosting for our esteemed brothers in science." He declined to elaborate. Let someone else swear and smash things!

"What the hell—?" said the camerman. He said it alone. The bright young thing was already hard at work unpacking the jeep. Thank heavens she had a challenging career, she thought.

"Let me help you with that, my dear."

The bright young thing paused in her labors and promptly had a religious experience. Suave, serious, and undeniably top of the tag-team broadcasters, the perfectly coiffed and suited vision in Egyptian cotton was actually talking to *her*.

She did what any gently bred lady would do. She tittered like a chipmunk and blossomed into multi-track dithering when Horgist tried to take Ms. Hathaway's makeup case from her hands. "Oh, no, please, you shouldn't bother."

"Why not? It's always a pleasure to help a girl as pretty and talented as you."

Talented? The bright young thing's surprise showed on her face. She knew that she was talented well enough. Her mother also said so. But the network cloutaholics with whom she worked were not so forward with their praise.

"Are you with ABC?" she asked. If this was the sort of geek a crazed Dr. Hack might hatchet, it would have to be over her dead body.

Horgist projected sincerity, at the same time side-stepping her question. "I'm sure ABC would be proud to have someone like you working for them. I've been keeping my eye on you, you see, and I'm impressed. What I don't understand is why your network brass are still keeping savvy like yours under wraps."

"They're—bringing me along."

"Well, they'd better bring you along double-quick, before you're snapped up by another network. It's astounding how your people can keep a mummified relic like Linda Hathaway on the air and a hot comer like you in the cellar. You know. . ." Horgist set down the makeup case and put one

arm around the gofer-turned-sacrificial lamb. "I've got connections. I could make you a star."

"Oh, I'm going to be a star. It's just a matter of time."

"Don't say that, honey. A matter of time can stretch itself
out into a matter of years. I know. Let me make your dreams
come true."

The bright young thing guessed what was coming next. She
might look like cream-filled spongecake, but Horgist was
righter than he knew when he said she had savvy. "And
what's my end of the deal?" Her frown and her tone made it
clear that she knew that her end of it was to be his.

Horgist flashed her the pearlies. "You're jumping to con-
clusions. I can assure you, love, I'm not after your body."
He made an odd gesture over his heart that was almost a
cross. "Promise."

"Oh." The bright young thing sounded disappointed. Horgist
would never know that her frown had not been Puritanical,
but pragmatic. She was trying to recall where she'd packed
her safety supplies.

"Trust me, and you can kiss oblivion *adios*. Why wait for
their 'someday'? Why not *now*?"

"Because my biorhythms said 1989."

"Your what?" Horgist's arm slipped off her shoulder.

"My biorhythms. Actually it's the new system, twelve-
curve programming, all verified by computer. I've got some
false intersections coming up this year, and if I put too many
big career changes on line now, I'll blow them all. So I'm
going to succeed in 1989—April or May—and I'd be a fool to
make my move before the curves all peak. Blow my circadian
differential to hell."

"Blow what?"

The bright young thing seized Horgist's hand. "Come with
me and I'll show you what I mean. I never travel without my
charts. Gee, I just can't believe that a big name like you
hasn't had his curves plotted. What *did* you say your name
was?"

On his lonesome, a chastened Sam decided to find a spot of
shade and sit out the madness. Not going? What was there to
stay for? It beat hell out of him.

"She can't treat you that way."

A shadow crossed his path, a shadow with a minicam
perched on its shoulder like a pirate's parrot. Sam immedi-

ately recognized a fellow cinematographer, though nothing
else about the disguised Gerial looked familiar. *Must be from
one of the other teams,* he thought.

"Ah shit, that's just Linda's way," he said.

" 'Linda'? You're on a two-way first-name basis with her?
Tell that to the Marines!" It was the best Gerial could do.
Murakh hadn't been as thorough with his infusions of modern
slang as he'd been with other gifts. "What's she without you?
Did she ever once stop and think what she'd look like if you
. . . *did* things with the lighting? The camera angles? We're
the image-makers, man! We're the ones who can make or
break those mike-suckers. She oughta kiss your cam!"

"Fat chance," Sam said. He didn't know who this bozo
was, but he had a depressing way with telling the truth.

"Not so fat as that." Gerial jerked his head. "Let's find us
a coupla brews and talk . . . possibilities."

Sam knit his brows. Could this be a subtle job offer from
the competition? He knew he was worth more than he was
getting, but that seemed to be classified information where
the world was concerned. Maybe not, though. His work
spoke for itself. Someone on another network might've noticed. He wasn't going to screw this up by acting too eager.

"Tell you what," he said to Gerial. "I'm willing to talk,
but first I'd better do a little unpacking of my own, if we're
really going to be staying here. I'm the game warden for our
camera crew." He laughed at Gerial's bemused expression.

"Keeper of the game! When we're not working, it's the
only way to unwind and keep the troops happy."

"What game are you talking about?"

Sam had Gerial accompany him to one of the jeeps, where
he extricated a thick, square blue box. Inside was the folded
board, the two decks of cards, the die, and the distinctive
round markers with their small compartments for collecting
the pie-shaped tokens in pink, yellow, green, brown, orange,
and blue. Gerial had never seen the like.

"You going to play a game with that now?" he asked,
excited.

Sam thought it over. It was the perfect ploy if he was going
to play hard-to-get with this headhunter. "Why not? I could
use a round myself. What color you want to play?"

"Blue."

The rumors began to fly. There was no way of confirming

or denying them, apart from bearding the formidable Ms.
Hathaway in her canvas lair. Linda Hathaway was the number
one top-ranking journalist among all the throng, an anchorwoman with star quality and star billing. True, there were
more anchorpeople than she alone at the site, but any fool
will admit the difference in status between someone anchor-
ing out of New York or L.A. and someone playing Walter
Cronkite in Keokuk.

Linda Hathaway loved the news. She mourned the days
gone by when ace reporters wore trenchcoats and smoked
cheap cigars while bringing desperate criminals to justice in
print. Not that she liked to smoke cheap cigars herself, but
the spirit of the crusade lived on in her bosom. The tatty
trenchcoat had been replaced by the smartly cut blazer and the
cheap cigar by the rabid non-smoker, yet Linda Hathaway
preserved both images in her mind whenever she faced the
cameras. There was an intensity about her, a hard air of
no-nonsense coupled with a basic goodness. In her earlier
days as an ordinary reporter she had never sprung the classic
question, ''And tell us, Mr. Smotz, how did you feel when
you heard that your daughter had been raped and murdered?''
Linda Hathaway knew what made an eagle and what made a
vulture, and she was one of the eagles.

She was also irascible. She was also gruff. She was also
impatient with stupid people, and her line of work thrust her
in with more than enough fools. The result was that she
would not speak to her co-workers any more than necessary,
and so it happened that one of the world's most articulate
people on-camera was a word-miser outside of the studio.

Dr. Hack was grateful for whatever quirky godling had
made Ms. Hathaway the way she was. She had been the one
to seek him out and inform him of The Secret, but once
having told him her news, she would not tell another soul.

''We'll be staying,'' she clipped. She had just yanked back
his tent flap and rifled the words inside. Dr. Hack, lying flat
on his cot and dreaming of doom, scrambled to his feet and
begged her to repeat those golden words.

''I said we'll be staying. My network. I just got a wire
from base. You can see it, then shred it. If we can keep the
others out of this, swell.'' She gave him the wire and watched
the professor grow incandescent with joy as he read it.

''Keep it quiet if you can,'' she said. She knew he would.
There were an awful lot of bad qualities hiding out inside that

funny little man, some going as deep as his bones. He wouldn't be the one to spread the news when withholding it would be so much crueller and more satisfying.

Ms. Hathaway was right, as usual. Dr. Hack told no one a thing about the contents of the wire. He not only shredded it, he burned it, and she wouldn't have been surprised to hear he'd swallowed the ashes. What she didn't know was that Dr. Hack armed with a delicious secret he could not tell was twenty percent chattier than Dr. Hack without a secret. He hinted.

So the rumors flew. Dr. Hack launched most of them. It didn't take the rival networks long to catch on that something was cooking. They ordered their gear unpacked and their tents unfurled once more. They nosed about, trying to get a second hint, a more specific hint about what was going on. Dr. Hack smiled, pregnant with mystery, and clove to his cute little remark about "our esteemed brothers in science." It drove sane men mad.

"What brothers in science?" asked the bright young thing.

"Do you suppose it's newsworthy, or just a ruse?" asked the moon-faced girl from NBC. She was running low on Johnny Walker, and she wanted to be positive about things before bringing in a fresh supply. That Arab boy, Abou or Ali or whatever his name was, would be honored to fill her order, at his own price. For her the question now was, could she tough it out dry? Dry for how long? Why wasn't that Hack bozo talking? The nerve, making a helpless woman go Scotchless for the sake of rumor!

"There's something behind it," pontificated a greying specimen from CBS. He shared the lady's anxieties. In his case it was bourbon, not Scotch, at stake. "Hathaway's in on it."

"You got proof or is this just one rumor bolstering up another?" asked a cynic from ABC.

"What is proof?" Kent Cardiff looked wistful. "And what is Truth, for that matter? Reality is subjective."

He wondered why they all suddenly decided they had important work to do on the far side of the camp.

Up on the black rock, Melisan joined Gerial and Horgist to compare notes. The three fiends were all out of mortal mufti. They were also out of humor. Horgist was putting the finishing touches on a vicious dressing-down, administered to Gerial with more vim than the succubus thought the yeller feller could conjure. The last tongue-lash hit and Horgist knifed into the black rock without a word of farewell.

"What's up his tail?" she demanded.

"He blew it, so he's taking it out on me. Said it was all my fault I didn't get the one I went after because my—my—" he struggled to recall the gibberish "—my intersections were peaking through the apex of my curves? Whatever. And he yanked me out of the game just when I was going to score my sixth piece, the piss-colored bastard!"

"Hmmm . . . Little Gerial's been playing games instead of snagging souls? Naughty boy."

"I suppose you've got a better tale to tell?"

Melisan stuck out her lower lip. "I would've, if not for *her*." She projected an image of the moon-faced girl from NBC and promptly shot it full of holes. "How was I to know that *he* was her lover? He looked like such a gimme! I almost had him, too. Then *she* walked in on us. He's a fast talker, I'll admit it. Before she could say a word, he shoved me into her arms and blabbed that I'd seen her special report on Color-Rating: Career Kill or Cure. Said I'd been so taken by it that when I heard she did unofficial drapings, I came right over. Next thing I know . . ." She flicked out a multi-sectioned plastic sleeve full of colored cloth scraps. "I've been swatched."

"Ix-nay, ix-nay, here comes Ura-lay," Gerial hissed. Melisan turned her swatches to ashes and put on a guileless face as the black-haired succubus climbed the rock.

"What are you doing?" Lura asked half-heartedly.

"Oh, just mortal-watching." Melisan cast her eyes non-chalantly toward the camp below. They happened to light upon Kent Cardiff.

Kent Cardiff reamed out his pipe and filled it with an aromatic blend that cut like a fragrant knife through the thin desert air. The tendrils of perfumed tobacco curved sinuously above his head before they slithered away towards the black rock. The auxiliary team from Marmota smelled Kent's pipe and sighed, to a man desperate for a smoke. There would be no chance of that until breaktime. Ms. Ferrabosco was strict about overseeing the diggers, and she followed Dr. Hack's directives religiously. No smoking while digging. Fallen cigarette ash might harm or confuse precious data, he said. The diggers held their own opinions on the subject, but Ms.

Ferrabosco paid them and it is hard to purchase cigarettes when unemployed.

The wisps of smoke entwined themselves around the jagged edges of the black rock and titillated the demons' noses. Murakh had told them of the blessings of tobacco centuries ago, chuckling merrily over the fact that so many mortals continued to smoke in the face of disgusted neighbors and depressed doctors. He even brought a sack of the weed and introduced them all to the pleasures of smoking, but between his visits they were forced to do without.

"Ah!" Melisan breathed deeply, holding the pungent smell of burning leaves as long as possible. "What I wouldn't give for a good drag of that!"

"What do you have left to give?" sneered Lura. Melisan exchanged a meaningful look with Gerial. Lura had grown bitchy of late. She spent more and more time away from the others, ostensibly tracking down a vulnerable soul. They had not told Horgist a word of their suspicions . . . yet. If Lura didn't straighten out, they might find themselves forced to mention the matter to their new chief.

"Enjoy it," said Gerial to Melisan. "You'll get a lot of it now. They're staying after all."

"Not really!" exclaimed Melisan, ecstatic. "Truly? What happened?"

"Damned if I know," Gerial admitted, "but they're almost totally unpacked. I picked up more than pieces during that game." Lura was too wrapped up in her own thoughts to ask Gerial which game he meant. "Something's up. Looks like we've got all the time in the world to catch a soul now. No rush."

"I'd like to nab one and be done with it," said Melisan, sidling up to Ms. Ferrabosco and peering down at the diggers. They had unearthed a dome-shaped structure that Melisan remembered well. If they moved a few yards to the left, they would turn up another one, and another, although not all in such good condition. Only the top of the dome saw the light at present. Melisan felt an uneasy chill shimmy down her wings. There were too many memories hiding beneath that dull brown dome, some of them already beginning to peep out at her. She didn't like it at all.

She crept back up the rock to crouch next to Gerial, eyes closed, but memory needed no additional prompting. In her mind's eye, the toiling diggers put on the coarse brown robes

of Quintus' monks. She recalled how she had laughed as she
watched them try to breathe life into their pathetic little
garden plot. Quintus told them to dig deeper and deeper still,
for it had been vouchsafed him in a vision that if they dug
deep enough, they would encounter fertile soil and no longer
need to depend upon caravans for charity from the corrupt
cities or hard bargains with pesky nomads.

Melisan knew that if the monks dug deep enough, what
they would find would be the remains of the temple of the
sacred prostitutes, with murals fit to gag a gorgon. Buried
fertility, indeed! How she and her lover had laughed over
that. Her lover . . .

She opened her eyes, and Kent Cardiff's face was the first
specific thing she saw.

Melisan knew one sure cure for banishing unwanted thoughts.

"Where are you going?" Gerial called. Melisan could
stand it no more and had bounded upright, spreading her
wings against the shining sky.

"To bum a ciggie, my love," she replied, struggling to
sound calm. The last spadeful of sand out of the pit had
revealed a curious scratch pattern on the wall of the structure.
It was his. She had forgotten that it was his.

"Are you insane?" Gerial demanded.

"Just aching for a smoke. Don't worry, I'll be a good
girl," said Melisan, and beating the air once with her wings,
she was gone.

She landed invisible behind Kent Cardiff's tent where she
put on the guise of a bright young thing, PBS style. Amiable
and intellectual rather than chipper and bouncy, she minced
on stylish tennis shoes to where Kent stood sunk in meditation. What is Truth? he asked himself, and it had gotten to the
point where the answer was, How the hell should I know?

"Good day, Mr. Cardiff," beamed Melisan over the rims
of her Grand Prix sunglasses. Her speech was as crisply
starched as her blouse.

"Eh? Oh, hello there," said Kent Cardiff, his keen analyti-
cal brain whirring like a gyro as he tried to place a name for
this pretty doll of a woman before him. She looked like she
belonged to his entourage, exuding a faint odor of Harvey's
Bristol Cream rather than more common liquors. But who
was she?

Melisan leaned closer, filling her head with the warm
tobacco scent that emanated from Kent Cardiff. Some men

seemed to carry bits of places around with them, scents that
made women think of the sea or the forest or the clean sweep
of an arctic wasteland or the tingling mysteries of undiscovered
stars. Melisan closed her eyes and saw an ancient library,
panelled with dark oak and lined with innumerable books
bound in morocco leather. There was also the russet smell of
brandy.

Suddenly she wanted more than a cigarette.

"I'm so pleased to be able to speak to you at last, sir," she
said, all smooth propriety on the surface. "Please don't try to
recall my name. You don't know it. I'm simply one of many
people working behind you, and happy to do it. Marguerite
Gounod," she presented herself.

"Charmed," said Kent Cardiff. He was never so right.

Melisan now began her weaving, shooting out filaments of
entrapment more subtle than the airiest spiderweb. She never
said a dirty word. She never leered or spoke an off-color
phrase. Her breasts were hidden by a clean white blouse that
betrayed never a whisper of their lush curves. And yet Kent
Cardiff found himself gazing at her innocently upturned face
and dreaming of waterbeds, aphrodisiacs, and black lace
fripperies drenched with the compelling scent of musk.

I say, said Kent Cardiff to himself, and suggested aloud
than he and Miss Gounod retire to his tent to discuss the
nature of the soul.

Oh, Melisan, Melisan, not again, thought Lura, watching
them pass into the tent. The succubus felt cold and sad,
weighed down with a dreadful melancholy that she could not
name. In the ranks of hell there is no need for a living heart, a
throbbing, pumping organ to force blood through demons'
arteries. Indeed, can demons bleed? No need for a heart at
all. A nasty, cumbersome, human thing is a heart. They say it
also serves as a catch-all for emotion, and demons—the best
of them—should never have emotions.

Then what was this stone that Lura felt somewhere between
her breasts? Her tears flowed with acid, searing her cheeks,
but she had no need to shed tears then. Why? She asked that
question, and groped for an answer, and lost it.

"I must be feeling sorry for Melisan," she said to herself.
That made her angry. Why should she feel pity for a fellow
succubus whom she despised? Self-pity was all right, a sanc-
tioned emotion of the netherworld, but this was something
else.

Lura hunched over and hugged her knees. The flap of Kent Cardiff's tent swayed back and forth gently, as if set in dreamy motion by amorous sighs. It was very quiet.

"Quiet, Melisan?" murmured Lura. "This isn't like you at all. Who likes to bite and kick and scream with passion? I've seen the marks you leave with teeth and nails on all your lovers. You haven't been this quiet about it since—My, how time flies."

The tent seemed to agree, shifting and dipping slightly against its ropes, bobbing like a tethered balloon. The succubus stared at the tent, fixing her eyes on the sighing, gasping, whispering flap, until the tent became the only real thing in her world and the surrounding tents, jeeps, people, ghosts, took on the indistinctness of blown dandelion fluff, a mist of whiskery petals.

Time. What is time to a demon? Eternity works both ways for those beings who have no clear memory of a beginning. After those first, most memorable demons, where did the others come from? It is written that they took life from human minds, but who is fool enough to believe what is written? Well, and if that is so, they spring from ideas, mortal or otherwise, and an idea is its own eternity.

Time. Like a blob of mercury in a sealed capsule they are tilted back and forth at the whim of unseen hands, and they must go tumbling back and forth, up and down as the capsule tilts, while helplessly they listen for the laughter.

Time, in whatever direction it flows, grants wisdom. The unseen hands lose their power, or lose interest. With time, the victim becomes the master, capable of tilting the capsule from the inside. Any demon can travel through time. No demon can command precisely when he or she will do it, though. The hands can return at any time, and sometimes they are not the same hands.

Lura watched as time tilted, the tent with Melisan and Kent Cardiff inside sliding away from her down an oblique chute into starlessness.

It was quiet. Lura floated free outside the world, watching the rainbow eddies of time swirl below her over the round, blue, featureless face of the globe. A silken cord wrapped itself securely around her wrist and shot off into a realm that was neither air nor space nor chaos, but the breath of time. At the other end of the string was a canvas balloon that sighed.

They landed on sand, among ranks of brown, dome-shaped

dwellings. Men in long, dirty robes passed back and forth in narrow passageways between the hovels, never exchanging a word. Away from the cramped rows of adobe domes the desert stretched bright wings of light and freedom. The men saw nothing of it.

The canvas balloon landed and blended into a dream that was brown and dome-shaped, with curious patterns scratched into the hard clay walls. The men in their long robes kept far from that place. Without appearing to do much work, they gathered up every bit of movable stuff around them, lashed the slight load to the backs of grey donkeys, and drove the beasts into the desert, their eyes set to the east.

The ghost of the tent wafted illusion around the modest brown dwelling. In all of her travels through air and space and other, Lura had never taken her eyes from it. In places where there was no air to carry sound, Lura had seen the sighs. Now they stopped. Lura waited.

Melisan appeared at the doorway of the hut and looked out over the deserted encampment. A flicker of alarm lit her eyes, but only for a moment. The soft grey shadows behind her darkened as a tall man joined her at the door, a young man looking older because of his beard, a strong young man in a dirty brown robe.

Lura could not hear their words. She had not been any-where near this spot when this lost day had first happened, over a thousand years ago. If she remembered—if she cared to remember—she had been bathing in a hidden desert stream, waiting for Atamar's command.

She knew the young man. He was the only one of Quintus' followers, besides Quintus himself, who was literate. Ambrosius Minimus, he called himself, making much of the joke. He would not give his right last name. The clustered demons were newly arrived on the day that Ambrosius scribed that bizarre pattern on the moist clay wall of his domed hut. His cell.

Melisan wore no wings. She had hidden them beneath layers of cloth and invisibility. The robe she wore was just as rough and filthy as Ambrosius', and her hair was cropped short, just below her ears. She looked like a very pretty boy, but the folds of her robe hung open and it was plain to see that Ambrosius knew her for female.

They spoke, slowly at first, then more heatedly. Lura watched the soundless mouths trade recriminations, saw

Ambrosius raise his hand to strike Melisan, then turn the blow against himself. She watched, detached as only centuries can detach you, as the young man tore himself out of Melisan's grip and ran into the desert, following the trail of his comrades and stumbling in his flight. And never for a moment did his heavy hands cease their punishment of his own flesh.

Melisan wept. *Ambrosius! Oh, Ambrosius, my beloved! Come back to me! Come back! I couldn't help it that Quintus died! I didn't know you loved the foolish man so dearly! You knew me for what I was, and loved me all the same—as I love you. Can't you forgive me? If I could, I would change anything—everything that I am for your sake, for the sake of love. I would give all the powers of Hell to have such love again!*

Lura startled. Out of the soundless past, Melisan's heartfelt cry broke the rule of silence.

"I didn't know that," said Lura, and the force of a spoken word tilted the capsule back again, toppling the brown dome and the demon and the memories of Melisan and Ambrosius back into the twentieth century. Kent Cardiff's tent strained once in an unexpected wind, then was still.

Lura's head reeled with vision. *Strange,* she thought, *so strange to see Ambrosius again, after all these years. You're looking good, my dusty friend, and more toothsome than I remembered you. Who wouldn't give her tail to change the past? What was I thinking of back in those days, that I never noticed how handsome you were, mortal man? What could have been filling my brain?*

Dark wings took the universe, and a beautiful, sad, proud, pleading face appeared inside Lura's eyes, not wavery like a mirage, but strong and sure. He was rock, Atamar, unyielding, and the heavy stone between Lura's breasts called out for him.

She cried out like a frightened kitten and hid her eyes, but his face was cut into the lids, into the glassy surface of the eye itself. Waking, willing, or helpless, she would see him. Her whole body shook with the certainty of it.

"I am cursed," said Lura to the wind, and the wind was hot and fresh from a secret hellmouth, and there it returned, taking her cry along. In a place where thrones are shadows and shadows are dreams, there was laughter, very dry.

Melisan came out of Kent Cardiff's tent with the same

prissy mask she had worn when she first went in. The white blouse was as spotless as before, and as stiff with starch. She had a satisfied look about her, and no blood on her lips.

Behind her, Kent Cardiff managed to keep walking on his feet rather than his knees only by willpower. Plainly Miss Gounod had made quite an impression on the PBS pundit. His lips hung slackly, never to hold a pipe firm again. At least not without physical therapy.

They exchanged a chaste handshake at the doorway, and Miss Gounod pranced gaily over the dunes, humming a marching song favored by the Girl Guides. Kent Cardiff waited until she was well on her way before collapsing backwards into the maternal embrace of his tent, there to pray for a speedy recovery.

"You haven't been smoking," said Gerial sternly when Melisan took her place beside him on the black rock. She had shed the disguise, but she had a mind to use it again, and soon. Kent Cardiff was precisely to her taste, something different, sophisticated, and yet wonderfully debauched under all that tweed and khaki.

"Filthy habit," smiled Melisan. "Makes you smell. And did you know that it can cause cancer, not to mention other respiratory diseases? Horrors! Are you trying to kill me, Gerial?"

"All right," said Gerial, who in spite of his mortal origins could be a sharp thinker. "Who was it?"

"Who was what?" Melisan's eyes were pure.

"Melisan, you're trying my patience. If you're playing wingsy-tailsy with a mortal, Horgist'll want to know. I've been talking to him, and this near-loss we just had, with all those reporters hot to leave, has made him nervous. We'd better center in on a soul." A green lizard crawled up onto the black rock and lassoed an unknown insect with a foot-long tongue. The bug wasn't halfway to the lizard's mouth before Gerial flicked out his sea-dark tongue and snapped up lizard, insect, and all. "—like that," he finished.

"Tell Old Yeller to relax," Melisan yawned. "The pickings will be plentiful and rich before the day is out. My new—friend—is an intelligent man. We discussed so many fascinating things, such as why the media's staying put. Kent has a theory, and I'll bet my toe-ring it's right. We won't even have to lift a finger for them to tumble in our direction." She clammed up then, and Dr. Hack himself could have taken lessons from Melisan on how to torment a friend with I-know-something-you don't-know.

None of Hack's victims were Gerial, of course. Gerial had a good, direct method for dealing with recalcitrant secret-keepers. He grappled Melisan with his tail and whaled the living daylights out of her. He had watched Atamar's ways with the succubi for a long time, and he was pretty good at imitation.

But he wasn't Atamar. Melisan wormed free of his hold and took to the air, dive-bombing the blue demon with everything handy, including her own flashing silver teeth.

The fight didn't last long. No demon can utterly destroy another demon. Which does not mean that it is impossible for a demon to be destroyed, but simply that it takes more than one other demon to do it. Knowing that their battle would be indecisive took most of the force out of it for Gerial and Melisan. She subsided to earth with a weary flutter and he even reached up to offer her a hand on alighting.

"Well?" Gerial panted as both of them got their breath back. A good tussle was painful, but it put other things back into perspective. Somehow Melisan's big secret didn't seem so important anymore, not to Gerial, and definitely not to Melisan.

"There goes my thunder," said the succubus, untangling her golden hair with long nails. "Why bother telling you? Here they come. Look northeast, precious thing."

The miniature cavalcade was unimpressive for a demon who had gaped to see helicopters whupping down from the sky and a flotilla of media vehicles surging over the horizon. Two jeeps? Big deal. Was it for two jeeps that Gerial had chipped a tusk? Must be true what they said, about how sex with a mortal unhinges a succubus. Lura and Melisan both were a bit ga-ga, and Gerial could remember a few of the down-home succubi who were also kind of scramble-brained. Mortals! Nothing but bad news for everybody since the Beginning. Mortals!

Then why had he felt such a curious yearning every time he remembered Steve's words? *In my dream, Gerial, you are mortal again.*

Melisan insinuated a probing thought into Gerial's mind and read his reactions. He felt the coolness of her mind-presence and jumped, "You don't know how annoying that is, Melisan!" he shouted at her.

Melisan didn't flinch. "Those are the breaks, Gerial. You should be grateful that I'm the only one keyed into your brain. Murakh once told me about this poor devil down there whose brain was an open book to a full squadron of succubi. Mind-reading's a gift."

"So is privacy!" Gerial was sore. It wasn't his place to question the work of the Master, who had decreed that all succubi could read the minds of certain other demons. He was grateful that whatever forces governed telepathy had made his mind sealed to all save Melisan. But he hated when she exercised her powers on him.

I ought to be glad she doesn't keep my mind under constant watch, he thought.

"Yes," Melisan teased. "You ought to." Before he could lash out at her, she went on as if she had done nothing wrong. "Do look closer at the jeeps, my friend," she said. "Closer. You'll be more than pleased."

Gerial's eyes were all right, but not telescopic. He saw two jeeps, the first with a single passenger, the second with two heads bobbing and bouncing behind the windscreen.

"What's the big deal?" he demanded. Melisan hadn't waited around to answer him. She was gone, and only a summons from Horgist would bring her to heel. Gerial growled and scampered away from the black rock to learn for himself the fuss over two miserable jeeps.

At the wheel of the first jeep, Yuri was enjoying his last few moments of freedom. Every yard of sand he traversed brought him closer to the end of his golden daydreams and back once again into the dull reality of politically important archeology. If you could have asked him for his opinion, and if Yuri could be persuaded that it was safe to give it, he would say that he understood little about politics and cared less. He grasped the essentials, always voting for the one approved Party candidate simply because it was easier than inventing excuses for not voting. He knew what was the opiate of the People (religion) and what the workers had nothing to lose but (their chains), yet past that point he was happily unconcerned about any event, person, or philosophy that predated the sixth century.

In the jeep immediately behind, the jeep that dogged him more closely than a hungry shark, sat Yuri's partner, Illya. Illya was an altogether different breed of fish. He wore thick, unflattering glasses because he had sacrificed his eyesight equally between the minute details of pottery shards and the dogmatic trivia of Marxist writings. He would argue for hours with backsliders who disagreed with him about how many proletarians could dance on the head of a pin, providing that the blood-sucking capitalist leeches would let them have the pin.

"The trouble with Illya," said one of their fellow-workers on a previous dig, "is that he sees Marxism in every happening, even those predating Marx."

"There is much merit in a Marxist interpretation of history," objected Feng Mei Ling, a comrade from the People's Republic. The discussion was taking place in the days before the great split between the two Communist superpowers. "Even in the Stone Age, the workers felt the beginnings of oppression and imperialism."

"And so they did, but who is to call it a foreshadowing of Marxism? In every action we can find the splinters of a hundred different philosophies, Marx's being only one among many. What I mean is, Illya thinks Marxism is the answer to everything, the cause and the effect of a universe!"

For some reason, they never heard anything more of that outspoken comrade after that.

Yuri saw the twin camps of diggers and reporters on the slight rise ahead. The black rock was edging free of the sand more and more as Dr. Hack's auxiliary crew wormed at the baked clay structure near its base. One end of it was visible in the form of a sharp, upthrusting ship's prow, or the deadly head of a black missile. A party of welcomers came around the jut of rock to greet the Russians, led by Dr. Hack and a cluster of jostling microphones.

Yuri opened his mouth to speak and nearly chipped a tooth on an over-eager mike. The second jeep halted and disgorged Illya and a third person, either male or female. This strangely sexed third party puzzled everyone, Yuri included, and he had been told that Sonia Mikhailovna was female. In the loose white native robes she wore, she might have been a too-pale boy. Her hair was short and unfashionable, her face clean of makeup. On closer examination she was too pretty to be a boy.

"—happy to extend a heartfelt welcome to our brothers in science," Dr. Hack was saying, keeping his face turned more towards the cameras than to the supposed brothers. He was doing his best to be warm, and it was miserable. The three

Russians stood all in a row and waited until he had relieved himself of every last sentiment. Only then did Sonia speak.

"On behalf of my government," she said in flawless, nearly accentless English, "I accept your welcome. Furthermore, on behalf of my government, I wish to hereby officially lodge a complaint with the United Nations, calling for the public censure of this expedition, which has not only shamefully violated the national heritage of of a sovereign Third World Nation, but has also usurped the site whose exploration belongs to these men."

"Huh?" said Dr. Hack.

His hopes of getting a translation were drowned by the forward surge of reporters towards Sonia. They weren't much closer to understanding her than Dr. Hack, but the fine, round tones of phrases like "public censure," "shamefully violated," "sovereign Third World Nation," and "usurped" were pure box-office dynamite.

Claim jumper, chuckled a voice in Dr. Hack's ear. I knew it! Glory, glory, they're back again, and they're all mine!

"Oh, shut up," said Dr. Hack.

He said it aloud, though not very loudly. But you know how it is, even in a group of hungry reporters. There will come an unexpected lull in the conversation when no one at all in the area is saying anything. It is in moments like that that small, privately intended comments sail forth to reach every ear, including those ears never meant to hear.

So Dr. Hack's grouchy "Oh, shut up," winged its way right into Sonia's grave, determined, dedicated face, and it came at the precise moment after Sonia had finished explaining that her government was going to be polite about the whole sticky matter of claiming the site.

As if on a giant pivot, the mikes all whirled around in Dr. Hack's direction, but the cameras were smart enough to split themselves between shots of Dr. Hack's pale, flustered face and Sonia's enraged, insulted one.

"I wasn't talking to—" began Dr. Hack. He looked around and stopped himself. If he wasn't snapping at the Russian, then to whom had he been talking? AMERICAN DIGGER GOES BUGHOUSE. HACK CAN'T HACK IT. BURROWING BRINGS BRAIN BUST. It was easy to think in headlines with so many reporters living at your elbow.

"Does your attitude reflect the general feeling of your team, Dr. Hack?"

"Does this mean you won't be a party to U.S.–Soviet negotiations concerning the site?"

"Are her allegations true about the theft of priceless relics rightly belonging to the Egyptian government?"

"Do you favor a get-tough policy in other facets of our relationship with the U.S.S.R.?"

"Will America back down?"

"Oh, shut up," repeated Dr. Hack, and this time he was universal in his wishes.

"You see? You see?" Melisan did a little caper of glee. "It's less than a matter of time now. It's a matter of politics! Remember what Murakh told us?"

Horgist, heavy with the desire to go back to sleep and shrug off the mantle of command, said, "No." Rather grumpily, too.

Melisan did not like her new leader any more than he liked the sulky, tetchy, unpredictable crew he had become forced to lead. Ambition, Horgist was learning, was a sword that cut two ways and could also stab. Only the constant rehashing of all the warnings he'd had about Atamar's treachery kept Horgist going. The end couldn't come soon enough for him, and then it would be ho! for the throne of Hell and a request for a slight vacation, possibly as the guardian spirit of a dormant volcano. Inspiring, creative, infrequent work, that was what Horgist wanted.

Melisan frowned and informed her leader that politics was the answer to every demon's fondest dreams. Politics, she said, meant less work for Mother. It covered all the bases when it came to the Seven Top Deadly Sins.

"You get a minor political conflict, like, say, an argument over candidates at a cocktail party," said Melisan, who only knew about such gatherings from Murakh, "and right away you generate a whole roomful of Wrath. Then you move on to elections, and you get the bunch that won't vote at all because they don't like either candidate and besides, they figure one vote's not important."

"Ahhh," sighed Horgist, eyes moist with yearning. "Sloth!"

"Exactly, my love. Then someone wins the election, and you've got the ones who voted for him swelled with Pride and the ones who didn't consumed with Envy. Avarice, Lechery, and Gluttony come after he's in office, and that's just what happens in a minor political situation! When you've got

Avarice and Gluttony working on the grand, international scale, you've got the way paved for all-out war, and when what they call National Pride shows up, you've got guaranteed Gehenna. Even—dare I hope to say it?—'' she lowered her voice reverently— ''Armageddon.''

''Melisan!'' said Horgist sharply. ''You're not going to try provoking that?''

''Me? Never, Horgist,'' sighed Melisan. She was one demon who recognized her own limits. Not for her the glory of promoting the mythical Final Conflict. Her sphere of influence was more homey and domestic, but it sufficed.

''Good,'' the big yellow demon said pompously. ''We don't want anyone at home taking us to task for exceeding our authority. I'm responsible for your actions now, you know.''

''I'm not the one who's been doing anything wrong!'' Melisan snapped. And then she very theatrically slapped a hand over her mouth to make it clearer that she'd just said something she didn't want Horgist to know. In a pig's eye.

''Oh?'' said Horgist, his brow rising. Melisan tried to look newborn. ''That's a funny way of putting it.''

''Funny? What's funny about it? Who said it was funny?'' Melisan chattered. ''Really, Horgist, the things you think are funny!''

His flabby paw seized her by the scruff of the neck and swayed her experimentally back and forth, as if gauging her weight before slinging her against the black rock. She wouldn't—she couldn't—die from the impact, but it would crimp her prettiness for awhile if she hit it face first. Even succubi scar.

''Dear Melisan,'' said Horgist while she dangled in the air. ''Let me put it another way. Do you know of anyone who *has* been doing anything wrong?''

''Th- that all depends on what you'd consider to be wrong,'' said Melisan. Inside her golden head she could feel her thoughts bobbling around like ping-pong balls. It had seemed like such a good idea a moment ago! Just a hint, a delicate intimation in Horgist's ear about Lura and what she might be up to. Not an accusation or a betrayal, but just a hint! And why not? It would keep Horgist occupied, too busy to bother watching the rest of them, just in case he should disapprove of Kent Cardiff. It had been known to happen, and a succubus must submit to the decision of her chief regarding the objects of her lust.

I can't do that, she thought. I can't let him find out about Kent Cardiff. There's the slimmest chance he'll want me to leave him alone, to seduce another, and I don't want to!

Not, she quickly answered her own worried thoughts, that I care about Cardiff. Care? Me? I never have and I never will.

She was only thinking about never because she chose to do so. A tall, handsome, bearded, draggle-robed man rose imperceptibly out of the dust of his Alexandrian grave, then subsided. Ambrosius slept well.

"I have no time to waste on philosophy!" roared Horgist, lofting her into the air like a slender javelin and catching her before she hit the ground. "Speak! If I find out you're hiding anything from me—"

She didn't dare. Everything came spilling out, including many a wild guess and theory of her own that now emerged as rockbound facts. Yes, Lura went her own ways with not a thought to seizing souls. Yes, she searched for Atamar, prisoner in his lavender bottle. Yes, she intended to release him and to join with him against Horgist and the others. Yes, yes, yes, anything you want me to say.

Horgist set her down as lightly as if she had been made of china. "Thank you, my dear," he said in his antique, courtly manner. "I won't forget this."

Oh, I wish you would, thought Melisan. I wish you would!

"What are you going to do . . . to Lura?" she asked shyly.

"Do?" repeated Horgist. It was impossible to read his thoughts, almost as impossible to guess at them. A one-eyed face does not transmit many emotions well. "Why . . . I don't know exactly what I'm going to *do*, or if I'm going to *do* anything *to* Lura, as you put it. It may be unnecessary. She may lose interest. And if we bring down our soul before she finds Atamar, the entire matter will be academic, for we'll all be happily back home again—if that's the way the bargain goes."

"You won't tell her I told you?" begged Melisan.

"I doubt it will come up in the conversation," Horgist grinned. His teeth looked like a single slip of bone. "If our Lura does nothing to interfere with our plans, if she makes no overt moves against our purpose, then we'll act as if we know nothing, and if we know nothing, how could your name possibly be mentioned?" He patted her wings chummily.

Why don't I believe him? wondered Melisan.

"Have you seen Gerial?" she asked, just to get her mind away from untranquil thoughts.

"Why?" asked Horgist, quick as a shark. "Does he have something to add to what you've told me?"

"Not a thing, nothing!" exclaimed Melisan. "He didn't so much as notice what Lura was doing until I pointed it out to him. He couldn't tell you a shred more about her." Except I think he thinks she's doing the right thing, Melisan told herself. "I simply haven't seen him around."

"He's been trying his hand on Dr. Hack, most assuredly," puffed Horgist, looking fatter than ever with knowledge. "A good man, fertile ground. Where else should he be?"

"I was wondering . . ." Melisan's voice trailed off. Horgist's eye glowed with interest in her every word. "You know, now that the Russians are back, I haven't seen him and I was thinking . . ."

"He wouldn't," said Horgist firmly. "Not again. We pacted to never say anything about it to Atamar the first time, when we lost our chance with those people, but I won't take the blame for a second failure if he's up to his old tricks."

What have I done? Melisan cried out in silent anguish. Every word from my mouth becomes a betrayal today! I never intended to mention Gerial. I never wanted to tell him about Lura. Why did I?

She shivered as an unseen hand traced the serpentine trail of her backbone from the nape of the neck down between her shuddering wings and ending at the spot just above her sacral dimples. Heebie-jeebies, thought Melisan. No one could be there, doing it. If Lura or Gerial were here, if they'd overheard, they'd be doing more to her than raising ghosts along her spine. And Atamar was gone. Heebie-jeebies.

She snapped herself out of it to plead for Gerial with Horgist. "I can swear he won't do it again," she said. "You know he was a lot younger then, when he loused us up, and still recalling his mortal nature. He fell off the black rock onto his head when we were horsing around and no one thought much of it, but it could have been what set him off with that atrocious book. Remember? Remember how groggy he was?"

"Well, he's had time enough to recover his senses and destroy that book," snorted Horgist. "And he hasn't landed on his head recently. I'm going to keep an eye on him as well

as on Lura.'' Coming from the one-eyed demon, this sounded
like over-reaching himself.

"You don't have to!" squeaked Melisan. Too much vigi-
lance on the part of her chief might mean he'd be keeping an
extra eye on her doings as well. She thought of Kent Cardiff's
tent and all her recent, gusty joys there. In a forgotten grave
in Alexandria the dust of ages shifted a bit.

"I'd rather be safe than sorry," said Horgist, folding his
arms. "It's only for our joint benefit."

"Horgist, relax!" sighed Melisan. "I promise you—I swear
to you—I beg of you to trust me when I say that I will watch
over Gerial—and Lura—and I'll tell you the moment I see
anything amiss. Any glimpse of the purple bottle. Any page
of the awful book.''

"Weelllll . . .'' drawled Horgist. A demon is born to
recognize the signs of incipient temptation. Melisan knew
instantly that Horgist was leaning and ripe to fall.

"Horgist, dear,'' she crooned, stroking the jiggly yellow
flesh, "you know I care for you. I worry about you, too. We
all see how hard you're working for the good of us all. You
have so many important chores to do. Tasks. Labors. Work.
Drudgery.'' She watched, well satisfied, as Horgist's face
grew paler and sadder with each word that took him farther
and farther from his beloved Sloth. "So why not leave this
one teensy job to me? You know I'm your friend. You can
trust me. Didn't I tell you all about Lura and Gerial? Haven't
I always been your closest ally? Hmm?''

He fell with the sodden plump of a rotten peach. "My
darling succubus, what you say is grimoire-true,'' he said,
planting a fatherly slobber on her forehead. "Do as you see
fit. And I thank you.''

Melisan giggled. Horgist attributed it to the strain of receiving so much honor and trust from her superior.

"Don't worry about a thing,'' she said to him. "You know
who's number one with me, fearless leader.''

He thought he did.

In a secret hiding place, the terrible book lay wrapped in
spells, keyed to be broken by a blue hand and none other. On
the flyleaf was the owner's name and address, the address
later scratched out and rewritten as a cheap Bloomsbury hotel
in London that catered to foreign students. The name was also
scratched out and rewritten, probably at the moment when the

proud owner realized that any Englishman finding the precious book would be unable to read the owner's name in Cyrillic.

It was Yuri's copy of *Das Kapital*, in English, bought originally to help him over the pitfalls of that unpredictable tongue. He had lost it on his first dig at this site, not that many years ago. He had not missed it.

Gerial undid the spells and took out the book. Reverently he raised it in the direction of the rising sun, then hunkered down with it, hunched over like a buzzard with a tasty scrag of meat.

He really believed that he had nothing to lose but his chains.

"Good book?" a deep voice inquired from above.

Gerial stiffened and screwed his eyes shut, cringing from the blow about to fall. "Gimme a break, Horgist, I can explain why I still have the book. I figured if the Russians ever came back again I could, y'know, plant it near where they'd dig, give 'em something they could recognize, get their attention so they wouldn't call it quits quite so quick, the way they did last—"

"You don't have to explain yourself to me, Gerial. I'm not Horgist."

Gerial opened his eyes a slit's worth. Steve grinned. The blue demon immediately sealed his gaze, groaned, and tried to escape, but something snapped around his ankle and wouldn't let go. It was Steve's hand.

"I can't force you to give me your hand," the boy said, "but there's nothing in the rules says I can't grab you elsewhere. See what a rotten influence you are? Hang around demons too much and you start finding loopholes in everything."

Gerial tried to shake Steve loose and had the usual luck. An attempt at dematerialization came to naught. He detected the faint aura of supernal power about the boy. A lot of Americans had it, Murakh said. It came from descent from the old New England witches. It wasn't much magic, but it was close enough for jazz.

"You are one weird mortal, you know?"

"We are surrounded by weird mortals—which I think is a redundancy, by the way."

"Yeah, but you're the weirdest of the bunch. You know what I am—"

"It is rather obvious."

"—and here you latch onto me like a bear trap. Most mortals'd take one look at me *au naturel* and run screaming. What is it with you? You play Satanist at school to impress the chicks or see too many reruns of 'Thriller' or what?" He got back into a crouch—an uncomfortable one, attached as he was—and glared.

Steve laughed at the blue demon's indignant questions. "You're angry because your appearance doesn't make the desired impression on me. I've been nothing but a disappointment to you from the moment you stepped into my mind. You honestly don't know me yet, Gerial?" He searched the fiend's face. "No, I see not. And you thought I was the innocent. Innocence is only a matter of not being able to believe in a possibility you can't imagine."

"Uh . . . okay."

The boy let go of the demon's ankle and took up a mirror-image squat facing Gerial. "You don't have to stay, but I'd like you to. I'd like to talk with you, Gerial."

"About selling me your soul?" The blue demon didn't know whether to be avid or apprehensive about the opportunity.

"With a one-track mind like yours, I'm surprised you didn't—what's the phrase?—*land* one of the Russians the first time they came here." Steve prodded Gerial's fallen *Das Kapital* with one finger. "You have a second chance with these three, but why do you need it? Why did your first try fail?"

Gerial got antsy. "Well, damn, we all got to arguing about the best way to attack them and—"

"I don't want the rationalizations you five have spun over the years. You can deceive yourselves, but not me. I want the truth, Gerial."

"All right, all right!" Gerial's tail twitched, avoiding an invisible rocking chair. "We all said we'd act in committee, but we never did. Lura went off and tried to nab some gink named Vlad and blew it. Made mistakes a novice wouldn't try. Horgist kept saying he was too tired. Atamar kept lecturing us on plan, plan, plan, and never did a damned thing besides. Melisan hung around that big mama—Sonia, the one who's back again—and thought no one knew. I did. I snuck off and followed her. This'll kill you, but Sonia's a real balletomaniac. Always travels with a bunch of photos and tapes, and when she's alone in her tent she pretends she's a *prima!* Hell, all Melisan had to do was offer to make her a tippy-toe star and she'd've been ours. Funny thing, Melisan never tried.''

"Funny thing. Why didn't you?''

Gerial shrugged, pretending indifference. "I wanted Yuri. You know, the Jew. I'd had a little experience with King Solomon, so I figured it'd be more of the same kettle of lox. But then I found this book of his, and got wrapped up in it. I just never seemed to get around to tempting him.''

"In the name of merciful sanity, how did you ever hear of lox all the way out in the Egyptian desert?''

"Oh, Murakh brought us some on one of his visits.''

"Murakh . . . I see.''

"Yeah, Murakh's been real good to us. He never stopped believing in us.''

"A demon keeping faith?''

Gerial heard the sardonic tone in Steve's voice. He glowered. "Yeah, keeping faith! What'samatter, you think maybe mortals got the market cornered on—?'' He stopped. His scowl slowly dissolved.

Steve traced a pattern in the sand. "Belief. It's not exactly in the job description, is it?''

"He should've got his butt barbecued.'' Confusion and realization fought each other on Gerial's face. "Gifts, okay, but all that *encouragement* . . . He said he believed in us! I heard him say it enough times over the centuries; his exact words! *Believed!* The Lords of Hell would've had my tail for a toothpick if I even hinted I believed in someone 'sides myself.''

"They are rather big on self in Dis.''

Gerial gave Steve a sharp look. "How would you know?''

"I did Satanism in school to impress the girls, remember?''

The blue demon looked long and hard at the boy's laughing face, a face made to hold back no secrets. "Who are you?'' he asked yet another time.

"A troublemaker like yourself. A tempter. We've had the same basic training, and we work on the same commission.''

Gerial wrapped his arms around his knees and thrust his head forward, the better to stare at Steve. "Uh-uh,'' he said. "No way. They couldn't have changed the basic model *that* much since we've been gone.''

Steve's smile changed to a look of compassion. Gerial felt an odd twinge in his chest. He wasn't used to seeing someone feel sorry for him. "Nothing changes in Hell, Gerial. There isn't even the chance to change. No repentance, no admission of wrongdoing, No change. Think again.''

"I'm trying." Gerial's forehead accordioned in concentration. He drew a blank. "Gimme a hint?"

" 'There are more things in heaven and earth, Horatio, than are dreamt of in your philosophy.' "

"You're . . . Shakespeare?"

Steve lost his balance laughing and landed on his behind. Still laughing, he handed the blue demon *Das Kapital*. "Here, Gerial; read. Read, think, try to open your mind to all the possibilities of existence. And when you have, I'll be waiting for you." He got up, dusted sand off his shorts, and walked away.

"Touched," Gerial said, tapping his temple. He went back to Marx. Somewhere in the back of his mind was the idea of writing his own version of the economic milestone, adapting it to the requirements of Hell. *Dis Kapital?* It had—Gerial heard Steve's voice again—possibilities.

7

When We Last Left Our Hero . . .

FAITH STROKED GEORDIE'S brow and waited. It had been two days since the arrival of the Russians, and still no helicopter came to take Dr. Hack's assistant back to Cairo. What need for that now? asked Ms. Ferrabosco lightly. The fever was broken, he was sleeping normally, he roused himself slightly to take food and drink. He was getting well.

Is that so? Faith wondered. Then why hasn't he said a word to us, any of us? Why does he seem to sleep all the time, even when he's up and eating? His eyes are veiled and dreamy, drowsy. They've turned inward, and I don't think they're the same color they were before. What's wrong with him?

She asked everyone that last question, and she got the same answer, by and large. Nothing's wrong with Geordie, silly child. It's just your imagination. He's eating and drinking and sleeping, isn't he? He hasn't got a fever, has he? He's only getting well.

Outside the tent, Faith could hear Dr. Hack being forcibly interviewed by Giuliana Caruso. All of her questions were formulated on the lines of "When did you stop beating your

133

wife?'' So far the best one she'd launched at him was, ''And how much have the American imperialist munitions billionaires promised you for provoking a clash with the U.S.S.R.?''

Faith took a wavering breath. It was hot in Geordie's tent and humid. Outside it was hot but dry. She and Steve Ritter seemed to be the only people in the whole camp who still cared about looking after Geordie. No fever, no worries, or so the others figured, and Amanda had no use for the handsome specimen if all he was going to do was eat and sleep. She and Don spent their free time dabbling with amateur spiritualism. They were building up their expertise, she confided in Faith, for a full-fledged seance or a possible devil-raising.

''Cute,'' remarked Faith. ''Trying to bring that damned black dog back. Really cute. Don't invite me.''

''Don't worry. We won't,'' flounced Amanda. She had other fish to fry these days, torn between a tantalizingly slow flirtation with an ABC darkroom man and the temptation to start courting one of the Russians. Yuri was scruffier than she liked them, but he had nice eyes.

''You might as well be dead,'' Faith addressed herself to Geordie, ''for all she cares. And you thought she was so special.''

It didn't bother the girl that she had peeked into Geordie's journal, and so learned of his true feelings for Miss Amanda Rhodes. The incident had been rationalized so many times in Faith's mind that one more mulling of it would have the unconscious Geordie begging her to open his personal diary and read it aloud to the camp.

She first noticed the journal on account of its lovely bindings, pure golden leather, but no title stamped on the spine. Intrigued—as anyone might be—she flipped the book open. She had been sitting beside Geordie's cot for over an hour and she was desperate for some amusement. She got it.

It was, at first glance, a very taut, professional report of the daily progress made by the tour, together with Geordie's kind-but-honest evaluations of the student diggers. Don's was briefest, ranging from ''Hopeless,'' to ''Rather hopeless,'' to ''Quite hopeless.''

His comments on Faith Schleppey were more gratifying. He admired her resourcefulness, her spirit, and her cheerful nature. Faith gagged. The man saw her as an overgrown Girl Scout. But then he wrote about Amanda.

Ah, Amanda. He waxed poetical on the subject. She was the tender flower, the distant princess, the acme of beauty fit to be worshipped from afar lest an impure thought sully her. Faith gagged again, in earnest. Amanda had led her to believe that she was anything but pure, purity no longer being the fashion. Yet here was Geordie, carrying on over her in a style that was popular in the Middle Ages, when you had to adore your lady from afar because if you did it from anear, you'd get her Daddy's sword in your belly.

"Don," said Faith, "isn't the only one who's quite hopeless. Who'd have thought that under your healthy exterior there beat the heart of a lovesick medieval schoolboy? Poor Geordie! Scared to approach her, weren't you? And there she sat, fairly smouldering with lust, ripe for the picking. Oh, my, if you only knew! If the cold showers could only talk!"

In his sleep Geordie smiled beatifically. The thin beard he sported was a funny color for a man of Geordie's complexion and original hair color, but come to think of it, what *had* been his hair color when first they reached the site? Not jet black, surely? Dark, perhaps, but not this midnight shade. Faith mopped Geordie's brow with a damp cloth and shook her head.

"Love is a bitch," she muttered. "It's making me see things."

Geordie's eyes fluttered open. The peaceful smile was still on his lips. It looked familiar, naggingly so. Faith puzzled on it, while outside the tent the interview/Battle Royal between Hack and Caruso reached its height.

"Hello, Geordie," said Faith.

"Peace be with you, child," said Geordie. He sat up. The sheet fell from him. Beneath it, his tanned limbs appeared to have grown still darker, brown instead of bronze, as if all of those days out of the sun had had an inverse effect on Geordie's normally fair skin.

Faith goggled and swallowed hard. She felt her cool, eminently rational brain sending out shrill squeaks of distress. Something is wrong here, she thought, fighting to remain calm while her mind sorted out the evidence of her senses. Geordie wasn't talking with Geordie's voice. He wasn't wearing Geordie's hair. He wasn't wrapped in Geordie's skin. What the hell was going on? Who ever heard of body snatching while the body was still alive?

Who was this and where was Geordie?

"Dr. Hack! Dr. Hack!" Don Swann's piping voice interrupted the harried professor's interview just in time. One
more pointed question and it would be the first time in
centuries that Roman blood was spilled on Egyptian soil.

"Yes, my boy, what is it?"

"He's gone!" cried Swann, flailing his arms about.

My God! thought Faith, hearing it all, staring at the smooth,
untroubled, alien visage before her. They know!

"Who's gone?" Giuliana Caruso asked in chorus with Dr.
Hack.

"The body—the—the remains—from the sepulchre. The
sarcophagus is empty. Me and Amanda were just passing by
when we saw this—this *glow* kind of floating over the box.
She screamed that it was maybe radioactive and ran away, but
I looked and—he's—Quintus—he's gone!"

No, he's not, thought Faith, hypnotized and falling into
that weird state of shock that lets disaster victims stand by
smiling while a brick wall collapses in on them in slow
motion.

"Why, bless you, child," said Quintus, and he patted her
hand.

The touch broke the trance. Faith let out a piercing scream
and ran like hell. She sprang for Dr. Hack's arms like a
jumping-mouse gone mad and clung to his withered neck
while shrieking, "He's there! In there! Geordie's gone and
he's in there!" If Dr. Hack hadn't set aside his principles of
nonviolence and slapped her, she might have gibbered her
way over the edge of sanity.

Giuliana Caruso took notes like mad. On her pad of yellow
paper the lone slap escalated into a merciless drubbing, underscored with an oblique hint that Faith Schleppey had courted
the beating by championing the cause of glorious Socialism
within Dr. Hack's earshot. What the hell, thought Giuliana.
When this is printed, it'll be in Italian, and that old fossil can
barely speak English. Whenever I ask him a question he
either splutters or barks. *Contadino!*

"Now Faith," said Dr. Hack while the girl rubbed her
scarlet cheek. "Go slowly. *Where* is Geordie and *who* is in
there?"

To her eternal shame, Faith burst into dry sobs, a trick
worthy of Amanda Rhodes. If she answered, they'd lock her
up, and if she didn't answer, she'd explode.

Her problems resolved themselves. A high wind sprang up

from the east, sending the flaps of Geordie's tent lashing and cracking, belling out and snapping back like the sails of a galleon. On the wind came the dry, sweet smell of summer flowers.

Not another tent stirred, baking silently in the still, odorless desert heat.

A mixed choir's voices swelled out of nowhere, doing a selection from one of Handel's greatest hits. Cool light poured from the tent. Faith heard the cooing of doves and the rustle of their wings, a sound soon drowned out by Giuliana Caruso's hoarsely garbled recitation of the rosary.

"Peace be with you," said the tall, slender, brown man who emerge from the straining tent. He raised his hands in a gesture of welcome and benediction. The wind subsided.

He passed among them, smiling and nodding his head, reaching out to touch their hands gently, to give a word of encouragement. His hands were crackly and dry, like a shucked-off locust skin, warm as wood left out in the sun.

He paused before Giuliana and took both of her hands in his. She had dropped her pen and pad long ago. Holding her lightly with his eyes he said, "You see now that you were wrong. But you would not be human if you were not sometimes wrong. It is a blessing to admit your humanity, and a power, a great power." When he released her, she was weeping.

They followed his progress with looks alone. No one felt like moving, let alone running after him. He wore a coarse brown blanket. It hung over his naked thinness in simple but elegant folds, evoking a garment midway between the robe of a penitent monk and the toga of a well-to-do Roman. It was no longer a blanket.

He stopped and turned to face the rise where the media people encamped, raising his arms as gracefully as if they were attached to huge, white wings. The sun cast a halo around him, outlining him with light. There was a growing buzz on the media hillock as they scurried from their tents like ants. Then came a rush of silence as one by one they recognized the dark face they had photographed so often in the sepulchre.

"He's alive," someone breathed.

"Or we're all dead," supplied someone else.

Lowering his arms, he smiled. "Let five come to me," he said, and resumed his easy pace toward the black rock.

Ambrosius' clay hut was nearly all exhumed. The workers were on a break. They huddled with the Russians, trading guarded stories about the dig for slugs of mind-bending vodka. No one was near the site.

He gazed at the hut as if recognizing an old, old friend. "May you have peace, Brother Ambrosius, wherever you lie. My need is greater than yours. Forgive me." With those words he took possession of the hut.

8

Once. or Maybe Twice. in a Lifetime

THEY WERE COURTED more assiduously than kings, courtesans, or publishers. Their every word was taped or scribed, then reviewed for hidden meanings and inflections. They were called The Five, The Chosen Five, The Five Elect, and most commonly Those Five Lucky Bastards. They were the court of Quintus.

Dr. Hack was chosen because he was the first one to reach the clay hut and attach himself like a leech to Quintus' shadow. Giuliana was the second, although she was not very cheerful company to have in such a small dwelling. She just would not stop crying, except to grab handfuls of sand and pour them over her head. Then she would invariably get a few grains in her eye and the tears would spurt again. Father Lewis was sent for at Quintus' bidding, and told to bring the scroll. Yuri crouched by the priest's side in the cool shelter of the adobe hut, mindful of Sonia's hasty instructions. She had single-handedly raised such a stink that Kent Cardiff had graciously bowed out of his chance to be one of the Five rather than provoke an international incident. Faith was the fifth, just along for the ride.

Outside the hut, the media waited. It was the daily hour of study, a time that Quintus set aside specifically for the chapter-by-chapter exposition of his scroll. Father Lewis had begun translation efforts on his own, and Steve had taken a stab at it before the British priest, but what could be better than the subject of a biography being right there to correct any minor flaws or oversights in the story of his own life?

"We now come," intoned Quintus, "to the end of my conversion and the beginning of my desire to enter the life contemplative. According to Ambrosius Minimus, who was of great help to me in the compilation of this scroll—"

And so he rattled on, giving them his life in modest tones, but how modest could he remain when the scroll came to tell of the countless miracles he performed before the eyes of his brethren in the desert? He knew how to hold an audience, now with a gesture, now with a tantalizing bit of reticence, now with a stirring adventure.

"We all thought Brother Titus was dead," Quintus smiled. "But at the urging of Ambrosius, I knelt beside the body and offered up a prayer, for I confess we needed Brother Titus very much. He was our brother-infirmarian, you see. And praise be, he opened his eyes and rose up and was evermore his old self."

"A miracle," breathed Father Lewis.

"Oh, I wouldn't call it that," disclaimed Quintus. But he made no suggestion of what he *would* call it.

"Speaking of old selves," piped Faith, "I have a question."

"By all means," said Quintus indulgently. "And I shall answer it if knowledge is vouchsafed me."

"Good," snapped Faith. "Where's Geordie?"

Quintus lost his grip on beatitude for a moment. "Geordie?" he echoed, looking puzzled. "Who is Geordie?"

"You are," said Faith.

"No, no, my child, that is not possible," the incipient saint replied. "I am Quintus Pilaster, until such time as it shall please the powers that be to free me from this earthly form."

Faith was having none of that. It was the same thing, just like the study hour, a regular feature of her days since the coming of Quintus. Every day she wedged in her angry question and every day he denied there had ever been a Geordie Burns. Then, like clockwork, Dr. Hack would barge into the conversation and decree:

"Don't bother Quintus, Faith. You should be grateful he's accepted you as one of us."

Oh, they were insufferable, thought Faith. The others would band behind Dr. Hack and urge her to leave off annoying Quintus with silly details, such as what had become of Geordie's—body?—soul?—likeness? It was hard to say what Quintus had usurped, or where he had stowed the things that made up Geordie. Geordie's *ka*, thought Faith. Maybe the ancient Egyptians were right about the nature of the spirit, and at this very moment Geordie's *ka* was wandering through the twilight without so much as a box lunch for company.

"Great inspiration, boss," Gerial said, his eyes on the hut. "They'll never leave now."

"What inspiration?" Horgist was testy. He hated sitting up on the black rock, much preferring the soft embraces of the sand, but in his new position as commander he periodically had to check on the troops. They were easiest to find on the rock.

"Having Quintus come back. What'd you do, reanimate the body? Alter a living one? Do a full-scale mock-up?"

"I didn't do a damn thing," Horgist growled.

"You . . ?" Gerial gazed at Ambrosius' old cell, his shins tingling. "Then was it one of the succubi who—?"

"The Furies know where Melisan spends her days, and it's no longer a secret what Lura's looking for. She wastes no time for the sake of our cause!"

"Then if you didn't bring Quintus back, and they didn't, and I sure as hell know I didn't . . ." Gerial didn't want to say it.

"Miracles make me puke," said Horgist.

Quintus raised two fingers in benediction, the signal that they were dismissed. Obediently the Five filed out of the hut to face the reporters.

"What did he say? Are you still going to call him Quintus? What proof do you have? Any new miracles turn up today, Doc? What did he tell you from the scroll today?"

Dr. Hack was the self-appointed spokesman for the Five. He sometimes answered every question, sometimes waved the reporters away with a knowing look. For the first time in his life, he was in a privileged position, and he loved it. Damned if he was going to let it slip, either. He had them all at an advantage. Yuri couldn't speak enough English to answer the questions, and in any event, he reported to Sonia alone.

Giuliana—well, there was no sense to be gotten out of Giuliana, and Father Lewis ran a close second. They would spend hours in silent contemplation after leaving Quintus' presence, and they did not like to be bothered with, "What did Quintus eat for lunch today?" or "Have you ever seen him use the khazi?"

Faith, the sole potential chink, was a tight-lipped sort. She would gladly answer questions, but her answers were not good press, not exciting or stimulating news. "Something's fishy here," said Faith, and that was all she would say.

On this day, Dr. Hack chose not to dally with the press. "Perhaps later, gentlemen," he purred. "Our interviews with Quintus do not relieve us of our normal obligations. I have to supervise the dig."

He left them gnashing their teeth, a sweet sound to his ears. The dig was an excuse. It had been pitifully easy work ever since the advent of Quintus. Why cast about for a likely place to excavate when you have an informant on hand, a man who knows precisely where you should dig and what you will find? In Dr. Hack's breast pocket was a small notebook with the fruits of his chats with Quintus written down in cypher. He knew where he could unearth, at leisure, the rest of Quintus' monastic buildings, a neighboring village that dated to the second century B.C.E., and a hidden temple to Zeus-Ammon that was built upon the foundations of an even older temple where lithe priestesses danced with rouged feet on midnight tiles and gave themselves to all comers when the dance was done.

There were even, Quintus confided, rumors of temple treasure. Just rumors, of course.

Of course, thought Dr. Hack. Still, no harm in trying.

Quintus himself came out of the hut when the sun hung low in the sky. Over-zealous reporters who tried to push their way into the hut for an exclusive interview were gently persuaded to desist. Quintus used a simple method in this. Any reporter who entered the hut without leave was immediately smitten with leprosy. So far, the technique had worked. There were four dejected inmates of an isolated tent, but there would be no more. The media had taken the hint.

"It is astonishing," sighed Father Lewis, dreaming of past and future talks with the saint, imagining himself at the core of a new band of apostles.

"I don't believe it," muttered Father William, shaking his head. "I know I'm supposed to be skeptical and cynical in this investigation, and it was easy enough when we were dealing with a well-preserved corpse, but when it comes to a potential saint who walks and talks back to me when I question his past miracles, being skeptical is ridiculously simple. It's almost a reflex."

Father Lewis said nothing in reply, only looking pained and sorrowful for his dear friend Father William. In one of his discourses, Quintus had elaborated on a vision of Hell, with special attention to the place of doubters. Scorpions figured prominently in it.

Outside the priests' tent, Giuliana Caruso was singing an old hymn as she went to wash the feet of CBS. She had decided on her own penance for a life of doubt and little faith. Each day she would perform another act of humiliation for one of the major networks. She was beginning to make them nervous.

"Double damn with nuts," growled Melisan from the rock, and shot a bolt of laryngitis through the songster's throat. Giuliana coughed, croaked, and went her way humming.

"Not nice, Melisan," chortled Horgist. "I liked the music."

"Stuff it in your ear," snarled Melisan. She had become moody. Lura coiled her tail tight as a top around her slender body and wondered what had gotten into Melisan lately. It didn't take too much mental strain to come up with the answer. Even now the golden-haired succubus smelled of pipe tobacco.

Gerial joined them on the rock, looking two shades too pale for a blue demon. Nobody seemed to be thriving these days. It was—and here they were all unanimous—all the fault of Quintus.

"How can we get anyone damned with a *saint* hanging around here?" grouched Gerial.

"Why should that stop you?" Melisan sneered.

"Oh, it wouldn't stop *me*," Gerial bragged, puffing out his chest. "But you know mortals. They'll do anything, so long as there's no chance the neighbors will find out about it. Neighbors have been responsible for more straight living than all the great religions of the world combined. I mean, moral imperatives are all very well and good, but there's more fear of gossip than G—well, then you-know-who."

"Such preaching merits a pulpit all its own," Horgist said, looking at Gerial slyly. "How is that going to look on your record, Gerial? Preaching in the desert?"

"We haven't seen our records in centuries," spat Melisan. "Why don't you come off it, Horgist. You're no better at leading us than Atamar ever was. I've got half a mind to bug out right this minute and help Lura look for that stupid purple bottle!"

Lura gasped. Gerial looked miserable. Horgist simmered and steamed. "You have half a mind," he said darkly. "That much is correct, Melisan. Court is now convened."

Lura edged closer to the towering bulk of the yellow demon and timidly touched his knees. "You're joking?" she piped. "About—about court? You would not—?"

"IN SESSION!" Horgist thundered, striking the earth with a heavy foot and sending Lura tumbling backwards. The black rock quaked beneath the demon's tread and a fissure the size of a hair opened, showing depths out of dreams. Black rock glittered like glass, beckoning to demon eyes as sweetly as green fields can tempt mortals. The three demons could not help but creep closer to Horgist's feet to steal a peek down into the depths his stamp had opened.

A wisp of mist arose from the black fissure and it widened imperceptibly. "Open rebellion," Horgist intoned, "against your superior. Lura, for subordinating our mission to your own desires, you are charged. Plead."

"My lord, all I've ever desired is the success of our mission."

"Is that why you seek a certain bottle so assiduously? Atamar's soul is already condemned. Confess, Lura! You intended to find him and release him, in the hope that he would overthrow me. If that isn't treachery—"

"Atamar is our true leader! You're the usurper."

"I never asked for this job. I curse the day it fell to me. You weren't asleep when we imprisoned Atamar. You were just as keen to believe Murakh's warning. We acted together, and we must abide by the outcome of our actions together. Part of that outcome made me your chief, and I won't stand for second-thought backstabbers."

"I would hardly think you'd take open rebellion so seriously," said a high, bright voice behind Horgist. "Isn't that how you all got your start? Hell is full of incompetent rebels."

Lura and Melisan pressed themselves against Gerial, who
was slavering with fear. Horgist wheeled around with a roar
to face the interloper. And yet, as he turned, he could have
sworn that he and the others had maintained invisibility. Who
could see them? Who could possibly hear?

"Calmly, now," said Faith Schleppey, holding up a small
shard of pottery on which were carved two rows of symbols.
"I think you must be calm."

Horgist sprang, but in mid-flight he felt hard fingers solid-
ify out of the air and push him back. Emanations of power
pulsed from the bit of clay, and the runes inscribed by an
inexpert hand were nonetheless binding. They smarted and
seared their track across Horgist's eye. The Word of Saving.
The Word of Binding. The Word of Ruling. The Word of
Submission.

Horgist fell back to huddle with the other three, a thick
sweat falling from his brow like melted butter. He felt very,
very cold. He clawed at Melisan in his terror, leaving long
scrapes across her rounded belly, but she appeared not to
mind. Her arms reached down to cradle and comfort him and
he whimpered.

"Good," said Faith. "We know each other, I see."

"Who—who are you, O Mistress?" stammered Gerial.

"Faith Schleppey. Pleased to meet you. You're staring at
me as if I had two heads. You're no treat for the eyes either,
kiddies. When I borrowed that stupid book, I never thought it
would turn out like this. But oh, am I ever glad it did!"

She laughed and reached into the pocket of her skirt, then
flung a well-worn paperback book with a familiar cover right
at the demons. It was Don Swann's tome on magic and
witchcraft. He'd been looking for it for days.

"That's tripe!" protested Lura, who grew bold enough to
pick up the book and skim it. "None of this would raise
celery, let alone demons!"

"I agree," admitted Faith. "But I didn't need to raise you.
You're already here. What I did need was to find you, then to
use you. Well, gotcha. Now as to using you—"

"You never found those runes in this book!" objected
Gerial. Lura had passed the paperback to him, and he had
found nothing more exciting in it than the preparation of
nauseating love-draughts. "No mortal now living could know
them! They were engraved on the tomb of Solomon, the true
tomb that lies in the Valley of Clouds, where death sleeps,

where shadows walk on the wind! Where—!'' His voice cracked and he hid his face under Melisan's wing, feeling the loss of exile.

"Are you mortal?'' asked Lura gently.

"Entirely so,'' said Faith. "None more mortal. I don't know anything about valleys in the clouds or tombs or runes. All I know is that I was told to copy these scratchings onto a piece of clay, so I did, and the next thing I knew, I saw the four of you having your little spat on top of the rock. I wonder how long you've been lurking around our camp, invisible? I never thought I was completely alone in the shower, but that might have been Don. Amazing what the right combination of words will do,'' she remarked, taking an admiring look at her handiwork. The runes rippled and seemed to run together like laughter.

The four demons felt the air around them grow tense with possibility, the way the atmosphere will hang unbreathing before a thunder storm. Another wisp of vapor feathered out of the fissure in the rock.

"Who showed them to you?'' whispered Horgist. "Who showed you the runes to tame us?'' His burning eye perceived a slow darkening of the sky behind Faith, a shadowed corolla that might have been real or a phantom of pain. "Who?'' he repeated.

Faith's shadow grew, seeping outwards. The girl's image became fainter, until she was less real than the shadow, a character stepping back into her part in a vision. She was in and of the shadow, where sand was a golden haze and Faith's hand closed on the neck of a small purple bottle.

She picked it up. She turned it end over end, studying it. She drew out the stopper.

Rage poured into the desert. Atamar was fire, a scarlet flood of flame. His perfect face was a mask of serpents, a writhing horror where uncounted lidless eyes stared, forked tongues hissed and flickered, fangs curved death. Faith stepped back; only a step. Her face was pale, but she made herself hold her ground. She held up the bottle and the stopper so that Atamar could see them. She spoke, but the shadow's vision did not let its witnesses hear the words she uttered.

Atamar's fires cooled. His face became again the cold absolute of beauty. As he knelt to the girl, she regained her reality. The shadow ebbed back, her black aura. The demons gazed on it as it underwent a new change.

The shadow spread wings that looked as if they sprang from Faith's shoulders, black as the wings of a bat, strong and broad as the wings of a dragon, ruthless as the wings of nightmare. Atamar had returned. There was a thin collar of iron around his neck and a little waterfall of silver chain. As casual and self-possessed as if she were going to air her pet poodle, Faith took the chain in her hand and tugged it lightly.

"Have you all met?" she smiled.

9

Heads Will Roll

"WELL, NICE GOING, everybody," said Gerial, flicking at the silver leading-chain that dangled from his iron collar. "We're really going to get to Hell this way, I'm sure. I wish I were mortal!" It was every demon's cry of ultimate despair. Coming from Gerial, it held a poignance the others could not imagine.

"Oh, shut up," Melisan answered. "You were in on it just as much as we were. If anyone's not guilty of treason it's Lura, and fat lot of good her innocence is doing her."

"Too true, too true," sighed Gerial. They were in Faith's tent, wedged in between her bedroll and her suitcase. Once Gerial leaned back too far and upset Amanda's array of lipsticks, mouthwashes, and perfumes. Conditions were cramped, but Faith insisted that they all lodge with her, unperceived by Amanda. She wasn't going to take any chances.

"Where is she, by the by?" Gerial inquired, scraping his tusks for lack of anything better to do. "Where is Lura?"

"With him," Horgist rumbled. He was stretched out inert on the floor and the two other demons present crouched on top of him. Since Atamar's return, he had lapsed into his somnolent ways again. The yellow fiend yawned sulfurously and slept.

"Still at it," said Melisan. "Still after him. She's a fool. He blames her as much as he blames us. I could almost hope we never get home again if it means having him always there to reproach us with what we did. We really didn't have any cause."

"We had our suspicions," Gerial offered, but it sounded lame. "We still don't know if we were right or not. We just had our suspicions." *And who planted those suspicions, Gerial? The thought came on Steve's voice. Ever wonder why? Open your mind, my friend, while there is still time!*

"Condemned by reason of suspicion," Horgist glubbered in his dreams. "You can tell you were once mortal, Gerial. It shows."

"Well, I hope he does forgive her," the blue demon maintained, ready to champion Lura's cause. Her image was in his brain, so small and forlorn, no longer the happy-go-lucky succubus he had know and loved (how well! how often!).

Gerial's fond hopes might have helped him comfort himself, but if hopes had wings and would fly out of the tent, they would soon crinkle up and blow away once they hit Atamar.

He perched on the black rock and watched the camp below him grimly, his talons digging deep into the stone, his eyes glowing the dull red of dried blood. He was still handsome—his stay in the bottle had not altered that—but his looks had turned brittle, as if bitterness had gnawed away at him from inside until he was only husk and hate. Behind him, scarcely daring to breathe, Lura sat tailor-fashion, absently playing with her braids and feeling as if she were strangling on a bone. Nearby sat Faith, apparently reading a sensational paperback on witchcraft. The book shielded her lips as she addressed the demons.

"I am not a marriage counselor," Faith said. "I never wanted to be one. Why don't you two make up?" She meant it lightly, but one glance at Atamar's face convinced her that this subject should remain off-limits. The iron collar held him in her power, yet Faith was not the kind of person to tempt fate by pushing her power to the utmost. She liked a safety net, a little margin for error.

"All right," she said harshly, trying to assume some air of command. "All right. Forget I mentioned it. Now report. Where is Geordie? What's become of him?"

Atamar's beautiful head moved slowly around, the head of a Greek statue coming to life. "He is not dead," he said. "I have scanned the camp and the countryside, to the limits of my realm, and I find the same number of souls abroad as before. He is not dead, O Mistress," he finished with a hint of scorn. The silver chain made a tinkling sound.

"Not dead, but *where*?" demanded Faith.

"Mistress mine," said Atamar smoothly, "I regret with all my heart disappointing you, but I must. I do not know where he is, beyond the fact that he lies within my ken. Perhaps it would help me," he added archly, "if you told me where you were keeping him before you misplaced him?"

Faith made a fist, ready to pummel Atamar. The demon did not flinch. It was all he hoped for. Let her strike him! He was bound by obedience to accept her as his mistress. He could not strike her back. But he could allow his skin to chill or heat to the point where human flesh would burn and die on contact.

"No," said Lura softly, seizing Faith's arm. With her eyes she begged the girl not to hit the demon, knowing well the sort of non-revenge Atamar practiced.

Faith misunderstood Lura's motives. "I wasn't going to hit him that hard," she said. "Don't worry, I won't hurt him." Atamar chuckled and off-handedly let himself grow until he was five times his original size. The image of his wings cast a cool shade over Faith and Lura.

Lura did not release her grip on Faith's arm. "Please," she whispered. "Please speak to me. Have Atamar do something else, go away somewhere. I must speak to you."

Life before this summer had dealt Faith few surprises. She had done well in the high school debating society and been voted Miss Congeniality. She had gone to the Prom with her cousin Albert. She was always spoken of as having a great personality. Now, confronted by a succubus or two, and arch-fiend, and a couple of minor devils, Faith Schleppey had what Hollywood likes to bill as the Big Break.

"Atamar, you search the camp for clues about where Geordie is. Maybe your eyes will help you more than your other powers. If you find him, I'll have no further reason to hold

onto you, you know." She did her best to sound cajoling.
Atamar remained unmoved. "Take the others with you to
help."

"*All* the others?" Atamar looked pointedly at Lura.

"Just the ones in my tent. I'm not pushing you two on each
other. I'm not the one around here peddling miracles. Oh,
and when you see Dr. Hack heading for the clay hut, make
yourself look like me and—"

"My Mistress seems to forget who it is that dwells in that
hut," said Atamar. "I met him once before, long ago, when
he was still a man. Now it happens that he might be a saint.
My Mistress will understand the reluctance of my—people to
bear the company of saints."

"Say no more," Faith dismissed his objections. "No one's
forcing you into bed with Quintus. Just tell Dr. Hack, as me,
that we've got a bastard of a headache and we won't be there
for study hour today. He'll be ecstatic. I only embarrass him
in front of Quintus. Now get along."

Atamar winked and dwindled down into a painful replica of
Faith Schleppey. There was not even the soothing hope that
the mirror lied. Atamar was no mirror. He was exact, and
Faith saw herself as she was. It was uninspiring. The transformed demon skipped down from the rock and away.

"I'm all yours. Which one are you? I think I'd better learn
the names of my demons if I'm going to do this right."

"I am called Lura," said the succubus, lowering her thick
lashes. "You know Atamar well, I would say. The other
female among us is called Melisan, the blue one is Gerial,
and the yellow one is Horgist."

"Colorful lot," remarked Faith. "What can I do for you,
Lura?"

Lura's tail wove in and out between her toes as she strove
to work up the nerve to speak freely with Faith. "How—how
did you find him?" she blurted at last. "I've been searching
for him everywhere, ever since we all—"

"I know what you did, you and the others," said Faith.
She felt kindly towards the succubus and was enjoying the
odd pleasure of sympathy for the devil. "Atamar told me
about it when I released him. My finding him was blind luck,
just the way your not finding him was bad luck. It's kind of
nice knowing that demons don't have it licked, you know?
But anyway, I had just stolen into Don Swann's tent to

borrow that stupid book of his on black magic—you saw it. More bad luck, just as I was going out with it, I saw him coming towards the tent with Amanda. I think the woman's getting desperate if she and he—But forget that.''

Lura cleared her throat and prompted, ''The bottle?''

''I'm getting there!'' snapped Faith. ''It's all connected. I took the book and gave it a strong slide out under the back of Don's tent, figuring to pick it up later. I said I'd just popped by to see how Don was doing. Some lie! Then, when they were out of sight, I doubled around in back of the tent and looked for the book. I found it, and it had found the bottle.''

The succubus looked wide-eyed, her tail trembling with suppressed rage. Of all the luck! Not bad enough that Atamar, and now all of them were at the beck and call of a mortal, but this chit was not even an adept. Chance, nothing but chance had given Faith the purple bottle. There was no justice in the world, thought Lura, and being originally from Hell she had a strong inherent sense of justice.

''Well, the rest is Aladdin,'' Faith laughed. ''I pulled the stopper as you saw, and Atamar streamed out. I thought I was going to die. I don't know why I didn't faint. He was terrible! But then he told me that he was beholden to me for freeing him and I could have one request of his powers, no soul attached.''

''The halidom of Hell,'' said Lura. ''Our code of honor.''

''Honor? In Hell?'' Faith considered. ''Well, why not? But to make it short, my dear, my one wish was that Atamar give me the means for controlling demons. Pretty sharp, if I do say so myself.''

''Most astute,'' said Lura, sharpening her nails on the rim of her iron collar. ''How ever did you come up with it so pat?''

''Years of reading fairy tales,'' shrugged Faith. ''Anything else I can do for you?''

''Free us,'' said Lura.

''No,'' said Faith. ''Not until Geordie's back and you clear out of here. Then I'll let you be free to hightail it smack back to Satan himself.''

Lura laughed and cried at the same time. It made her sides ache and her face smart, for free emotions have always been discouraged in demons, but she couldn't help it. ''By Dis, Mistress, what the hell do you think we've been *trying* to do?

For years! For centuries! Do you want us gone so badly? It's easy, Mistress. Just give us a soul. One small soul.''

Careful questioning by Faith revealed the whole story. "I see," she said at last. "So that's the price of your ticket home." Faith shook her head. "Incredible." She asked Lura to retell the part of the tale that described Murakh's kindnesses over the years.

"Really incredible. I'd never peg a demon for a Boy Scout. I guess it takes all kinds, even in Hell. Say . . ." She looked around suspiciously. "This Murakh isn't here right now, is he?''

"You'd see him the same as you see us, Mistress." Lura gestured limply at the rune-scribed shard.

"I'll let you loose after Geordie's back—trust me on that—but I won't have your pal try springing you before then.''

"Murakh respects the rules of magic as much as the rest of us. He must. The holding you've laid on us will remain until you lift it. There's nothing he can do.''

Faith cradled her chin between two fingers. "I wouldn't bet the ranch on it. From what you've told me, your bigwigs are torked with you for losing Quintus. Then you messed up on the rest of the monks. You didn't get any of the Russians either, the first time around, did you?''

"We tried," Lura said miserably.

"It just doesn't add up." Faith gave Lura the once-over. "You can't tell me that this desert monastery was the only one entirely inhabited by perfect souls. Not one monk among them who'd fall for you? Russians are human, too, and Dolf Lundgren can act his cute little buns off before he convinces me otherwise. You had all the delights of Hell at your disposal, and you couldn't catch one soul? Not one?" Faith clicked her tongue. "If I were your bosses, Lura, I'd ask you whether you really wanted your present job. And if Murakh's such a respecter of rules, why is he playing on the white line just to bring aid and comfort to a bunch of screw-ups like you? What a clutch of greenhorns you are, even Atamar.''

"Mistress," said Lura with an edge in her voice, "I would be more charitable if I were you. One day you may be compelled to release us, and on that day it would not be good to have a demon angry with you. Don't speak ill of Atamar.''

"Mmm," said Faith. "And of Murakh?" Lura didn't answer, but she took the diamond pentacle from her breast and flung it to the wind.

The raspy voice of Giuliana Caruso rang out like the notes of a rusted bucina. She was preaching repentance to the camera crews. Somehow she had found a case of Pretty Good Stuff in the supply tent and had dragged it away. Now she used it· for her pulpit and drew her audience by threats to demolish the liquid gold with a pilfered pick from the dig site.

"Fun at last," chirped Faith, grabbing Lura and shinnying down the rock. "Let's watch!"

In the gathering crowd, Steve bumped shoulders with Gerial. The blue demon's collar and chain had been disguised as a throat mike. "Long time, no see, friend," Steve said, playfully tugging the chain. "Is this some of your doing?" He pointed to the entabled Giuliana.

"I'd put it down to your side," Gerial mumbled. "We don't do reformations."

"So you've finally guessed . . ."

"I've had a lot of time to think." Gerial gave his collar a ringing snap of the fingers. "What I don't get is why you're here at all. None of your guys bothered to show up when we went after the monks, but maybe you thought they should go the whole temptation-rejection route for their spiritual good. You didn't show a whisker for the Russians either. Then again, they don't believe."

"You're confusing belief with religion, Gerial. Your own faith never had a name."

·"Then why are you here? Just for the fun of lousing up our last chance to get home?" His shout was swallowed in the rising volume of Giuliana's sermon.

"No, Gerial; to give you all a final chance to truly go home again."

"Home . . ." Gerial's eyes filled with searing tears. Steve touched them, and they fell as ordinary drops. "The Valley of Clouds. But—but my sin—" His brows came together, his eyes dried. "You're taunting me with the impossible!"

"I'm offering you what you refuse to see. That wasn't my purpose when I first came here. I was supposed to keep an eye on Dr. Hack. He's a good man who's had bad luck."

"And you're supposed to jerk him back from the abyss?" Gerial sneered.

"Your team doesn't do reformation, ours doesn't do intervention. I can only do for Dr. Hack what I can do for you: show him that there is always another way."

Gerial snickered. "I showed him another way. Got him
shacked up with Ferrabosco. How's that for an abyss?"

Steve was not distressed. "The love of a good woman
might be just what the man needs. Thank you, Gerial. You
and your friends have been doing my work for me."

"In a pig's ass!"

"Wherever."

"I oughta pop you one!" Gerial swung at Steve and missed.
Steve laughed and vanished. None of the bystanders noticed.
There was too much else going on.

The joint was jumping. Few hearts are brave enough to
stand between old newspapermen and their liquor. Fewer still
would defy the thirsty hordes of the electronic media. Giuliana,
as a former journalist, should have known better, but the
flame of new zeal burns with a hard, bright, blinding light.
She swung the pick overhead and preached Temperance.

"If she smashes that booze," said a soundman, "she
dies."

The crowd took up the sentiment. It had been a long affair,
this coverage of the Marmota, Inc.'s newfound saint. What
had started out as a nice feature on the discovery of Quintus'
corpus had spread like bread-mold into days and weeks of
new wrinkles, angles, and spin-offs. Every newsman's dream,
a story to be milked *ad infinitum*, was right there in camp
with them, and yet they were all—to a man, to a woman—
heartily sick of it.

"Oh, for an assassination in Cairo!" moaned Sam, the
cameraman. "Oh, for a hijacking! A terrorist attack! An
anti-American rally or two!"

"Get that dumb broad off the booze box!" raged Linda
Hathaway.

The rhubarb-rhubarb of the crowd went up a notch. Dr.
Hack emerged from Ms. Ferrabosco's tent smoothing down
his hair and hastened to see what was up. Ms. Ferrabosco
came, too, trying to pretend it was business as usual. Her
blouse, however, was inside-out. Don and Amanda, in match-
ing burnooses, streaked to the scene. In the confusion no one
noticed Faith Schleppey acting most peculiar. For one thing,
she held an invisible *something* in her hand. For another,
there were two Faith Schleppeys.

Father William noticed it first. He'd have blamed the sun if
he hadn't just come out of his tent. Before he could tap one

Faith or the other on the back and ask what in heaven's name
was going on, the ground beneath the multitude rose and fell
once, majestically, like the back of a sea-serpent.

"Peace, peace my children," intoned Quintus Pilaster from
the black rock. He made a gesture of calming the earth. The
tremor responded to his command by subsiding immediately.

Giuliana took a flying leap from the booze crate and
crawled to Quintus' feet, but she could not climb the black
rock. In dribs and drabs the crowd shifted towards the lone
figure on the crag. He was bathed in an unspeakly sweet
radiance.

The real Faith dropped Lura's hand. Her mouth hung open.
She'd never seen that many teeth in one mouth before.
"Murakh," she breathed.

The demon on the rock met her eyes. His smile broadened.
He knew she could see him for what he was, and it only
seemed to amuse him. Faith sensed that this fiend would not
be so easy to bind as the five she held thralled. His power
streamed into him from direct contact with Hell itself. Her
runes would shatter against him. He knew it. He knew he
could reach down and destroy her, if he liked. He made
certain that his smile conveyed this knowledge straight to her
heart.

Lura clutched Faith's arm. "Free Atamar," she whispered.
"He is the most powerful of us all. He—he will protect
you."

"Why should he?" Faith whispered back. She shook with
fear. "I made him my captive."

"Murakh made us worse than that. He made us all fools.
Atamar must have realized it first, and Murakh knew. That
was why he influenced the rest of us to turn on Atamar. Free
my lord, Mistress. It is our only hope."

Faith nodded, swallowed, and spoke the words of release.

On the black rock, the demon in Quintus' skin ringed
himself with an aurora. "Peace," he whispered.

"Peace my ass!" shouted Faith Schleppey. Or was it Faith
Schleppey? It was the one without an invisible hand-hold,
that much was certain. "And peace your ass, too, my friend,"
she went on, each step towards Quintus sending ripples of
change down her body, peeling it, filling it, brushing aside
the plain, pert face of a girl and replacing it with the un-
equaled features of a prince of Hell.

"Show yourself!" boomed Atamar. The last vestige of

Faith Schleppey fell from him, a snake's discarded skin. He loomed like endless banks of black thunderheads across a leaden sky. "Show yourself, for I know you! Show yourself if you are unafraid!"

Afraid, Atamar? Quintus' voice rasped from his throat, his lips never moving. *Of you? Not now. Not ever.*

"Then you are a greater fool than you ever took me for, Murakh! I will name your offenses against us before the Lords of Hell! I will see that you get the punishment you deserve for having thwarted all our endeavors here! I will have justice!"

Quintus' face split wide. Flaps of skin petalled away. The newspeople panicked, ran, trampled one another and got nowhere. Invisible walls held them, contained their terror and turned it back on them. Atop the black rock, Murakh tore Quintus' hide from his body and discarded it.

Foolish Atamar. I protected you as long as I could, you and these other misfits; not for yourself, but for Lura's sake. Poor creature, I hoped there was a chance to salvage her, but she would love you past the limits of reason. There is no hope for you and yours. There never was from the first! The pursuit of Quintus was a test, and you failed, as my princes suspected you would. You seek justice from Hell, yet Hell metes out only judgment!

Murakh's claw closed on an invisible string and pulled.

The earth lurched again and chasms opened red mouths to draw down frantic mortals into sure oblivion. Light cracked in arcs of flame, burning down the heavens. Wails of terror cut through every throat, every heart, and the sound of panic tumbled headlong into the sudden, merciless gorges of the desert.

Afterwards, they say, it was quiet.

It was not.

The ones who found themselves still intact, still on the surface of the earth, could not stop screaming or sobbing or calling on and on for their homes and mothers. Some would not open their eyes for a day afterwards, rolled into armadillo balls that bit and scratched at any effort to unroll them.

The desert floor was smooth, untouched.

The case of liquor was unharmed, intact.

The quake, when time gave the others a chance to seek rational explanations, was found to have been local. Ex-

tremely local. Entirely local. Not one seismic institute around
the globe had picked up on it. Not one native of the nearby
village could recall feeling anything.

Here were the missing, as the survivors could count them:

Dr. Randolph Hack	Father William Stanhope
Ms. Faith Schleppey	Father Lewis Freeman
Ms. Amanda Rhodes	Quintus Pilaster
Kent Cardiff	

There were four others, but no one bothered to count them.
No one had known they were there.

PART III

1

Holygate

"I FOUND HIM."

"Who?"

"Come and I'll show you."

"Hey, how about that? He's dead again."

"Yeah, dead and back in his sarocphagus. I just came by to get one last snap of it, and there he was. Like nothing happened."

"Nothing did happen."

"I wouldn't say that."

"You'd better. That's the word going down from Hathaway, and there's one woman with a clear head. We're making a pact. All of us. Destroy all film. Destroy all stories. If we tell this the way it was, they'll send us far, far away. I've got better things to do than plead at a sanity hearing."

"I don't like it. I mean, it *happened*. We *saw* it!"

"So tell it your way. But no one else will back you up. Have fun at the squirrel farm."

A pause. "What about the parts of the story that've been sent out already?"

161

"I dunno. Pray someone on the other end of the line had
sense enough to delete the wilder parts. If not, wing it."

"What about the people who're missing? What're we going
to do there? We can't pretend *that* didn't happen. They're
gone."

"Earthquakes happen. We can release that story, but the first
word out of anyone about a big, bat-winged Adonis, and we all
swear under oath that it was acute alcoholism, sunstroke, and
plain insanity. That goes for anyone."

Another pause. "Well, when they see Giuliana Caruso
back home, they'll buy the insanity story."

"Sure they will. Want some coffee?"

"Yeah, let's—"

"What are you waiting for?"

"Where's Quintus' scroll?"

"What do you care? Ferrabosco from Marmota's got it.
Look, you can see her from here, going over it with her head
digger. The quake stirred up their site plenty."

"Oh. Because look at this."

"A scroll? Where did you—?"

"In here. In the sarcophagus. Quintus had it in his hands,
like the other one."

"Well, what do you know?"

Gerial felt strong hands slip under his arms and help him to
his feet. "Are you all right?" Steve sounded genuinely
concerned.

The blue demon touched himself gently. "Yeah, I—I think
so, but—" He searched all around, using all his senses.
"They're gone. They're gone and I'm still here. He didn't
take me. I'm alone." He felt tears rise and was unable to stop
them. His cheeks were wet, but the wetness neither burned
nor froze. "Why?" he asked plaintively.

Steve put his arm around Gerial's shoulders. "Murakh took
the demons for punishment."

"They didn't do anything! And if they did, he should've
taken me, too! We've been in this together from the first."

"You didn't hear me, Gerial. I said he took the demons."

"So what do I look like?" Gerial tore off his mortal
seeming. A transient gofer saw, goggled, ran like sixty, and
swore off Nutrasweet for life.

Steve crossed his arms over his head and swept them
down, transforming himself into a creature so hideous that

Gerial's belly quivered. Ruined lips on an eyeless face asked, "And what do I look like now? But we both know what I am." The arms swung back and Steve was a boy again.

"You know what *I* am, too!" Gerial shouted. "This is no dream. You can't tell me I'm mortal."

"I can't tell you anything, Gerial. Murakh took mortals with him, too. For spite, I think, or for a cruel joke, or perhaps he doesn't even realize he's taken them. True demons have always been able to overlook mortals until they want something from them. They find them insignificant."

The blue demon could not understand. "I've always found them fascinating. I mean, it could be 'cause I used to be one, but the others . . ."

"Your friends were just as fascinated by mortals and their ways as you. Too fascinated. Too easily distracted. Much too easily swayed from their purpose. Remember what I said about bad influences, Gerial?"

A stern look hardened Gerial's features. "Is that what Murakh hauled them off for? That dirty frog-jammer! He can't do that to my friends! Look you, I'll make you a deal—"

"We've tried that."

"Shut up and listen. All this cosmos needs is more wisemouths. You chase Murakh, get my friends back, I'll promise you we'll let this whole batch of mortals go free—no trials, no temptations, *nada*. No matter if we have to keep out of Hell for eternity."

Steve shook his head. "No deal, Gerial. If I could follow Murakh into his realm, don't you think I'd have done it? One of the mortals he's taken is the man I was sent to save."

"Why can't you go after him? Scared?"

"Bring Murakh back into the world of men and you'll see how scared I am of him. But I am forbidden to trespass on his precincts. There is only one force in all creation that is not bound by limitations of place and power."

The blue demon hunkered down for an epic sulk. "Here I went, thinking you guys could go anywhere you felt like and expense the trip, too! Big help you are. I sure as heck can't do it. I'm barred from Hell."

"They are not in Hell."

Gerial's chin came up. "Say what?"

"If I show you the way into the realm where Murakh rules and holds your friends, will you agree to enter it willingly, find them and the mortal wanderers, and lead them safely out?'' He raised his hand to forestall any precipitous reply. ''Think it over. You can say no. You would place yourself in danger if you accept, and there is nothing I could do to help you until you return to the face of the world.''

The blue demon folded his arms across his chest. ''So who needs your help, flyboy? Just show me the way.''

''Come,'' said Steve. He extended his hand.

This time Gerial clasped it warmly.

2

What Place Is This?

"ARE WE IN Heaven?" asked Father Lewis.

"Are we in Hell?" trembled Dr. Hack.

"That damned, illusive Pimpernel," Faith Schleppey chirped. She couldn't resist. From the look of things, it might be long before she felt like joking again. Wherever they were, it wasn't the most conducive atmosphere for merriment.

The terrain underfoot and the sky above were alike in their deathly bleakness. Sky? There was no sky, but whatever was up there needed a familiar name and sky came closest. It was high, distant, unreachable, and a deep, ghastly grey. It wasn't the roof of a cave; that would be solid. It was only a dull grey void where warm winds moaned and swirled and met in half-drowned claps of sullen thunder.

The pave beneath their feet was also grey; grey and rocky. The loose stones were just the right size to annoy. Too small to be crunched down as gravel, too large to be sidestepped, they rolled out from underfoot at the slightest pressure and sent the wanderers tumbling.

"We can't just stay here," said Father William.

"Quite so," Kent Cardiff agreed. His face was impassive,

succinctly British. It heartnened the others to look at him, so elegant, so phlegmatic. One had the notion that should all the hosts of Hell descend upon the party in all their evil splendor, Kent Cardiff would take brisk action immediately, whip them into line to the last devil, and have them singing hymns and fetching *chota pegs* to the Sahibs. Ah, Empire!

"Go?" Dr. Hack's laugh rang thin in the alien air. "Where do you suggest we go? This is the end of the line. The damned don't have anywhere to go. We're already in Hell."

"I don't know about you, sir," said Father William severely, "but Hell is where you find it, when you want it, and I don't want it. We are not in Hell. Now shape up and use your brains. We are *somewhere* and we got there *somehow*."

"Somehow being via earthquake," supplied Faith.

Father William appeared to agree with her. "I would guess we are not far beneath the surface of the earth. Well, a road works both ways. We'll just have to find our way out of this cavern."

Gerial materialized at Father William's elbow. "I can help!" The American priest nearly made the Olympic trials cut-off for the standing high-jump. The blue demon saw a clutch of faces regarding him with anything but hail-fellow-well-met.

"Uh . . . hi, everyone. The name's Gerial."

"That voice!" Dr. Hack aimed a quivering finger at the blue demon's tusks. "I know that voice! You were the one who told me to try my luck with—" He became aware of the others, blushed, and retreated. "You tempted me," he finished lamely. "And I fell for it. Dirty, filthy, loathsome, disgusting Lust! That's why I'm in Hell now. I should've known. I never got something for nothing in my life. Why should it all change now?"

Gerial tried to make amends. "It's not as bad as all that, Dr. Hack. It wasn't all that dirty—I've seen worse. And she liked it, and she liked you, and if you still respect each other afterwards . . ."

Dr. Hack wasn't having any of it.

"You didn't do anything really *wrong*." Not for our lack of trying, Gerial thought ruefully. Our hearts were never fully in it. What's sin without sincerity? No danged wonder . . .

"Ha! Is Lust one of the seven deadly sins or isn't it? I leave it to the experts!" Dr. Hack dragged the two priests into the conversation.

"Well now . . . well now . . . " Father Lewis clasped and unclasped his hands.

"Of course it is!" Father William snapped.

"Hey, what's the big idea calling them experts on sin?" Gerial demanded. "I'm the demon around here. I've had more experience with Lust than they'll ever—"

"We will take your higher qualification on faith, sir," Father Lewis said quickly.

"Good. You believe me about that, maybe you'll believe what I was first trying to tell you. You don't belong down here. I'm supposed to help you find your way out."

"A little out of your ordinary line of work, isn't it, old chap?" Kent Cardiff inquired. "Beastly decent of you."

"Lead on, MacDuff," said Faith.

"Get us *out* of here!" Amanda squealed. The two priests added their votes to hers. Gerial looked to Dr. Hack to make it unanimous.

Dr. Hack shook his head and shut up like a clam. He knew where they were. He knew that he, at least, belonged here. Hadn't he led a life of envy? Hadn't he played the opportunist with Quintus? Hadn't he been unworthy to be one of the Five, forcing himself into Quintus' hut not for virtue's sake, but merely to make reporters pay some attention to him? He had rejoiced in Geordie's fall! He had dreamed of causing that fall, and evil intentions could condemn you as sure as actions! He was evil. Worse, he was growing proud of being so evil. He deserved Hell.

They counted noses and found that they were six. The sheer height of the grey cliffs looming up behind them was enough to convince them all that there was only one way to go, down and away from the shifting slopes. The rocky slag seemed to end in a bleak plain many yards below. Across the plain, far away, Gerial could see a gentle yellow glow.

"What is that?" asked Faith, straining to see.

"It looks like a valley," said Father William. "I think that's what it is."

"Why is it shining like that?"

The American priest shrugged. His white hair was dusted grey with pumice. A little wind whipped up and puffed large clouds of volcanic ash from between the rocks, gritting everyone's eyes and making them cough.

"Maybe we're not as far from civilization as we thought," suggested Father William. "We might as well aim for the valley. It will be a start."

"A start!" shrieked Dr. Hack. "We have no food, we have no water. We don't know where we are or where we're going, but fine! Let's fall in behind our leader and go marching like good little soldiers into the valley—the valley— " He began to titter like a monkey—"the valley of death! Oh, excellent! Quite excellent. Come see the deadmen marching off to Hell!"

Gerial turned to Amanda, whose long legs had proven themselves functional and not just ornamental. "Does he go on like that all the time?" he asked. "Or is he just trying to depress me?"

Amanda Rhodes had said nothing directly to the blue demon so far, beyond her generalized shriek demanding a way out. For all that, her presence had exercised a certain nebulous restraint on Gerial. He had not picked his nose or belched once since coming into her presence. Somehow he sensed it would not be the Done Thing.

"Is he bothering you, too?" Generation upon generation of thin blue blood and thick green money rose to the occasion. The hour brought forth the woman.

Since Amanda's tumble into the chasm with the others she had examined herself for hurts, found none, and turned her attention to Father Lewis. The British priest was not holding up well under the strain of being in this uncanny place. The brave front he had put on when Gerial appeared had cracked long since. He looked ready to bawl like a baby. Amanda had been trying to soothe him when Dr. Hack's croaking of doom broke the spell. Now Father Lewis was shaking, Gerial was in a funk, and Amanda was furious. Nose-to-nose and toe-to-toe she confronted Dr. Hack and said:

"How would you like a fat lip?" Faith gave a little squeal of delight.

Dr. Hack tried to chuckle off Amanda's threat. "Now, Amanda—" he began, and offered to pat her pretty head with a father's kindly concern. She slapped his face hard and stalked off. Dr. Hack retreated into his black shell.

"Amanda," Faith whispered, "I didn't know you had it in you." Amanda ignored her, returning to care for Father Lewis.

"Thanks," Gerial hissed. Amanda gave him the freeze, too. The blue demon hesitated, unsure of whether this snub was a rejection of his leadership or his dubious social standing. There were only a few demons in Debrett's.

"I say, shall we?" remarked Kent Cardiff, offering to start the trek down from the cliffs. After two steps he skidded on the rocks and took several yards on his back, feet in the air. His smart khaki suit disintegrated to beggar's rags. He appraised his cuts and tatters cooly. "Frightfully unsettling," he stated on surveying the damage. The others trudged cautiously down to catch up with him.

Father Lewis leaned heavily on Amanda's arm. The desolation all around them had sapped every drop of color from his face and he looked older than Father William in the queer ashen light. Before they had gone a hundred feet he was panting, and there was a disquieting wheeze deep in his chest.

"I—I really think—I ought to—sit down. Just for a minute," he faltered, clutching Amanda's wrist.

"Hey! Everyone wait up!" Amanda relayed obediently. "Let's take five."

Father William was impatient. They were nearly off the scraggy slopes, in spite of slips, slides, falls, and— he didn't like to admit it—Hell. The broad expanse of the featureless plain beckoned, and he thought he heard the sound of human voices wafting up from the distant valley. Impossible to be sure so far away, of course, but still. . . .

"What's the matter?" he demanded. "We've only just started! We can't stop every two minutes simply because someone's picked up a little scratch."

"Old Scratch," giggled Dr. Hack. He gazed almost joyously into the steely sky. Darker swirls played at weaving trellis work of shadows against the void. It looked like rain, but he doubted anything as prosaic as water would fall from those hellish heavens.

"Oh, get out of here!" Amanda yelled. "Just go, all of you, if you can't take the time—two lousy minutes!—to wait for Father Lewis to feel better."

"Father Lewis?" Father William dropped his impatience and looked concerned. The British priest was still clinging close to Amanda, eyes staring and mouth agape, like a fish. He jumped at every sound, even the smallest, and when Father William approached him he curled up into a knot of shivers.

"Go away," he whispered. "They don't want you Father William. It's me they're after. Here, take the girl away with you—" he pushed Amanda into the American priest's arms.

"It's not right, expecting her to suffer for what I've done. And now I've dragged you all down with me, the innocent along with the guilty. Ha! Did you hear that? No man's foot makes that sound. They are coming closer, and we must march on, march on, march on to meet them. Save—save yourselves! Save—!" He shrieked and broke away from them racing down the last few yards of rocky incline and shooting off across the barren plain.

"Lewis! Lewis!" shouted Father William, and ran after him. Amanda, Faith, Kent Cardiff, and Dr. Hack stood stunned, watching the two figures dwindle in the distance. Dr. Hack tried to smother a burst of toneless laughter.

"Hey! Hey, come back here!" Gerial shouted after them, semaphoring with his tail. The two priests ran on. Gerial stamped his foot. "I might as well have stayed topside for all the respect I'm getting down here."

"No fear," Kent Cardiff said tersely. "We shall find them again once they tire. Best fall in and follow them at once. Off we go, then." He straightened his shoulders and stepped smartly in the best tradition of Lord Baden Powell.

"Nobody listens to me," Gerial groused, and let PBS lead the way. He didn't even have the satisfaction of seeing Kent Cardiff take a wrong turn and get them all good and lost.

They did not speak for a long time. They left the rocks behind them and blazed across the flat, endless plain, their faces set towards the gently dipping valley. In the flatlands it should have been easier going, but a few miles of trudging through the waste took the heart out of a person. They walked over what looked like grass, long dead grass that crunched and crackled at every step like the bones of birds. On the slopes, at least there had been some element of surprise, the sense of not knowing whether your next step would hold firm or give you an impromptu bouncing down the mountain. Here there was nothing to break the monotony, nothing to mark the distances. The valley shimmered and teased them, now undulating closer, now drawing away like the outgoing tide.

The warm air around them grew tropical, heavy with unshed rain. They forged on and winds blew up, but they brought no relief, slamming masses of thick air against the marchers' chests like hammer blows. A few drops of moisture fell and clung to the sere grasses. Breathing became harder. Faith felt as if she'd been locked in a greenhouse, although there was nothing remotely green or living for miles.

"I really have to sit down," she announced. The others—
Dr. Hack excluded—agreed that they should take a break.
They threw themselves full length in the rustling grass, heed-
less of the sharp, dry blades that poked through their sweat-
soaked clothing.

"I feel like Dorothy in *The Wizard of Oz*," sighed Amanda.
"You know, when she comes to the poppy field. But there
aren't any poppies. Oh, I am so tired!"

Kent Cardiff gave a subdued cry of joy. He had located
his spare pipe and tobacco pouch. All was officially right
with the world. He tamped down a load of shag and prepared
to enjoy himself.

"Mind the match," mumbled Faith, watching him through
half-shut weary eyes. "One lousy spark on this dry stuff and
we've had it."

"Dear girl, I know a bit better than that," Kent smiled
indulgently. He made a great deal of lighting up, then extin-
guishing the match with a glob of well-bred spit. Then he
settled back to enjoy his pipe.

Gusts of sultry wind came from the mountains, bringing
with them a last gasp of powdered rock and blending the
fragrant pipe-smoke with the ashes into a thick, reeking veil.
Faith lay at ease, staring up into the depthless sky, when
gradually she became aware of the thin, impenetrable sheets
of mist blurring her vision. She sat bolt upright and peered
into the miasma surrounding her. She could not see a foot in
front of her. Worse, she could not see a soul.

"Amanda!" she called. No answer. "Mr. Cardiff?" Again
none. "Dr. Hack!" A high-pitched squeak, like a bat laughing, fading, silence. "Hey, where are you?" Not even an
echo.

They couldn't have just picked themselves up and gone
ahead without me, Faith told herself reasonably. Dr. Hack
might do something like that, but not Amanda and not Mr.
Cardiff. Gerial wouldn't either. He's not like a real demon.
None of them were. They were just like a bunch of kids
playing a game because someone bigger made them. They
didn't like it, but they played anyhow, because they had to.
Gee, I wonder where they all are right now? I wonder where *I*
am! I haven't been asleep, have I? No, I know I haven't. So
then what . . . ?

A sound—the most incongruous sound Faith could imagine hearing in such a place—cut through her thoughts. A low,

sensuous, mechanical, purring sound it was, a sound she had
heard only infrequently in real life, but with nice regularity on
television.

"Lotus," said Faith Schleppey aloud. And the low-slung
sports car knifed throught the fog, headlights glowing, and
came to a smooth halt beside her.

"Get in, darling," said Geordie Burns, holding open the
door.

Oh, how white the car was! White as the ghost of an
iceberg, and no wonder Faith's thoughts turned to ghosts.
There was no doubt about it, there was Geordie, a little pale
and a little worn, but Geordie for all that, and the whole affair
was rock-bottom spooky. She pinched herself once, and felt
it, but who could trust such a remedy for dreams? She might
just as readily dream that she pinched herself and dream that
she felt it and dream that she wasn't dreaming after all.

"You're looking . . . well, Geordie," she said. The car
was skimming through the rustling grasses like a swallow.
The only sound was the inobtrusive murmur of the exquisitely
engineered motor. Geordie grinned at her and made no reply.
Faith sighed, leaned back in her seat, and tilted her face
upwards. Through the sun roof she watched the misty sky
execute its eternal arabesques.

"Geordie," she persisted, sitting up. "Geordie, listen,
what's happened to you? Where have you been?"

"Hey, angel, why worry? I'm here now." He took one
hand from the wheel and slung his arm comfortably around
her shoulders. "Relax, baby. Everything's gonna be all right."

It was worse than watching Geordie on his sickbed, worse
than the moment she realized that she wasn't looking at
Geordie Burns' face anymore, but the face of Quintus Pilaster. This was Geordie, Geordie alive and well and looking
like himself, but it wasn't Geordie at all. Not with those glib
lines slipping slickly off his tongue. Not with the cold charmless
charm of high-speed living.

"Get your hands back on the wheel," snapped Faith.
Geordie ignored her. She reached up and stuck her nails into
the offending hand and was pleasantly surprised to hear Geordie
utter a yelp of pain and anger.

"Hey, all right, sweets, if that's how you want it," he
sulked. "No fooling around. Okay, you want it, you got it."
A wicked yellow gleam came into his eyes, a sidelong sly

look as his hands tightened dutifully on the steering wheel. He jabbed his foot down and floored the gas.

Faith's head snapped backwards and her body sank an inch into the buttery soft leather bucket seat. The hot air of the plain whipped through the car like a lash, searing her cheeks. She wanted to protest, to call Geordie off, to promise him anything, anything he wanted, if only he'd stop this crazy steeplechase, but before she could get out a word, it was over.

"End of the line, love," said Geordie, slamming on the brakes. She was still shaking her windblown curls out of her eyes when he grabbed her roughly by the shoulders and shoved her out of the car. She sprawled on her face on a tarry pavement. Behind her she heard the mocking purr of the white Lotus as it drove away.

Faith picked herself up and rubbed her hands, which still smarted from the fall. Her knees were skinned, too, and she was mad enough to bite— to bite—

HONEST ARIEL'S

SANDWICHE SHOPPE

PIZZA TO GO   CALZONE

WE DELIVER

The red neon sign over the silvery diner blinked on and off through the fog. It diffused to a cinnamon-colored blur, fizzled, and went out for good. There was the sound of an irate voice from within, a loud clump, and the neon staggered into action again.

Faith looked at the diner from up, down, and sideways, but it was still the same, still as real as Geordie and the white Lotus, a relic from the prime days of American Highway Culture, a bright metal tribute to technology and stale Danish, the great-grandpappy of the golden arches. Here, a diner, in the middle of Heil.

"I never thought I'd say this," remarked Faith to the diner, "but I agree with Dr. Hack. This has got to be Hell. There's simply *got* to be better taste in Heaven!" With that reassuring thought, she stamped up the steps and swung back the aluminum door.

Inside, the diner looked true to type. There were four tatty booths with cracked, red-vinyl padded benches to either side of the door. Directly before her, a mottled formica-topped counter stretched the length of the establishment, complete with low stools set along it at intervals, their plastic seats patched with colored masking tape. Behind the counter was the kitchen door, the blackboard with the soup de jour scrawled on it, the pastry display cases, and Honest Ariel.

He was leaning on the counter, a cup full of cigarette butts at his elbow, a fresh king-size smoldering in his mouth, his eyes rivetted to the pages of a scandal sheet. At his back, extended to their full spread, a pair of glorious wings the color of summer rose and fell in the feeble breeze generated by the overhead fan.

Faith sat down on the stool directly opposite her host. It gave a squawk of agony and promptly listed to starboard. Honest Ariel sighed and folded up his paper, letting Faith get her first full look at his face. It was flawless. Not even Atamar could come close to this model of physical perfection. There was simply no mortal room for improvement, and then there were the wings—!

"Yuh?" grunted Honest Ariel. "Whaddaya want?" He said it all without bothering to remove his cigarette.

"Um . . ." said Faith. "I'd—I'd just like some directions, if you please."

"Whadduzis look like, lady, a fill-em-up station or what?" demanded the proprietor, swatting imaginary flies with his folded newspaper. "Whaddumeye, a Boy Scout or something? Who you think you are, commininta a nonesman's place of business and wasting his time and don't buy nuthin', huh? Where do you—?"

"Coffee," said Faith punctually. "Cream, no sugar."

"Huh," grunted Honest Ariel. "We gotta cover charge here, girlie. A minimum."

"Okay, okay," Faith raised her hand. "Piece of pie with that."

"Huh," grunted Honest Ariel a second time. He pushed his paraphernalia to one side and produced a sopping, stained rag with which he swabbed down the counter space in front of Faith. This Herculean labor done, he shambled off to bring her order. "Whakinda pie you want?" he yodeled.

"Surprise me," said Faith. He obliged by giving her a hunk of pastry that actually looked palatable. A tentative

mouthful confirmed it: It was edible; tasty; a confection
worthy of Brillat Savarin in his heyday.

"Like it?" asked Honest Ariel, wings aquiver with sus-
pense. Faith could only make muffled sounds of ecstacy in
her throat as she crammed her mouth with pie. "I baked it
myself," said the proud master of the Sandwiche Shoppe. He
looked like a giant butterfly. Whorls of pale green and deep
crimson swirled and flowed, forming and destroying random
patterns in the fragile tissue of his wings.

Faith finished the pie and washed it down with the coffee.
She wasn't expecting miracles of the brew, but it was in
every way as good as the pastry she'd wolfed down, if not
better.

"You know," she told Honest Ariel after dabbing her lips
primly on one of his tattered grey paper napkins, "if this
weren't Hell, if this were somewhere on earth—New Jersey,
say—and I found a diner that looked like this, and then it
turned out to serve food that tasted like *that*, I'd pinch myself
black and blue to find out if I was dreaming. So how do I
prove I'm not dreaming in Hell?"

Honest Ariel's wings drooped. An inch of ash from his
dangling cigarette fell into Faith's empty cup. Morosely he
cleared away the dishes, dumping them with a crash into a
green plastic basin under the counter that already brimmed
and reeked with unwashed plates and cutlery.

"This ain't Hell," he said when he finished. "I kinda wish
it was. Sometimes, ya know?"

"Well, if this isn't Hell, what is it?" demanded Faith. "It
can't be Heaven. Is it Limbo? Purgatory?"

"Nah," said Honest Ariel eloquently. He brought them a
brace of cream-cheese-and-olive sandwiches, two fresh cups
of coffee, and took up a chummy seat across the counter from
Faith. "We're in Parvahr," He stressed the last sylable.

"Oh, goodie," said Faith coldly. "That just makes it all
clear as crystal. What in hell is Parvahr?"

"Geez," Honest Ariel scratched his head. "I dunno, ya
know? But this is it, girlie. I been here five, six thousand
years, maybe more. It's not so bad, really, oncet ya get used
ta it. I do pretty good, ya know?"

"I am appalled," said Faith Schleppey, drawing herself up
to her full, insignificant height. "Shocked and appalled that
a—a man of your culinary talents is wasting five or six
thousand years of his life in a sinkhole like this when the

world awaits a taste of your pie, let alone your coffee! And these cream-cheese contrivances—brilliant. And what do you do? You sit here in a tacky aluminum diner in the middle of Parvahr and vegetate. I am apalled.''

"Ah, lay offa me, woudja?" snarled Honest Ariel. "You think I like it here? You think I wouldn't clear outa here in two minutes flat if—"

The bell over the door tinkled flatly. Three creatures with the faces of birds and the bodies of lizards shambled in. They were wearing evening gowns fit to grace a coronation. Strands of diamonds reposed garishly on their scaly bosoms. They set up a loud clatter with their pick-sharp beaks and would not shut up until the harried Honest Ariel slapped menus down in front of them. Faith gave them a nervous sidelong glance.

"Is that your usual run of clientele?" she asked.

"That's them," grunted Honest Ariel. The creatures were arguing among themselves over what to eat. Two of them became enraged and leaped at each other, clawing gusts of feathers, sinking their beaks into the foe's weak spots. In the midst of the conflict, something large and green and hairy ripped the diner door off its hinges and lubbered in, slodging its fatty bulk into one of the booths. Four smaller versions of the same noseless abomination hopped after it and packed the other side of the booth. They reeked of ammonia and cotton candy. Honest Ariel was about to bring the green things their menus when the large one lost interest and flung itself onto the one bird-lizard that wasn't fighting. It squawked once and succumbed. The big green monstrosity lugged it away, followed again by the four tiny disasters.

Honest Ariel said a very foul word. The fighting bird-lizards ignored him. The one in the red dress was pressing the advantage. Drawing back its head, it plunged its spear-like beak through its opponent's throat. There was a gush of blood that sprinkled everything inside the diner as the loser thudded to the floor. The winner wiped its beak on a paper napkin and ordered a ham and cheese on white, trim the crusts off.

"Ah, scroomall," swore Honest Ariel, blotting the blood off his wings with the dirty counter-rag. "Ya see that? How'm I gonna get a classy rep if these punks keep messin' me up, huh? And you catch those others? They siddown, then they don't order nothin', just pick up a quick bite and go. Some nerve!"

"Especially since their snack might have been your paying

customer," commented Faith. The bird-thing had finished its sandwich and slunk out of the diner without bothering about payment. It left the body of its victim behind as collateral.

"Oh, for—!" Honest Ariel was at the end of his rope. "Now whaddoo I do? Last time this happened, I tossed the body before the health inspector could slap me with a fine, and I got inta big trouble with the next of kin. They wannit ta eat it themself."

"Mm," said Faith, green. She cleared her throat and considered Honest Ariel. He had the face of a saint and the mouth of a stevedore. He cooked like an angel and served it to the devils. He sat in a ghastly, cheap-looking diner in the middle of nowhere and talked about getting a classy rep. She had the certain feeling that if she could figure out Honest Ariel, she could figure out Parvahr.

"Say, Ariel," she said almost casually. "Mind if I ask you a personal question?"

"Shoot, sweetie," he shrugged, then muttered, "Damn it, I guess I'll hafta tip the garbagemen extra for hauling this one away. Heavy bastard." He was trying to hoist the dead bird thing into a battered silver trash can behind the counter. It went in headfirst, leaving only a pair of clawed feet in open-toed sandals visible.

"Ariel, dear," said Faith, "are you dead?"

Honest Ariel glared at her. "Boy, you got your nerve! Go around calling me dead. I'm just as alive as you, toots, and don't you forget it!"

"I thought you had to be dead if you were in Hell," said Faith, trying to placate him. "I just asked to find out whether I was alive or what."

"Look, lady, I told ya; this ain't Hell, it's Parvahr. You can't be dead to be here. It's like—like you know how sometimes you can't make up your mind about something, so you go someplace to think it over? Well, that's Parvahr," he finished, smiling.

"What on earth could it take you six thousand years to think over?" Faith demanded.

"Oh, you know." Honest Ariel shrugged again, this time with his wings instead of his shoulders. "Good. Evil. Siding with the angels or signing with the competition. Going all the way with chaos. Holding out for order. Stuff like that. You know, the universals. Want another sandwich?"

The bell over the door tinkled again and a blue, tusked face peeped in. "Hey, Ariel, still here?" Gerial hailed the proprietor.

"Yo! Gerial! Getcher fuggin' butt in here, ya sumbitch, an' havva cuppa Joe." Honest Ariel slammed a full cup onto the counter. "Man, it's been a long time. What kept ya away?"

"Oh, this and that. A little trouble with the bosses." Gerial sipped the coffee as neatly as his tusks would permit. "Hell's off limits, but I didn't know I could still drop in on Parvahr."

"So where you been?"

"Don't ask."

"Awright, keep secrets. Screw you and the horse you rode in on." It was said with a smile so wide that the surgically attached cigarette fell out of Honest Ariel's mouth and into Gerial's coffee. "Ya wanna hunk of pie?"

Gerial declined. "We've got to go." He took Faith's hand. "Put her stuff on my tab."

"You shittin' me? You ain't paid squat on your tab since Hammurabi got jugged for jaywalking."

Gerial and Faith were out the door. "Later, Ariel."

"Yeah, later. I got nothing but later." He swabbed the counter with his rag and lit another cigarette.

Father Lewis ran and ran, always hearing the crackle of approaching horrors behind him over the dead grasses. The featureless plain gave him no place to hide, nowhere to go. It betrayed the British priest as surely as if it had been a blank sheet of snow white paper and he a blob of ebon ink splat in the center. Still, knowing his flight to be hopeless, he ran.

The black rock jutted slightly out of the grasses around it. He caught his foot on it and thought he was falling forward until he realized he was toppling down into darkness. He was racing headfirst down a slippery tunnel with the hot winds of Hell on his face.

The fall of Father Lewis ended in a gorse-bush. He found himself face-first down in the prickles, struggling to get free. His hands and cheeks were bleeding generously when strong hands yanked him out of the bush and set him on his feet. Father Lewis looked around. He was in the heart of a misty forest near an ancient oak and the only other soul nearby was the silent old man, face like a cragged Welsh mountain, who had helped him up.

"Whoever you are, thank you," said Father Lewis. He felt strangely revived. The moist green air of the forest blew through his brain and cleared it of all thought of demons and eternal vengeance. In the shade of the timeless oak tree, heavy with the pearls of mistletoe, the world had lost knowledge of sin.

The old man looked at Father Lewis steadily from under his shaggy white eyebrows. His hair and beard were lambent white, the color of lightning, and his eyes brooded darkly, like thunderclouds. An owl perched in the branches of the tree above his head.

Father Lewis grew uneasy under that hard stare. He felt like a schoolboy called upon to recite a lesson he hasn't studied. "My name is Lewis Freeman." For some reason he didn't want to mention his clerical calling.

"Priest," said the old man. His voice reverberated in the arched vastness of the forest as in a hall of stone. "Priest, why come you to disturb my meditations?"

"I—I didn't mean to," Father Lewis faltered. "I don't even know how I got here. I was running away from something; running across a flat plain, and then I tripped and fell down a sort of passageway and came out here." He gestured towards the gorse-bush, then froze. There was nothing but forest all around. There was no tunnel; there was not even the gorse-bush, although he still had the scratches.

"Do not fear," the old man intoned. "I shape it. I change it when the shapes tire me. No man can meditate forever. I'm glad of your company. Sit with me and talk." He stroked the air and a thick walnut-wood table appeared. Another stroke, and it was set with two silver goblets studded with jasper. Father Lewis sat down slowly on the massive chair that suddenly awaited him. The old man took the place opposite.

"I am Merlin," he said, and a ghostly page in Pendragon livery was at Father Lewis' side, pouring the wine. "Welcome to Parvahr."

Father Lewis felt himself grow gradually calmer. He had relished the tales of Arthur since boyhood, and here he sat, sharing a drink with the greatest wizard of the age, just as if they were chums at the local public house. He finished the first measure dreamily, listening to Merlin talk. The page poured him a same-again. He proposed his host's good health, raising the goblet high.

"DON'T DRINK THAT!"

A russet-headed blur scooted into the forest clearing. The page and the owl took flight simultaneously as the girl knocked

Father Lewis' goblet from his lips. The wine splashed over
Merlin's robes. The wizard rose in anger, snatched a stem of
mistletoe from the overhanging oak, kindled white fire from
the shining berries, and hurled it at Faith.

"Oh, for—!" Gerial did a swan-dive into the earth behind
Father Lewis' chair and came up between Faith and Merlin's
fireball. He batted it away bare-handed. It fizzled out in the
forest's damp depths. "That smarts." Gerial sucked his singed
paw and rounded on Faith. "I can't take you anywhere!"

"You're not supposed to eat or drink anything in Hades or
you have to stay here!" she countered.

Father Lewis stared at the empty goblet horror-struck. "But
I've already drunk some! A full cup!"

"You dumb broad, why don't you use your ears for something more than hanging your specs on? This isn't Hades!"

Faith was chagrinned. "I forgot."

"Yeah, you forgot all that 'don't eat or drink' stuff pretty
good in Honest Ariel's, too. Think I didn't get a look at what
you put away? Your hips are gonna remember it real good.
Calories count everywhere, baby: Hell, Heaven, or Hacken-
sack!"

"Call me a dumb broad again and—"

"Now, now, children . . ." Father Lewis tried to make peace.

Merlin snorted and cleared away the table and all it held
with a pass of his hands. He turned his back on his three
unasked visitors and walked right into the heart of the oak
tree. It split to receive him and closed with booming finality
once he was inside.

'And here I always thought it was only Nimue who could
shut him up in that thing," Father Lewis mused.

"I can think of a few people who could use lessons in
shutting themselves up," Gerial mumbled.

Faith cocked a snook at him.

Night fell over the plain, night with borders, night with
limits, night that shrouded only Father William in darkness
and stars.

He had been loping after Father Lewis for a long time, he
could not say how long. He was tired, but some hard streaks
inside him would not let him admit how much he would like
to stop and rest. Father Lewis needed him and he was the
only one who could help his friend, but to help him he would
have to catch him first, and that meant not stopping.

The darkness forced him to stop. He felt almost grateful for the sudden nightfall. Panting, he sank down in the whispering grasses. He would try to pick up Father Lewis' trail in the morning. It might not be too hard. Father Lewis was a beefy man. He'd trample down the dead grasses, and Father William had sharp eyes. With a yawn, he composed himself for sleep.

He was jabbed awake by a set of prongs in the small of his back and awoke to look a pig in the face. No, not a pig, a pig-faced demon that snorted and slobbered with yellow foam clinging to its flaccid lips and ochre tusks. Its body was man-like, but covered with the short, bristly, parti-colored hair of a boar. It held a scarlet pitchfork in its hands and shoved it at Father William. He gave a yell and scrambled to his feet, but the pig-demon was gone.

He was standing in the middle of a circle of flames that blazed and crackled without a break in the infernal curtain. He could feel the searing heat, and he thought he noticed an imperceptible drifting in the wall of fire, drifting closer to him, coming nearer by millimeters, but still coming on.

Tighter and tighter drew the noose of flames. Father William felt his hair begin to crispen and sweat trickled down his neck, but it was the cold fear-sweat. Beyond the ring of fire he thought he saw the pig-demon again, prancing, taunting, posturing obscenely. There were other demons, too, demons in every shape and form, demons with the faces of beasts, demons with the wings of angels, demons with neither faces nor wings, demons that were the shapes of nameless fears that had dogged Father Lewis and all his race from the moment a glimmering of understanding had broken upon their newly formed brains.

The demons yowled and jeered and beckoned. The fire burned thin. It could not have been wider than two inches. It was easy to see the demons through the flame, the way a man could see fish through deep water. But the fire was very real, very hot, and no matter how thin a curtain of flame burned, it was made of the flames of Hell, which can consume utterly.

Father William looked to right, to left, above and below and saw no help, no possibility of help. And then, strangely, his fears all left him. The very fact of his helplessness seemed to reassure him that there was only one course open to him, and it was a course he cherished and welcomed wholeheartedly.

Father William knelt to pray.

They were stabbing at him through the encircling inferno.

They were reaching in for him with their charred, cracking, scaly paws. They were not immune to the flames, these demons, and the stench of their burning flesh and fur was choking, yet still they grabbed for Father William. A man's hand that ended in a falcon's talons brushed his left ear, drawing blood. A jabbing lance with a white pennon blazing at the tip just missed his head. The wailing, slobbering, tittering song of the demons rose and fell and rose again to crest in a wave of pure chaotic noise, true pandemonium, but through the incoherent babble Father William could still make out intelligible words, pleas, promises, horrible promises. He prayed on.

And they were gone. He was kneeling in the middle of a polished hardwood dance-floor in what looked like an abandoned nightclub. A lone baby spot shone down from the light grid above the stage, illuminating a swarthy man who wore dark glasses and aimlessly played a guitar.

"Where—" began Father William. "Where—?" He could not fit the right words to form the question. Where was he? Where was Father Lewis? Where were the others? Where . . . Too many questions to be asked. And where were the demons?

"Parvahr, man," drawled the whisky-voiced guitarist. "Don' mind me. Have youself a seat. 'Bout time we had showtime." He struck a melodramatic chord. On cue, every spotlight blazed white-hot, shining on the lonesome player and on the banquet table spread between him and Father William. A pair of lithe wenches, as supple as snakes, writhed sensuously to the low, tremulous, suggestive music that the musician seduced out of the rosewood belly of the guitar. They danced and brought fresh delicacies out of thin air. They danced and poured wine.

"Pretty fine show," said the player. Without smile or apology he segued smoothly out of the Oriental melody and into the jingle for a crowd-pleasing mouthwash. Father William winced, but the dancing girls never missed a step. Back and forth and back again the blind player went from songs that held the soul of the man who wrote them to tasteless, mindless, deathless ditties proclaiming the virtues of floor wax and roach killer. "You like my show, man?" Father William's host asked, giving him a big old down-home grin.

"What is all this?" demanded the priest wildly. The dancing girls twirled, their rose and saffron veils like wisps of fragrant smoke in the air. "I was asleep, dreaming terrible dreams. Maybe I'm still dreaming. Where am I? Who are you? For God's sake, stop tormenting that poor guitar and answer me!"

"Well, hey, man, I'd like to oblige, but I don't think I better leave off playing, you know? Later. Hey, I can talk and play. Always could. No problem. Where you? I told you, man. Parvahr. Not a little slice of Heaven, but then it ain't Hell either, so don't kick."

"Parvahr," repeated Father William. "Where is Parvahr? Are we near any large town? I've got to get help to find my friend, and the others."

The musician gave a rich chuckle deep in his throat. "Oh, Parvahr's near everywhere, man. You can get here from there, but getting back . . . That's something else."

"Ridiculous!" snorted Father William. "If I got here somehow, it stands to reason I can get back by retracing my steps."

"Sure, man," sighed the player. "If you know the steps that got you here. Now me, I know how come I'm here, and I could get out easy if I wanted, but I'm not so sure I want. You like my music?" He went from plucking out a cheap imitation-flamenco ballad to an elegant rendition of something by Vivaldi.

Father William decided that the man was mad. However, he had mentioned knowledge of a way out, mad or not, and so might be worth humoring. And then there were those two dancing girls who lightfooted their way through the mazes of sweet sound traced by the old rosewood guitar.

"You play very well," said Father William gruffly.

"Think so?" Light reflected from the musician's dark glasses in starpoints. "You not the first to say that. I hear it five, six times a day down here. Yeah. It be easy for me to pack it up and get it out of here, man, knowing I'm that good, but then you know what I think? I sit back and I think, I'm good, but *how* good? Who says I'm good, man? Anybody what got some real connections? No way. Just a bunch of drifters, like you, they come by, say I play good, they go on. They no better at what they supposed to be doing with their life than I am. Why should I listen to them, go back, maybe get a kick in the teeth when I try to play my music, huh? I don't want no kick in the teeth, man. I had enough of them before I came here. It ain't so bad in Parvahr, you know. You get used to it. If you don't, you know how to get out."

"If I knew that," said Father William, "I wouldn't be here." The guitar stung the air with a mocking trill that set his teeth on edge. "Will you *stop* that infernal tickling!" he shouted.

"Hey, okay," grinned the musician. "But you won't like it." He lifted his hand from the strings.

The dancing girls poised on the silence, their doe-eyes wide with betrayal that slowly heated to anger, flaming yellow behind their thick black lashes. A wild, impossible wind began to blow through the deserted nightclub, a wind that sent their torrents of golden hair, their rose and saffron veils, streaming out into fans of brilliance behind them. Blurred brilliance, brilliance that shifted shape, brilliance that sprouted harsh plumage from their slender arms, arms into wings, wings that beat rapidly into the wind and formed the wind and were the wind. Their wings grew as their bodies dwindled, their long legs drawing up into strong, short, taloned feet meant to grasp and tear and ruin. Only their faces remained, faces of women, faces of harpies. With a savage scream they fell upon the delicately laid table and devoured the dainties, grossly befouling all they could not eat, making the smoky stale air hideous with their stench. Father William cried out like a kitten and hid his head. The blind guitarist laughed and applauded, then took up his instrument again. At the first chord the harpies blinked to lissome dancing girls again.

"Best show you ever find in all Parvahr, man," said the musician, playing a lost lament of Amadino.

Gerial stuck his head in. "Yep, he's here all right!" he yelled to whomever was still outside. "Come on, Father William, the bus for home's loading."

The American priest didn't need a second invitation. He nearly knocked Gerial over as he ran out of the unearthly cabaret. Gerial clicked his tongue over the poor manners of some mortals.

"Hey," he called to the guitarist as he was about to go. "Play 'Melancholy Baby'."

"I don't do requests, man."

"Neither did I, and look where it got me," Gerial said as he closed the door behind him.

"Mr. Cardiff?" called Amanda, groping through the smoke. Her hand lit on a khaki-covered arm.

"Right here, dear girl. Where'd you think I'd be?" Kent Cardiff asked pleasantly. "No need to panic, is there?"

Amanda hesitated. She had, like the others, gradually become aware of the impenetrable mist surrounding them, and she had been the first to call out to the others, but none answered. None until Kent Cardiff, and she had called his name the last of all. The fog was lifting and in its place a gritty drizzle was falling. The barren plain looked like the most dismal of city streets in a November rain. As far as they could see, they were the only creatures there.

"Where do you suppose the others are?" Amanda asked. "Faith!" she called tentatively. "Dr. Hack!" She got up and squinted at the horizon. No sign of Father Lewis or Father William either. She called their names anyhow.

"Frightfully sorry," Kent Cardiff said crisply, "but I haven't a clue. Fogs do strange things to people, you know. Alter sight and sound, or so I've heard. Not like the old, dependable London fogs, not a bit. But we're not in London any more, are we?" He sighed. "Not even a sight of that demonic chap—what was his name?—Geritol?"

"Gerial. He abandoned us. Maybe Dr. Hack was right. This is Hell and Gerial was just sent to get our hopes up when we shouldn't have any."

"I wouldn't misjudge the lad. If he really wanted us to lose heart, he could've left the job to Dr. Hack. Old Gerial struck me as a bit of all right. Not much to look at before teatime, but not the true demonic type at all; inside, that is. I rather miss him."

"What shall we do?" Amanda wondered miserably. The rain was cold and penetrating. Her hair hung in strings and she had to keep wiping droplets out of her eyes.

"Press on," Kent Cardiff said matter-of-factly. "Nothing else to do for it. Here now, chin up. I think I see a ray of hope on the horizon, eh?" He gestured towards a muzzy yellow glow not too far off. It was the hidden valley.

"I still wish I knew where we were," Amanda panted as they trudged onwards through the soggy grass. "And I wish I knew where everyone else had got to."

"Mustn't fret," Kent replied. "It'll all come right eventually."

"My, aren't you chipper," Amanda growled. "Is this the famous British pluck that defeated the best of the blitzkrieg?"

"I couldn't say, actually." Kent shrugged. "I was raised in Canada."

"Well, you tweedy phony!" gasped Amanda, standing stock still and planting her hands on her hips. "Where did all this Oxonian English spring from, then? You unmitigated ham!"

"Dear girl," answered Kent Cardiff, "at least now we shall be able to understand each other better, as one phony to another."

"I beg your pardon!"

"And well you might. Come, come, if I play the Britisher more than I am strictly entitled to—and I *have* been British at heart since before you were weaned—don't you also play the wicked, wicked society girl?"

"I resent that."

"We all do," Kent Cardiff stated calmly. "Your behavior's been the talk of the encampment since we arrived."

"My behavior is no one's business but my own. If you think you're going to impose your stupid outdated moral values on me—"

"Oh, please, let's not have a row. We never once criticized your actions *per se*. It was simply that you were so loud about being so frightfully, frightfully evil. You overplayed it. I don't know why, but I for one got the feeling that you wouldn't be cheering half so stridently for lust and lechery if you weren't perhaps the *best* behaved little girl around. You might even be a virgin."

Amanda colored hotly. "That's a rotten lie!" she bellowed. "How dare you call me a virgin?"

"Awfully sorry, dear girl. Had no idea it was an insult. Although . . . ," the light of insight touched him, " . . . perhaps it's considered more of an insult to be a virgin these days. Well, no matter. Virgin or not, step lively. We're almost there."

"I am not a virgin," grumbled Amanda, stomping after him, "I am *not* a virgin." But she knew that saying so would never make it so, and she was ashamed. Amanda Rhodes, scandal of her set, and not only a virgin but firmly and foursquare on the side of the angels.

If this ever gets back to my friends, she thought, I'm ruined.

"Phoenician influence. Definitely Phoenician influence," decreed Dr. Hack, examining the inscriptions on the clay walls of the temple. Above his head, carved in high relief, a fish-faced god gaped down at the inner court of the temple.

Dr. Hack was deliriously happy. He had, he reasoned, dozed off in self-defense against the noxious fumes of Kent Cardiff's pipe and the obnoxious behavior of Amanda Rhodes. His cheek still smarted from her slap. Where did she come to strike her superior, that spoiled little rich-girl tramp? For that matter, where did any of them come to dare treat a man of Dr. Hack's learning with such disdain and contempt? Ignorant barbarians. He'd only had a run of bad luck, that was all, but now . . . now he would come into his own. He had discovered the temple.

Whose temple, or what it was doing there, or how he had gotten there were all confused in Dr. Hack's mind. But none of that mattered, he told himself. He was here, wasn't he? How did it matter how he came to be here? Possession was nine-tenths of the law, and the stray tenth was self-possession. It was his temple, his discovery, and it was a find of such glory as to be worthy of the noble Dr. Hack.

He had wakened from his torpor under the arched lapis gate that led to the inner court of the temple enclosure. Beasts, birds, and fish sparkled in the strange, overcast light, their portraits picked out on the enclosure walls with carnelian, lapis lazuli, jade, agate, and gold tiles. The actual temple structure was even more magnificent, the pillars beneath the fish-faced god alternated nephrite and pink marble with golden capitals chased with gems. The terrace before the temple entrance was a mosaic of laughing girls and grim priests, their eyes diamonds undimmed by time, their limbs of inlaid ivory, their veils thin slices of opal, serpentine, and turquoise.

Dr. Hack finished his study of the inscriptions and admitted himself stumped. The characters looked akin to Phoenician, but they made no sense if translated as such. There was, however, one word that called to him, a word so very close in sound to the true Phoenician that it simply had to mean what he thought it meant: treasure-house.

"The treasure-house of a lost god," Dr. Hack breathed, looking up at the fish-faced deity on the plinth. Some forgotten artisan had painted the sandstone sculpture with stripes of Mediterranean blue and green, but the slack lips were tinted blood red. The obsidian eyes appeared to follow the good professor's movements.

Dr. Hack satisfied himself that he had paid enough homage

to the god of archeology by straining his eyes over the inscriptions. Scholarship had been satisfied. Now it was time to step within the precincts of the temple—of the treasure-house, he hoped—and prove his theory. Hadn't there been talk of just such a buried fortune in a temple of sacred prostitutes near the very site of Quintus' monastery? Hadn't Quintus himself mentioned it during those sweltering sessions in the hut, poring over his scroll? Dr. Hack rubbed his hands, already seeing the divine Ms. Ferrabosco bedazzling in the golden panoply of centuries-dead harlots, and no foundation garments.

It was cool and dark inside the temple, pitch dark and redolent of mold, strange in such a hot climate. Dr. Hack was in a cavernous, square room, its thick stone walls unbroken by any door or window apart from the one he'd entered. Something cold glittered on the far side of the chamber.

Dr. Hack blundered forward towards the glitter in the dark, cursing himself for being without a flashlight or even a match. He began to lose his sense of direction. The glimmer grew faint, and when he turned back to orient himself from the temple entrance again, he could not find it. Something came up suddenly behind his knees, the edge of an ancient bench perhaps, and he windmilled his arms vigorously to keep his balance, but fell anyway in a crash and tinkle of broken glass and jangling metal.

Flat on his back, Dr. Hack saw the solid blackness of the chamber roof begin to glow with dawnlight, and for one senseless moment it seemed to him to be a perfectly normal thing for a ceiling to do, to change color like the night sky in the hour before the sun. Yes, yes, of course, why not? All black, that vast and endless roof over his head, Dr. Hack's own personal sky. Why shouldn't it lighten with the dawn? Why shouldn't he enjoy the coming light? It filled him with hope, and hope was not the sole, unique province and birth-right of the Geordie Burns' of the world. Somewhere, some-how, in his private part of Hell, Dr. Hack had found a morsel of hope.

"Excuse me, honored visitor," a voice of melodious sweet-ness piped from above, "but you are sitting in my foot-bath."

"Pay no attention to the wench," a hoarse, blustering voice slammed down like a lid on the first one. "She'd never think of washing her feet if I didn't nag her to it constantly, and then it's done only with a damp rag."

"It is still my foot-bath, Gerha'ar," said the first voice petulantly. "Whether I wash my feet or not is my own business. It's still mine, and I don't want him sitting in it. It was a gift from the Liege Ruler of Heaven."

"May he live forever," intoned the hoarse voice, then added in a mutter, "Stupid jackass! Didn't die a minute too soon to suit me."

The light from above increased and Dr. Hack could now see the people who were speaking. Moreover, he could see where he was lying, smack on his backside in a gold dish studded with rubies, any one of which would have ransomed a soul. The most beautiful young girl in the world was giving him the most disgusted look in creation. Beside her stood a corpulent, bald-headed, triple-chinned being in a white gauze gown and an inlaid torquoise collar. He rubbed his fat hands together, making little popping and squeaking sounds, while he talked.

"Honored guest," the fat one made a modest bow towards the prone Dr. Hack. "If it would not too much inconvenience you, we should be pleased were you to rise from that most unworthy seat and accept one more befitting your obvious rank and prestige."

"Oh," said Dr. Hack, and scrambled out of the foot-bath. The girl immediately seized it and bore it away in triumph. He could not see where she went. Shadows still lingered in the corners of the chamber, shrouding any possible doors.

"She'll be back," said the bald one. "It is almost the hour of the dance, and she takes an awfully long time to get ready. I don't think she cares about it anymore. I can't fault the child. For the first thousand years she performed her functions punctually, but the second thousand made her spirits sag, and the third saw her moping through the rituals, and the fourth—"

"You didn't say the first thousand years, did you," stated Dr. Hack. Not since that voice had first come to him in his solitary tent had he seen so clearly the slender thread he walked on above the pits of madness. "Thousand."

"Thousand, of course thousand," huffed the fat man. "But she's shaped up again, recently. You won't be disappointed. Except if you expect clean feet. Ah!" A tinkle of silver ankle bells chimed across the red, white, royal, and gold floor tiles. "Now."

Her dance was the dance of promise, the dance of passion.

Her hips undulated as if her entire body had gone suddenly liquid from the shoulders down. Her tiny white feet stamped out her own accompaniment, setting her silver bells jingling in hard time. They were her only ornaments, her long, black hair her only dress.

Dr. Hack was speechless. Now he thought he recognized the temple and the god. One of the many faces of fertility, the rich, fecund, swelling principle that man took for his first god, although he gave it other names. Astarte. Isis. Kore. And this was the dance, the dance to call up the dormant desires of the male and spin his brain until the only thing he lived to do on earth was sow and sow and sow his seed into the mystery of a woman.

He felt himself grow hot. Thoughts that had not troubled him since his distant adolescent years came back to plague him. His mind reassured him that he was too old for such foolishness, but the twists and turns and ripplings of the dance made more powerful forces inside him cry out that he was young. Young! Unsteadily he stretched his arms out towards the dancing girl and lurched across the tiles.

The last gasp of his reason said, Temple prostitutes were compelled by custom to accept all comers, for the greater glory of the god and the increased fertility of the land. SEE: *Sympathetic Magic*, Vol. IV.

"Oh no! Oh no! Go away! Please, please, go away you horrid old man!" The temptress shrilled like a piglet caught in a gate. She cringed away from Dr. Hack and ran back into the sheltering darkness. Dr. Hack sighed, released from her enchantment.

"Dear, dear," sighed the fat one, folding his plump, ringed fingers over his paunch. "Thought we almost had it there. Pity. Well, it can't be helped. Not your fault, honored one. Will it please you to have some wine while Tiamat dresses?"

Torches sprang to life on the walls of the square chamber. Piled gold coruscated and flashed in the light. Crowns and armlets, torques and brooches lay piled pell-mell, in some places swept into tidy heaps of wealth, in others rolling free across the floor. Tiamat's gold foot-bath had been the poor cousin here. Besides the ornaments there were common household objects—common in Phoenician times, that is—made ludicrous and gaudy with gold and jewels. Treasure-house.

Tiamat the dancing girl returned, calmer, and wrestled a gold table planked with topaz from one of the piles. She set

up the bench—gold also—that had tripped up Dr. Hack,
fetched a mahogany stool inlaid with mother-of-pearl, and
plunked down a homely clay jug of wine and two chipped
terra cotta cups. Motioning the gentlemen to sit and refresh
themselves, she took a humble station on the floor, beaming.

"You see?" said the fat one. "Tiamat's a good girl. One
of my favorites. But she never could quite go the distance.
Dances like a dream, doesn't she? Ah, don't be modest with
me, honored one—" he wagged a sausage-like finger at Dr.
Hack. "I could see the wanting in your eyes. I've seen too
many of 'em. Come and go, but we're still here, and all
because Tiamat can't bring herelf to do what's expected of
her, but she can't make herself go into another line of work."

"Oh, shut up, Gerha'ar. You give me a pain," said the
girl. Dr. Hack assumed that the fat one must be one of the
temple eunuchs for Tiamat to be so bold. Would she dare
address a priest like that?

Gerha'ar shook his head and made clicking noises with his
tongue. "No respect," he commented sadly. "No respect left
for me at all, and I do so try to keep up appearances. We
must make the best of our lives here in Parvahr, but little
Tiamat makes it difficult. You understand, honored visitor,
that once upon a time—the first time my reluctant handmaiden
refused to perform her holy function—with a dropsical
Canaanite wine-merchant, as I recall—Where was I?"

"The first time she refused," prompted Dr. Hack.

"Just so! The first time she refused, I might have spared us
both all these years of torment by the simple expedient of
striking her dead on the spot, after spectacular agonies, natu-
rally, to bolster the faith of the unbelievers. But I didn't. She
was my favorite, the girl with the most promise of any in the
temple corps. The Liege Ruler of Heaven, Zemuz IX, had
gone so far as to send her tokens of esteem before her first
performance."

"My foot-bath," mumbled Tiamat.

"Oh, be quiet!" snorted the fat man. "I am sick of you
and your eternal foot-bath! May the Earth-frog swallow you
both and belch your soul to the winds of perdition!"

Tiamat laughed. "That's not even vaguely scary," she
jeered, then turned confidentially to Dr. Hack. "You should
have seen him in the old days, honored guest. Then, could
that guy curse! When his maledictions were coming thick and
fast in the sanctuary, I saw grown men keel over dead with

fright. Very impressive. That's why I decided to enlist in the temple service, especially after he cursed Zemuz VIII. Now there was a curse!''

"Really," commented Dr. Hack drily.

"Oh, yes," replied the girl sincerely. "Plague of locusts. Devoured him right in the royal palace bath-house, down to the bones. Was that a curse or was that a curse? But he's fallen off lately. I'm not even scared of him anymore.''

"You could be, you know," said Gerha'ar sulkily. "You could try, at least in front of company. What do you think your flippancy is doing to my reputation?"

"You haven't had where to hang your reputation for seven thousand years!" screamed Tiamat. "Even if I would've submitted to this one—" she pointed to Dr. Hack—"you'd still be stuck down here in Parvahr, because what the hell could you ever do to get out?''

"No more nor less than you, girl," puffed Garha'ar. "No more nor less than any in Parvahr must do to leave."

"Leave! My God, there's nothing I want so much as to get out of here, and you say you know how?" demanded Dr. Hack. He collared Gerha'ar so eagerly that the fat one's turquoise collar came off in his hands. The white gauze vestments began to slip from the chubby shoulders. Tiamat gasped.

"*Sacrilege!*''

"Huh?" grunted Dr. Hack.

"*Sacrilege!*" shrieked Tiamat again, raking her cheeks with her fingernails and flinging herself down to writhe among the piles of gold on the temple floor. Lightning cracked beneath the stone roof, riving the dome, crushing it inward like an eggshell.

The gauze robe lay in a pool of whiteness at Gerha'ar's feet. His iridescent scales throbbed with light and life of their own, his membraneous wings hanging in sea-green folds from wrist to hip, flaring out like a translucent cape when he raised his arms. Whorls of blue and green flowed over his sagging cheeks while his slack lips parted, revealing the small, uncountable rows of needle-sharp teeth gnashing angrily within the scarlet mouth. His finny tail lashed back and forth, mashing precious vessels and goblets to gold dust.

Dr. Hack screamed and threw himself down beside the grovelling Tiamat, waiting to die at the hands of the god whose person he had profaned. The earth heaved and trembled under his belly, or perhaps it was just his belly that heaved and trembled. There was an eternity of imagined deaths he passed through, but when he felt the temple floor buckle once, then subside, and he was still alive, he gathered the courage to look up again.

"It's all right, quite all right," said Gerha'ar, pinching together the snapped ends of his collar. The fishy body was once more discreetly covered with the white gauze gown, the mighty tail tucked out of sight somehow. "I understand that accidents do happen. It's not like in the old days. You'd have been dead by now for doing less. It's true, the years do mellow one."

"Some god!" sneered Tiamat, regaining composure swiftly. "If you'd have slaughtered us both on the spot, you'd have been out of here!"

"Yes, I suppose so," admitted Gerha'ar. "Maybe someday I will wipe out you and him and everything for miles around. That should be decisive enough to get me out of here. But I just don't feel up to Armageddon today. Will you both excuse me? It's time for my nap. Help yourself to anything, honored guest. There's food and wine on the sideboard, and there's Tiamat, if you like. And if she lets you." A glare from the dancing girl indicated plainly that she was not going to let anyone.

"Wait!" Dr. Hack called after the retreating god. "Please, you have to tell me. How can I get out? If I kill her, would that be good enough? If I kill you—?"

Gerha'ar chuckled and it was the sound of waves breaking on the beach. "You can't take another person's path out of Parvahr," he smiled. "You made your own way in, you must find your own way out."

"But how?" Dr. Hack moaned. "How?"

"I've got my own problems," Gerha'ar replied. "Tiamat, if you're not going to serve this fellow, study the obscene mosaics in the turquoise chamber while I'm snoozing. I will quiz you on them when I awake and you *will* be graded."

He left, his hidden tail sweeping the floor. The dancing girl paused only long enough to drag her foot-bath out of Dr. Hack's reach. Frazzled, the archeologist sat down right in the middle of the floor and sobbed.

"There, there," Gerial said, patting him on the back hard enough to dislodge a chicken bone. "Take it easy. We've found you again."

"Don't cry, Dr. Hack." Faith gave him her handkerchief. Even in Parvahr, she was prepared. "We're almost to the valley. Gerial says it holds the easiest way out for us." Father Lewis and Father William nodded agreement.

Dr. Hack rubbed the tears away brusquely, acting as if they had never fallen. He stood up on his own, snubbing all offers of help with a harsh. "I can take care of myself!"

"Glad to hear you say so, Doc." Gerial beamed. "That's half the battle to getting out of Parvahr."

"The other half would appear to be knowing what you want in the first place, then acting decisively on it," Father Lewis contributed.

"I know what I want." Dr. Hack picked up one of the thick gold bracelets littering the temple floor and stuffed it into his pants pocket. "There! Decisive enough for you?"

Gerial stroked his chin. "Decisive," he allowed. "Second-degree Avarice, but decisive. Seems I recall I started out that way. Wish you better luck than I had."

Dr. Hack pulled the bracelet from his pocket and dropped it. "Let's get out of here!" He stormed past them all, making for the lapis gate. The others followed him, leaving Gerial to bring up the rear.

"Who's supposed to be leading this group anyhow?" the blue demon shouted after them. "No respect for the danged proprieties," he muttered, trailing out. "No respect at all."

3

Down In the Valley

"You know," remarked Kent Cardiff as he and Amanda shinnied down the brush-strewn sandy slopes of the yellow valley, "I confess I'm not too frightfully keen about this place."

"Awk," said Amanda. It didn't strike Kent Cardiff as either a polite or a logical reply, but he had to keep reminding himself that the girl was American. She was also upset, waving her arms about in a most undignified and unflattering manner. Kent Cardiff regretted that his dear Marguerite Gounod was not present to give Amanda a few lessons in the art of ladylike deportment.

"Would you stop gawping at me and use your eyes?" shouted Amanda. "Over there! Is your neck made out of leather? Look!"

Kent Cardiff looked.

"Awk," said Kent Cardiff. It struck Amanda as just the right thing to say.

The black castle brooded over the floor of the valley like a deadly spider in a yellow bowl. Its proportions were fit for Titans, its chill aura so insidiously penetrating that Kent and Amanda, yards off, began to shiver. Its towers soared up to pierce the dusty grey of the sky. One spire in particular surged heavenward like a great black rocket, its topmost parts hidden in the upper reaches of darkness. The moat was dry, the drawbridge was down, and a single amber light burned in the highest window of the sinister turret. The dry yellow bones of a dragon sprawled before the gate.

Kent Cardiff and Amanda picked their way cautiously across the valley floor and unconsciously linked hands, like children. The dragon bones gleamed with a sulphurous light, the eternally grinning fleshless jaws forming a grisly gateway that they had to pass through in order to cross the bridge. The bones creaked and swayed menacingly above their heads, tilting and shifting slightly with every step they took, constantly threatening to topple in upon them. Kent Cardiff stumbled over the lower jaw-bone. The smallest dragon's tooth was taller than he was by a head.

"Let's get out of here," hissed Amanda. "We're looking for a way *out*, not a prison."

"Hardly qualifies as a prison," said Kent Cardiff. "This thing's dead, y'know, and the gate's wide open. Beastly, poorly run prison, if it is that. Should at least have a live dragon."

They entered the gateway. All was shadows. The black walls of the castle seemed to inch surreptitiously around and behind them in a flanking motion, like the double sweep of two black scythes. There were no windows, no source of light, yet they walked on into the blackness and found that they were able to see as clearly as if a thousand candles lit the gloom.

"I think I see a light," said Amanda.

"I see several," amended Kent Cardiff. He paused to fill his pipe, not spilling a flake of tobacco in the dark. The flare of his match was blinding.

"Maybe we should go back," ventured Amanda. The black castle made her skin crawl. There was the uncanny feeling she had that the structure itself was gloating over its prey.

"Well, we shall, if you insist," shrugged Mr. Cardiff. "But it seems a pity, rather. Those lights just ahead might be our companions, mightn't they now? Why, they've all come on ahead of us, drawn by the valley, and once in the valley there isn't any place other than this old pile to go to, is there? Do let's have a go and see if it's they."

Reluctantly Amanda allowed Kent Cardiff to persuade her.

They walked towards the lights. Dimly she sensed that they were passing from one room to another, then ascending a winding stair, and always the vagrant tongues of light danced before them like will-o'-the-wisps that lure benighted travellers to drown.

A cornice of icy white marble sprang up like a mushroom, bizarrely out of place in an edifice of darkness and shadows. The flickering lights were still, no longer leading Kent and Amanda on. They had come to the end of their search. A round obsidian table, chased with arabesques of steel, studded grimly with black opals filled with evil fire. Four bowls of blood-red lacquerware, each filled with a queer, oily green liquid on whose surface a single scrap of fire twinkled. An iron chair with a seat of stone. Geordie Burns standing to the right of the high seat, Quintus to the left, and in between Murakh, resplendent in the full regalia of a cherished Prince of Hell.

"Welcome to my domain," said the demon with his incredible smile. His pearly claws curled lovingly around one of the red bowls. "I am surprised to see two of you. I have judged—It doesn't matter what I judged. I was mistaken. Two of you. Two who for one reason or another were exempted from a short sojourn . . . " he raised the bowl—"here."

Murakh tilted the red bowl towards Amanda. A pit of oily green light spilled out at her feet, eating away the fabric of black stone, pitching her vision into a void she had to follow down, down, until at the bottom of it all she could just make out the wavery figure of Faith Schleppey sitting in an ancient diner with a winged man beautiful as song.

"Parvahr," said Murakh, and set down the first bowl to pour out the second in a cascade over Kent Cardiff's impassive head. Then he righted the bowl, and all the awful radiance flowed back into it like a moving picture run in reverse.

"Merlin," mused Kent Cardiff coolly. "And Father Lewis. They seem to be getting along, rather."

"Parvahr," said Murakh. Geordie Burns moved like a zombie to clear away the first two bowls and hold them stiff-armed in front of him. Murakh smashed the third bowl to the floor. Amanda yelled as its contents splashed upwards, splattering a picture of Father William administering a severe lecture to a pair of indifferent dancing girls, while in the background a black guitarist shrugged and played and smiled.

Green rain fell from the ceiling to fill the third bowl. The flame pirouetted on the slimy surface as if nothing had happened to disturb it. The bowl itself skimmed through the air to Murakh's waiting hand. He passed it to Quintus and seized the fourth bowl.

"Parvahr," he said, and breathed fire over the liquid until Dr. Hack cowered before the wrath of a fallen god. The fire consumed the seeing and Quintus cleared away the last bowl. "Parvahr," leered Murakh.

"Thanks ever so, I believe we've gotten the idea," said Kent Cardiff crisply. "However, it might be courteous of you to explain what you mean by Parvahr. Clearly it's where our companions are, and in a variety of situtations ranging from the pleasant to the unbearable, but we require more specific information, if you don't mind . . . " Kent Cardiff's voice trailed off. He wanted very much to observe the proper forms of address, but what honorific did one use with Satan? "Your Infernal Highness," he groped.

Murakh laughed. "Oh, I like you, Mr. Cardiff," he said with his crocodile grin. "If it were up to me, I would even overlook your little trespass. But that is not my jurisdiction."

"Trespass?" snapped Amanda. "If we're trespassing, just show us the way to go home. And as for those—" she jabbed a finger at the four bowls—"we'll thank you to return our friends to us as you found them."

"Yes," Murakh's voice was a caress. "Be sure you won't have to warn me again, sweet lady. Delicate lady. Tender lady, still untouched by man." His eyes were knowing, mocking. Amanda cringed. Kent Cardiff put one arm around her and gave her a reassuring squeeze, but it didn't help.

"See here, sir, I'll thank you to leave the young lady out of this," he said, an aggressive tilt to his chin. "She's perfectly right, y'know. You and your minions haven't a glimmer of holding our friends in durance vile legally. And if I'm not mistaken, the Devil's got quite the healthy respect for legality."

"Father of Lawyers," smirked Murakh. "But you flatter me. I am not our Lord Prince Saithann. No, nor any of his first-ranking princes, viceroys, generals, or lieutenants. I, alack, am merely Murakh, Commander of Vengeance and Lord of Parvahr."

"Well, sir—I mean, Your Lordship," Kent Cardiff settled on the way he would address the demon—"as I also understand it, one must be dead to fall into your clutches, mustn't

one? And I doubt we are, nor are our companions. Illegal
detainment, m'Lud, is beneath your power. Release them.''

Murakh rasped with laughter. Geordie and Quintus flashed
obedient, mirthless smiles and laughed like dolls. Ha. Ha.
Ha. Each syllable fell hard and sharp as the blade of the
guillotine.

"You are correct, Mr. Cardiff," Murakh admitted good-
humoredly as he wiped the scalding tears from his eyes. "I
am bound by the strictures of Hell to release you and your
companions from my realm." He snapped his fingers. Geordie
and Quintus flipped the bowls upside-down abruptly. Four
slippery streams of thick greenness dashed themselves to the
floor in a choking burst of smoke. Faith, Father William, Dr.
Hack, and Father Lewis lay starfished at Murakh's feet in the
dark beneath the iron table. One by one they clambered out of
the shadows and exclaimed with wonder and fear to be re-
united with Amanda and Kent, but in such a place and with
such a patron.

"Where—?"

"How did we get—?"

"One moment we were at the valley's rim, and suddenly—"

"Where's Gerial?" Dr. Hack bleated. "Where's that
damned—?"

"Shut up." Faith tugged urgently at his shirt, using it as a
choke collar. "No names, okay?"

"Why not? He said he'd get us—"

"I said *shut up!*" Faith tried to jerk him by the shirt again,
but Dr. Hack stepped out of reach. Prissily he smoothed the
wrinkles from his garb.

"This is going on your record, Miss Schleppey."

"You can take my record and—"

"I trust—" Murakh's voice sliced definitively through the
babble of their voices—"that now you are satisfied. I shall
go even farther, and all in the name of the honor of Hell. I
shall give you free and clear directions out of here. It's very
easy, but of course it must be easy to leave Parvahr. My
kingdom hasn't got the pull of Hell. All it takes to leave
Parvahr is one step; one very sure, irrevocable step."

"I've had my bellyful of riddles since I've come here!"
barked Father William. "What do you want us to do? Speak
plainly, if you can."

"My good man," said Murakh smoothly, "there's no
riddle there at all. I said step and I meant step. The topmost

step in the staircase that brought your intrepid friends this far
into my castle to seek you. Leave this room and find that
stairway again, then follow it upwards. At the moment you
set your foot on the last step, you will leave Parvahr. All of
you.'' He looked meaningly at Geordie and Quintus. ''They
shall go as well,'' he promised with an innocent smile, his
heavy eyelids lowered.

Kent Cardiff thought matters over and decided he would
lose nothing by shaking hands with Murakh. He extended his
own and said, ''Dear sir—Your Lordship, I mean—we're
ever so grateful that you've decided to be so beastly decent
about all this. And I can assure you that I shall henceforth
speak of you and your—ah—infernal associates—with great
respect. I might even suggest a special on demonology to the
network brass. Properly handled, we could winnow out the
sensationalism and give the public a firm grounding in—''

Murakh held up his hand and shook his head modestly.
''Don't trouble yourself, Mr. Cardiff. I shall be more than
amply rewarded for what I am about to do. Now go, all of
you.'' He smiled, and as the smile spread across his face, his
face itself appeared to spread and thin away until he was
gone, leaving only the suggestion of his features in the black
stone walls of the castle.

''Uh . . . hello, everybody,'' said Geordie Burns, rubbing
the back of his muscular neck and trying to work the kinks
out of it.

''Geordie!'' Faith yelped. ''Where have you *been?*''

Geordie shrugged. It was still a mystery to him, and the
one party who might have explained it all had smiled his way
out of existence. The body of Quintus was also gone.

''He can give us a blow-by-blow travelogue later,'' said
Dr. Hack severely. ''Meanwhile, let's get out of here before
that creature changes its mind.''

''Oh, Murakh won't change his mind.'' Gerial stepped out
of the same wall that had swallowed the leering demon.
''That's not his style.''

''Who is this?'' Geordie asked. He got his answer right
away.

''Gerial!'' Faith squealed, delighted. She embraced the
blue demon, who went violet with embarrassment and did his
best to untangle himself from the girl's arms.

''Never had anyone glad to see me,'' he mumbled.

''Well, of course we're glad to see you! I don't trust that

Murakh past square one. He's the same one who diddled you and your friends for centuries, isn't he?''

Gerial, shamefaced, allowed that this was true.

"So why shouldn't we be happy to have you back? You're one guide we can count on. He's going to get us home, Geordie, isn't he wonderful?'' she added for the benefit of a very bewildered Mr. Burns.

"Yes, I can just about see the halo on him now," Dr. Hack remarked drily.

Gerial champed his tusks. "S'matter? You don't feel a demon-guide is *worthy* of you, Hack? Ever stop to think how much good an angel'd do you down here? They're okay, I guess, if you can stomach their grandstanding way of getting stuff done, but they sure don't know this territory."

"And you do." The words dripped sarcasm.

"I know my place, that's what I know! I—I even know what I want, for the first time in centuries, which might be more than you know, Mr. Hotshot Archeologist. And I know that Murakh can do more harm with the truth than with a hundred lies. It's all in what he *doesn't* tell you, not in what he makes up. So, what *do* you want? Out? Quit wasting time and find those f-verbing stairs.''

" 'F-verbing'?'' Amanda looked at Kent.

"Demonic reticence in the matter of vocalized obscenity is something I never expected to hear. Fascinating, from both a linguistic and a theological point of view. Psychological, too, perhaps. Do you concur, Dr. Hack?''

Dr. Hack's reply used the f-verb in all its glorious permutations. Dr. Hack was sick of inaction. He bolted from the chamber and the others followed him. All was black around them and Kent and Amanda noticed that they no longer possessed the weird ability to see in the dark, like cats, the way they had been able to do when they first entered Murakh's black castle. Amanda groped ahead of her with outstretched hands, feeling now the smoothness of the wall, now a pinch of someone's clothing, now the touch of warm human flesh. And sometimes—sometimes in brief moments of panic, she thought she felt the touch of flesh that was not warm or human or even monstrous.

"Hey! This way! I've found the staircase!'' Geordie Burns shouted. The others stumbled towards the sound of his voice and to the last man they managed to encounter the stairs by

tripping on the first one and falling forward, barking their
knees on the rough-hewn stone.

"Remember," cautioned Father William, feeling for the
wall with one hand. "This may not be a continuous ascent.
There could be landings. First one in line call out if the stairs
end. We don't want to lose anyone on the way up. We must
all be together whenever we aren't on the steps."

"I think I see something," said Faith. "A sliver of—"

"I'm on a landing, Father William!" yodelled Geordie.
"Hey, everyone, there's a landing here. I'm waiting for you.
No one go past me."

"A sliver," said Faith when she reached the landing, "of
light."

They huddled together on the landing and their eyes were
drawn like mothflight to the four lines of brilliance that
defined . . .

"It's a door," said Amanda. She dared to go nearer.
Behind it she could hear voices raised in laughter, deep,
gravelly voices, and the clink of glasses.

"Party, party," mumbled Faith. "I'm glad we're not in-
vited. I wouldn't want to see whatever's celebrating its birth-
day back there." She recalled the green, shapeless, hairy
thing from Honest Ariel's and shuddered. She wondered if he
would ever do the one irrevocable deed that would decide the
direction of his life, for good or evil, and lift him from
Parvahr.

"Let's go on," said Father Lewis. He was feeling more
like his old self since his short interview with Merlin. What
had they talked about? It was hard to remember everything,
the way sometimes a man awakens from a vivid dream that he
can never recollect afterwards. He knew they had spoken
about Arthur, and he had given the ancient mage all he knew
of Albion, but specifics eluded him. The only fact to stick in
his brain were the last words Merlin had spoken before the
unseen hand slopped him out of the mystic forest and onto the
black castle floor.

"So they are all gone now, are they? And I am here,
spending my days thinking. . . . Thinking! What a poor excuse for a wizard I am, sir, who holds the power of the skies
and the dark reaches of earth in one hand, who could crook
my finger and lift Albion free of the morass that drags her
down, and who instead does nothing. My meditations are as
false as my motives, priest. My mother was a nun, my father

was a devil. My blood pulls both ways, and for a time I
served my mother's side, but the reward I had for that was to
let the maiden Nimue seal me in that storied cave at the roots
of the oak tree. And when she died, and the spell of her
binding lifted, and I could have come out and rescued Albion
once more . . . I did not. My blood tore me, priest, as it tears
me now, telling me I should serve good—no, evil—no,
good—no, myself. So I did nothing, and that is why I am
here.''

And Father Lewis remembered what he had said to Merlin
then, his brain bemused by the old wizard's special wine.
''It's no fault of yours, Merlin, sir. Someone should either
make the rewards of good better or the punishment of evil
worse. Poor planning on a grand scale, I call it. Nothing but
poor planning.''

They found the next flight of steps upwards and resumed
the climb. The air grew thinner, with a tang of mint and
moisture that was pleasantly refreshing, yet disturbing to the
mind. Geordie, still in the van, shouted down that he had
come to another landing. No light shone there, and so they
went upwards.

''Light!'' called Geordie.

''Another door?'' asked Amanda wearily.

''No,'' said Geordie, considering the matter. Even his bronzed
muscles were feeling the strain of constant ascent. ''No, it
looks like daylight.''

''Ah! Thank heavens!'' sighed Dr. Hack, putting an extra
thrust into his step and scrambling past the others on the
staircase. Geordie grinned and allowed his superior to get by.
With a shout of triumph Dr. Hack leaped from the last step
onto the sandy wastes around the black rock.

''We're home! I mean, we're back!'' crowed Dr. Hack,
letting the sunlight warm him. The rest of his party wasted no
time in joining their exclamations of joy with his. Only Faith
was unmoved.

''If we're back,'' she said slowly, ''we're the only ones
left. Where did everybody else go?''

The desert wind filled the silence that followed with a low,
grating whine. They all looked about and saw not a sign of
Marmota, Inc., or the massed might of the high priests of
media.

''We— we must've been gone a long time,'' said Dr.

Hack. "Oh, it doesn't matter where they are, Faith! It's not such a far walk to that Arab village. You know the one."

"How long could we have been gone?" wondered Amanda nervously. "I mean, it could've been years! Wherever we were, how do we know how they reckon time? It could be . . . more than years," she finished in a terrified whisper.

"Ah, yes, the legend of Ogier the Dane," Kent Cardiff announced, pinpointing Amanda's anxieties but doing nothing to relieve them. "A common enough motif in world folklore, with representative tales coming from as far away as Old Ireland—the story of Olsin MacFinn, for example—and Japan—the fisherman and the Sea King's daughter. The hero goes trotting off to Fairyland or the sea bottom or wherever you like and thinks he's only been there a month or two. Then he has the yen to pop in on his parents again, only when he returns he finds that thousands of years have passed and everyone is dead. Whereupon he breaks some taboo laid upon him by his supernatural sweetheart and immediately crumples to dust himself."

"And they lived happily every after," tagged Faith. "Well, if we have come back thousands of years later, I'd say architecture's taken a giant step backwards. Must be a nostalgia craze; clay huts are making a big comeback."

It was true. The sands near the black rock were teeming with a cluster of baked mud hovels, all looking brand-new. On a rise just to the west, a group of men in harsh brown robes sat in a semi-circle at the feet of a tall, ascetic-looking man, a man whose face was an old friend to every one of the fugitives from Parvahr.

"It's Quintus," said Amanda softly. "Quintus and his monks. We haven't gotten out yet. We're only on another landing. Look, past where they're sitting. Another flight of black stairs."

"Illusion," said Father William. "Interesting, but why would he pick this one? It won't keep us from going on."

"Maybe the monks will attack us," suggested Faith. "Or maybe—"

Leathery wings flapped in the air above them. Two broadly pinioned shadows stooped across their faces. Atamar and Melisan soared on the hot breath of the wasteland, unperceived by the gathered monks. The sands bubbled and churned. Horgist, Gerial, and Lura boiled up from the desert floor in a gust of brimstone. The light of greed filled their eyes as they contemplated the newly arrived monks. From somewhere far below a voice that rang with hate and envy roared like a brazen trumpet. The words were the tongue of Hell, but their meaning was clear.

"Oh," gasped Amanda. "Poor Quintus!" She bit her fist and stared at the hungering demons the way a bird will freeze before a deadly snake.

"It's all happened already, Amanda," Geordie's voice was gentle, comforting. "We can't change the past. Let's go on to the next flight of stairs. The sooner we're out of here, the better."

Everyone agreed. They trudged through the sands, past the demons, past Quintus and the monks, and no one seemed to note their passing. They reached the twisting black staircase unchallenged.

A warm breath tickled Amanda's ear. "Don't feel sorry for Quintus, honey," Gerial whispered. "We never got him. Just take a closer look at our faces, wouldja? Too evil for words. Overdone. Melodramatic."

"Phony," Amanda breathed.

"Twice as phony as all your wiggles and jiggles, you betcha." Chuckles from an invisible source wreathed Amanda's head. "Don't get angry, sweet thing. It takes one to know one. We didn't really want to be what we were, and it showed to everyone but us. But you can't change the past."

"Is that why you're invisible? Because you can't meet your past self without the world exploding or something?"

"Heck, the world doesn't need metaphysics to make it explode! Get real. I just realized that Murakh may be watching us, and I'd kinda rather not have him see me, if you get my drift. Might make him have second thoughts about overlooking me when that quake hit. Come on, you've got a lot of climbing to do, and I don't mean social!"

"Up yours, darling."

"I love it when a woman talks dirty." Gerial's voice faded into heavily overdone lecherous laughter.

"Be careful," Father Lewis cautioned, studying the corkscrewed flight. "It just goes straight up, with no walls around it. Through the air."

"Impossible," Father William grunted, tilting his head back and trying to peer past the clouds that hid the upper reaches of the naked stair. "What's holding it up? There have to be walls!"

"If there's one thing I learned in Parvahr," Dr. Hack sighed," it's that nothing is impossible." He got on his hands and knees and crawled up the winding stair like a crab, taking no chances.

"Don't look down," Geordie advised. That was good counsel. Faith forgot herself for a moment and stole a glance back, over the edge. The monks were ants, the clay huts walnut-shells.

She felt an irresistible desire to lean farther over the edge of the steps and watch Quintus directing his men. They trickled off in smaller groups, doing various tasks with tools made invisible by distance. She leaned out further . . . and fell.

Falling, she closed her eyes, but the rush of air as she plummetted down was full of voices, and behind her fast shut eyelids a host of bewildering images fluttered from scene to scene like the jerky movements of an old silent movie. The demons at their torments . . . the monks beginning to feel the presence of otherworldly forces . . . the murmurs of dissatisfaction . . . the strange young monk who shared Brother Ambrosius' cell . . . the exodus . . . the temptation of Quintus . . . the moment of triumph when the sensual delights promised him by the demons snapped his holiest resolutions and sent him howling across the desert to embrace the world, and women.

Tragedy. The first woman he sees is the jealously guarded property of a Syrian shepherd with a bad temper and a heavy crook that proves to be harder than Quintus' skull. He is sorry, he says when be brings the body back to the remaining brothers, but he thought the man was mad. He leaves his olive-wood staff as a peace offering. They bury it with Quintus in the strangely untenanted sarcophagus that Brother Fabius found while digging the well. Before they bury him, Brother Ambrosius tucks a scroll in beside him. The monks pray, then wander back into the desert.

And now the desert is racing up to meet Faith Schleppey's fall with a ruthless thirst to feel her bones crack on impact with the sand that looked so deceptively soft and pillowy. She opens her eyes to escape the visions, but still they come, faces of the demons who realize that Quintus died without having actually sinned, and the intention to sin is not good enough. Below, the same cavernous voice dooms them with curses too obscene and hideous to translate into mortal terms. Exiled they shall be until they bring down a soul. Exiled and confined to the place of their failure, until the world's end, until the earth shall crack.

"Whoof!" Strong arms broke Faith's fall.

"You wanna watch your step, lady?" Gerial demanded, cradling her tight. "You knocked the invisibility outa me."

"You—you saved my life, Gerial."

"Yeah, so what? Think it's a favor? Maybe I know you're in for really rough times down the road and I'm making sure you live long enough to do some awesome suffering." He began to carry her back up the winding stair. "Maybe I know your hair's all gonna fall out, or your teeth are gonna turn on you, or every pair of good nylons you buy's gonna get runs in 'em the first time you try 'em on. Misery, baby."

"Gerial . . ."

"Yeh?"

"Stop trying to be evil."

"Trying? Me? Look, I'm a demon—"

"Not a very good one, by your own admission."

"Yeah, but it's *what I am:* I can't be anything but this, even if I can't do it well. You got brains, huh? You tell me, then, what else I can be but what I am!"

Faith put her arms around the blue demon's neck. "I think you can be one of the nicest beings I've ever known," she said, and planted a chaste kiss on his cheek.

"Oh, for—!" With a grunt of disgust, Gerial pitched her through space.

"Ow!" Faith shrieked. Geordie looked at her quizzically. "What's the matter? Did you fall?"

Faith touched herself all over, then felt for the sand beneath her, but there was no blood, no broken bones, and no sand, in that order.

"I thought I fell—"

"I guess you did, then," said Geordie. "You must've tripped on the top step. We're on another landing."

"Oh, no!" Faith groaned.

Geordie put up a good front about it. "He can't keep this up indefinitely. He'll have to let us get to the end of this staircase some time or he'll be—"

"—in violation of the honor of Hell," Kent supplied. "He wouldn't dare. Cheer up. I have the feeling that this is the last landing before the top. It's so well appointed, after all." So it was. The landing was in the shape of a trim Regency salon, and the delicate gilt chairs and sofa looked most comfortable.

"Well, they do claim that *facile est descensus Averno*,"
beamed Mr. Cardiff. "The descent into Hell is easy, y'know.
Perhaps this is their way of making it all the easier. One
would pause here and be tempted to continue on downwards."

"I'm not," said Faith Schleppey. "Where's the next flight
up?"

"Your zeal is admirable, young lady," said Father Lewis
cheerfully, "but give a man a chance to catch his breath. I've
got a pair of legs that're a day older than yours." He collapsed onto a brocaded settee.

"I think I smell fresh air," said Geordie. He nosed around
the salon and pulled aside a heavy red velvet curtain. A set of
black steps winked at him. "Found it," he announced.

"One more flight," complained Dr. Hack, slipping his
weary feet out of his shoes and blowing between the toes to
cool them. "And how many more will we have to scale?
The demon lied, you mark my words. We'll spend eternity
climbing flight after flight of steps, going up and getting
nowhere."

"Dr. Hack, you wound me," smiled Murakh, lightly de-
scending the steps behind the red curtain. His appearance sent
the worthy archeologist toppling backwards from his seat.

"What are you doing here?" asked Father William imperi-
ously. "You released us!"

"Well, I'm not here to try to get you back, if that's what
you fear," purred Murakh. He was dressed in his leisure suit
again. A portfolio of fashion sketches was under one arm.
Several of the designs fluttered out, showing the curvaceous
nether regions of adolescent models tightly encased in quality
denim.

"Then what are you going here?" demanded Geordie.

"Why, it struck me that I wasn't the proper host when last
we met," the demon said mildly, his lips twisted into a
disquieting smile. "I should have at least told you how far
you'd have to climb to escape my influence. But never mind.
This is the last flight to the surface, so be of good cheer, my
friends. Your worries are almost over. I envy you. I and my
comrades envy you."

"I hope," said Father Lewis officiously, "that none of us
shall ever have to associate with you or your comrades in the
future."

"As for that," shrugged Murakh, "who can say? But
you've certainly associated with us enough in the past. Quite

enough. So much so that I understand some of you are on a most intimate footing with a handful of my kind. A disgraceful handful, however, but I mustn't sit in judgment. All that I have come to do is bid you farewell." He leered and turned to go, then stopped and faced them as if he had just remembered something. "Oh, yes, there is this: You mustn't be upset by anything you should happen to see on this last flight of stairs. It passes through a region reserved for the punishment of demons, and the sights there are most unpleasant, but they can't hurt you. Pass through, just pass through, and you'll be back in your own world in the blink of an eye. May the four winds guide you." He bowed his way back beneath the red velvet curtain and vanished.

Dr. Hack jammed his shoes on and leaped to his feet. "I'm still tired, but I'm not staying here one second longer," he announced.

"Same here," Father Lewis grunted, getting off the settee.

Geordie held up the heavy drape while one by one they ducked into the darkened staircase. Only Faith lingered on the landing.

"Gerial?" she called in a whisper. "Gerial, is it true what Murakh said about this being the last flight?"

The air shimmered blue before her. Gerial took shape, nodding. "I told you, Murakh doesn't need to lie. I'll leave you here. You'll be all right. I don't need to get out of Parvahr by the same route you do. You understand why I'd rather not go up . . . that way?"

"Sure. I heard what Murakh said."

"Well, see ya in the funny papers." Gerial grinned and gave Faith the thumbs-up sign.

Talons formed out of the air, closed over his paw. He blanched pastel as a harsh voice boomed, *Where have you been hiding, Gerial? What power protected you when I pulled the final string and brought your comrades down? Ah, never mind that now. I have you. I have you all!*

Gerial's wail of despair blended with Faith's useless scream as the blue demon was dragged through the rip in space and disappeared from sight. She stood frozen only an instant, then shot through the still-swaying red draperies.

There were walls on either side of the steps, and after the first turn that took them out of sight of the curtained archway below, the travellers were in blackness once more. Geordie took deep breaths as he climbed. There was still the promise of fresh air, even in these hidden regions. And Murakh had said it was not far to go.

The wailing began. If all the torments ever inflicted on the innocent were ever brought together and the shrieks of protest and confusion were combined, it would only reflect a tenth of the anguish deep-throated in that wailing. It rose and fell and dashed itself against the walls of the staircase, then trickled in at their ears and flooded their minds with reeling images of agony.

Purple and green light flickered in the shadows. The stairs broadened out and flattened into a gently sloping incline. The lights grew brighter, slithering down the black stone walls like glutted leeches, curling into poors of horrible radiance at the travellers' feet. Amanda screamed, and her scream came back to her coupled with the howls and whimpers of inhuman voices. The pit of torment opened suddenly, in a soundless explosion of pity and terror.

Horgist roiled through ever-changing shapes that probed his senses with spasms of pain that reached into every recess of his being and drew out fresh agonies.

Lura and Atamar, bound together by invisible shackles, played mirror to each other's sufferings, for a torture applied to the one hurt the other, and they fought a losing battle to conceal the excruciating punishment each underwent. It was useless. Lura cried out, and Atamar's cry of rage against any creature that dared to harm his beloved made her cringe more than the initial pain of torment. Then unseen forces turned their exquisite cruelties on him, and it was Lura's turn to suffer while she watched them scourge her lover.

Gerial sat hunched in darkness that clung to him like the thick, gelatinous folds of a jellyfish. Around him a host of phantoms played a drama of betrayal and remorse, of Gerial the mortal as he once had been, blessed and trusted guardian of a place so holy that when his greed and treachery destroyed it, it did not leave so much as the stain of memory or myth in the primitive sub-brain of man. The wisdom of Solomon had blessed it, the Valley of the Clouds had graced it, and Gerial alone had befouled and annihilated it. Sealed in his memories, he suffered.

"I told you not to be afraid," Murakh's voice seeped from the stones. "They are only being punished as they deserve."

"For *what*?" shrieked Faith among the shadows and the weeping. "What in the name of hell could they have done?"

"Yes," murmured Father Lewis, his eyes fixed on Horgist. He remembered that face, the black dog, the upraised scroll, but even as he trembled with the memory of his last encounter with the yellow fiend, his heart ached for the torments the demon now underwent. "What sin could be enough to add punishment to beings whose existence as demons is supposed to be punishment enough?"

"Sins?" echoed Murakh, and his cackling laughter ran in sadistic counterpoint to the cries of his captives. A taloned hand materialized, pointing to each demon as Murakh's voice intoned, "Gerial, the blue one, still yearned for his human life. He sought it wherever he could." A copy of *Das Kapital* flashed on the wall. A circle of cameramen bent in friendship over a boardgame followed. "And he treasured compassion." Images of Gerial seeking the Parvahr-straying mortals, catching Faith in her fall, carrying her up the stairs, receiving her kiss.

"Atamar and Lura," Murakh went on, their names falling like thunderbolts, "have loved without lust, loved long and secretly, loved and sought to deceive all around them with a show of hate and pure carnality, but love remained. That is why Atamar failed, and kept the others linked to him in failure. And Lura has felt pity. Horgist, my friends—" he indicated the twisting yellow demon—"suffers least. His sins are trivial: softness, reluctance to seize power, lack of overweening ambition . . . nothings, really."

"Nothings?" wondered Geordie. His stomach felt strangely empty, then full of a vague aching feeling when he looked at the demons in their suffering. Amanda was crying. Faith was biting her lower lip and trying not to cry.

"Oh, but I have saved the best for last!" exclaimed Murakh. "I keep her separate from the others. It is not yet time to frame her punishment, you see. We must wait, but it should be any moment now, any moment at all . . . "

A shriek stabbed through the blackness, a shriek that reduced every other sound to hollowness. The darkness parted like the unfurling wings of nightmare and Murakh stood triumphant before a moss-grown altar to dead gods on which was stretched the swollen body of Melisan, her golden hair tumbling over the edge of the stone, her breasts grown full and round, shimmering like twin moons, her belly arched and heavy with something still unborn. But it would be born, and soon. She writhed and struggled against the ropes that bound her and she shrieked again with the pains that rippled through her.

"Melisan," drawled Murakh. "Every sin we deem a sin in Hell is on her head. Remorse. Love. Devotion. Repentance. She would not even name the father of her child. That might have saved her. It will not save the child."

A rising orange moon melted the castle walls into a grove of raven trees whose naked branches clawed the windswept sky. Lost souls gibbered and clacked in the branches. The mortals flocked together in a circle of moonlight while the demons shrilled their terror into the storm.

"The hour comes," said Murakh, gazing at the hungry moon. "You had better go. The way lies straight before you. Touch nothing as you pass. All things here hold a touch of Hell, and that would be enough to hold you fast here forever. Go."

The wind and the demons howled in unison. Melisan screamed again, and a bolt of moonlight flooded her face. Kent Cardiff gasped.

"Marguerite! Marguerite!"

He sprang like a tiger and struck Murakh a stunning blow to the head. The vengeful demon staggered from the altar and pitched into a tree. Kent Cardiff did not wait to land a second blow. He was at Melisan's side, undoing the ropes, sweeping her into his arms, running for the black stairs.

"What is he doing?" squealed Dr. Hack.

"I don't know," said Faith, "but it's sure become popular."

Father Lewis had gaped at Kent Cardiff's exploit and wasted no time in asking for reasons. He was on top of Horgist, tugging at the yellow demon's bonds, freeing him, dragging him towards the stairs. Father William and Amanda flew with one impulse to rouse Gerial from his morose, self-inflicted prison and half-carry, half-drag him after Father Lewis and Horgist. Geordie Burns drew his utility knife and slashed the shackles holding Atamar and Lura. Old tales of the power of earth-iron against the forces of witchcraft sprang to mind as the simple blade bit through what looked like steel. Atamar seized Lura as soon as he was free and spread his wings, soaring for the stairs, Geordie running after. Dr. Hack let out a strangled cry and darted for safety, Faith hot on his tail.

Behind them the darkness seethed with all the rage of Hell and Murakh cheated. "You shall pay for this, mortals! You won't even have the comfort of death to prepare you! By all the legions of the damned, your own actions have condemned you! Your deeds have made you free and clear for my prey, and I will have it!''

"Oh, shut up," mumbled Faith Schleppey. She felt a warm breeze on her face and heard Geordie's voice shouting that they had broken from the darkness and were home.

4

Wings

"HOLY COW," SAID a young nothing from ABC. "Where did you people spring up from? Cheez! Where the hell is that camera? No one's going to believe this one."

"Where is everybody?" asked Father William, surveying the campsite. Only eight tents were left standing. There was no sign of the huge media settlement. Excavation of the clay huts had stopped. Ms. Ferrabosco lounged out of earshot in the sun before her tent, coaxing a tan. Giuliana Caruso sat at her feet, writing.

"Mostly gone, now," said the young nothing. "Are they ever going to be pissed! What a story, and when I think I was mad 'cause they dumped me here to bat clean-up—! I could fall down and kiss their feet for it. This'll make my name. First on the scene to interview the earthquake victims who survived the fury of nature itself. Film at eleven if I can find that damned camera-jockey. You wait right here." He sprinted away towards one of the remaining tents.

"Do you think he noticed us?" asked Horgist, edging closer to Father Lewis. The British priest patted Horgist's lubberly paw.

"Perhaps not. Or then again, perhaps he did. But it's not so easy to shock a media man. Not like a silly old priest from fair Albion's foggy shoes, eh?"

"I said I was sorry," grumped Horgist. Father Lewis laughed and patted him on the back.

"We must know," said Atamar, his arms still protectively wrapped around Lura, his wings sheltering her from the sun. "Most of our powers were forfeit for our offenses. Murakh told us that we had made ourselves the outcast of Hell centuries ago, soon after we lost Quintus. Even then, the Lords of Hell suspected that we would fail. We are the flawed, the imperfectly evil, the misfits. They gave us that last mission to see if their suspicions about us were true. We did not fail them in that respect, at least. Quintus died innocent. Quintus' death . . . That was when the change began, for most of us. For Melisan, it came somewhat sooner, although only Lura knew, and she refused to betray her friend." He smiled tenderly at the black-haired succubus he embraced. "Of course they left us our powers then, but now—"

"Hey, come on over this way, you guys, okay?" called the young nothing from ABC. He had rounded up the other young nothings from CBS, NBC, and FOX as well, creatures so low on the scale of media evolution as to be invisible to the naked anchorman. They were the dregs, gofers for gofers, plankton, left behind as a safety net just in case one final scrap of news should turn up, which no one important thought possible. An earthquake seldom gives back what it gulps down.

"Come on!" the young nothing called again, wig-wagging his arms. "I found the camerman, but he says he wants to shoot you here. Could you get it over here and we'll—*Oh, my God!*"

The young nothing, flanked by his equally obscure peers from the rival networks, felt the desert floor plummet thirteen stories. He tried to talk, but only whistling sounds came out. He saw the demons.

"What," croaked his comrade from NBC, "are they?"

"We can't," said CBS's contribution to young nothingdom, "be seeing things. Could we? A touch of sun . . . "

They gave up trying to rationalize the demons almost before they began. Cameras, microphones, and shorthand pads littered the sands like autumn leaves as the last of the media bravos scooted across the dunes like startled rabbits; rabbits that could pile into a jeep and burn rubber all the way to Cairo.

"So," shrugged Gerial. "We're visible. I guess."

"An understatement," moped Dr. Hack. He gazed at the fallen cameras with true longing in his watery eyes. His last chance, gone.

"Dr. Hack! Geordie! Faith! Amanda!" Steve Ritter's hearty greetings sounded sweetly in their ears. He came from his tent with Don Swann in tow. Don's eyes lit up as soon as he laid them on Amanda. "I knew you'd be all right. We all knew you'd be back." He embraced them all, one by one. The clawed, winged, tailed, naked presence of the demons did not seem to bother him in the least. "Welcome!" He gave Gerial an especially warm hug, and a palsy-walsy punch in the arm. "Knew you could do it, friend."

"Ow," Gerial said, rubbing his shoulder. "You smite too danged hard, y'know?"

"Sorry. Tradition."

Don was not quite so self-contained. He goggled at Atamar and didn't wait to check out any of the others in detail. "Oh, Ms. Ferrabosco!" His voice scaled untold heights as the color fled his pockmarked cheeks. "Ms. Ferrabosco!"

"Stupid twit," said Faith. "What does he think she'll be able to do with a clutch of demons? Sign them up with Marmota, Inc., as guides? Or as clients?"

"I don't bloody well care what she tries," cut in Kent Cardiff. He knelt on the sand, cradling Melisan's head in his lap. She groaned and twisted her head from side to side, tangling her lank blonde locks, clenching her fists with each fresh wave of birth-pangs. "Marguerite," crooned Kent Cardiff. "It's all right, Marguerite. I'm here, love. I'm with you. Someone get her a bed and some water, damn it!" he added in another tone entirely.

"A baby?" marvelled Steve, crouched down beside Melisan. He stroked her sweating brow and acted as if it were the most everyday thing in the world to witness a winged succubus about to give birth in the middle of the desert.

"Yes," returned Kent Cardiff, on the defensive. "And I won't have Marguerite troubled any longer. We shall be married as soon as she feels up to it. If she'll have me." He squeezed her hand. She gave him a wide look of amazement, gratitude, and love until another spasm made her wince and dig her claws into his arm.

"Well, isn't that fine," grinned Steve. "You know, the few cases where a mortal and a succubus had issue are—"

"Nooooo . . . " Dr. Hack whimpered, clutching his sandy head in his hands and sinking to his knees. "Through Hell and worse than Hell I've been, and now that I think I'm safely back where things are sane, what do I hear? One of my Marmota brats discussing the gestation of succubi as if he learned it at his mother's knee!"

Steve looked at the good doctor incredulously. "What's wrong with that?" he asked. "That's exactly where I learned it."

Dr. Hack took a gunfighter's stance and enunciated each syllable distinctly. "I don't care if you paid cash up front, Ritter. I don't care if I lose my job. I don't care if you're hiding a yard-long forked tail in your shorts. I want to know what you are and I want to know why you are here and I want to know *now!*"

"Oh," Steve shrugged. "Fair enough. I'm here to save you from doing something stupid, Dr. Hack. With your immortal soul, I mean. See, you're a good man who's had bad breaks, and you were all set to sell your soul for a little luck—which of course isn't any more a hellish commodity than a heavenly one—and everyone I knew thought that'd be a real shame, so they tapped me to come along with you on this dig and keep an eye on you and try to help you make the right decision without direct intervention—I can't intervene directly with mortal creatures, just supernatural ones; it wouldn't be fair otherwise—and you were almost damned for a minute there, but fortunately—"

Dr. Hack howled like a baboon and fell full-length on the sand. Ms. Ferrabosco and Giuliana Caruso were just in time to witness his collapse.

"Dr. Hack," Ms. Ferrabosco said severely. "This will not do."

"Santa Maria!" Giuliana gasped. She crossed herself for the first time since she'd grown too big for her Mama to drag to church. She was regarding the massed demons, Melisan above all.

"Oh," Ms. Ferrabosco said primly. "Are the pains close together yet?" Melisan yelped. "Apparently so. Well, don't just let her lie there, you stupid men. Get her into my tent and put her on the cot. We are not about to deliver a baby in the midst of all this sand. It's too messy and it will never do." Kent Cardiff scooped Melisan up and dutifully bore her into Ms. Ferrabosco's tent. She was on the point of following them, when Dr. Hack scrabbled at her leg and would not let her go.

"Am I—" he sobbed "—the only sane man left? Don't you see what she *is*? Don't you see the rest of them?"

Ms. Ferrabosco sniffed. "What a ludicrous question, Hack. Certainly I see what they are. My eyes function perfectly, thank you. I haven't the faintest notion of what to *call* these newfound creatures of yours, of course, but at the moment that is a purely secondary concern. Something is about to be born. I surmise it will be a baby. I could be wrong, but crises leave little time for conjectures. Geordie, sweet, see if you can't scare up some coffee for Dr. Hack. It will soothe him. I am a great believer in the lesser-known benefits of caffeine." She swept grandly into the tent.

"You were never crazy, Dr. Hack." Atamar's voice offered gruff comfort. "It was only me, trying to work you over into our hands I'm sorry for it now."

"Me, too," said Gerial.

The media folk, seeing that Dr. Hack and his group were not being rended, bitten, slimed over, or consumed by the demons, began to come out of hiding, like a colony of gun-shy rodents. First their beady little eyes gleamed from the shadows of their tents, then their moist noses emerged, and finally their equipment.

Lura tried extending the hand of friendship."We were only doing our job, Dr. Hack. And not very well, praise be. We'd like to thank you for making it almost impossible." Her smile was irresistibly radiant, entirely sin-free. She helped him to stand.

"She's *butt-nekkid!*" the young nothing from ABC squealed in ecstasy, and led the advance troops from the media tents.

"Demons," moaned Dr. Hack.

Demons, whispered the desert.

Dr. Hack shot an accusing look at Atamar. "Cut that out!" he barked. "You said you were sorry you did it before, so lay off me!"

"I didn't say anything," protested Atamar.

I did, said the desert. But you won't live long enough to repeat what I say.

The black rock creaked, shifting forward, then groaned backwards in a hidden socket. Irresistibly it began to rise from the sands, a curve of black rock like a scimitar of darkness against the luminous blue of the sky, a moon of black madness climbing the heavens, a demon-prince's ruthless smile.

You shall want weapons, little ones, Murakh hissed. His face swam across the sky, purging the brilliant blue to steely gray. It would be wrong to have you die unarmed. Take.

A broadsword sprang into Dr. Hack's hand. He stared at it as if it were a third monstrous arm he had grown overnight. It thunked to the sand, and he needed two hands to lift it again.

Swords are for men, the demon chuckled. Boys must find other arms.

Bows and a rain of silver-tipped bamboo arrows fell rattling over Don Swann's bowed head.

When he looked up, he found a microphone in his face. "You're the kid-Satanist, right?" a reporter demanded. "Do you really believe you can kill supernatural creatures with silver, or is this just an empty gesture on the part of Hell to make you believe you've got a chance?"

"Ever done any archery?" Another mike shot up. "What's your uncorrected eyesight? Corrected? Ever done any target-sports of any kind? If you survive this, are contact lenses an option? Hard, soft, or gas-permeable? Tinted or clear?"

A leather sling appeared in Geordie's grasp.

"Does this obviously symbolic allusion to the story of David and Goliath put you under any additional strain, Mr. Burns? Do you feel able to live up to the role that has been thrust upon you? Are you at all familiar with King David's later career?"

A second inquisitor added, "Ever play the harp? Visit Israel? Do any composition of sacred music? What are your thoughts on sheep?"

Amanda and Faith hefted the small, elegant throwing daggers that were their lot.

Giuliana Caruso's nostrils flared, scenting battle. She cast aside her penitential attitude and sank a claw into each of the girls' shoulders. "How deeply do you resent the flagrantly pro-male mind-set which has condemned you both to use weapons far inferior to those assigned your masculine counterparts? This is typical of the entire history of male-female relations from the time of the inglorious Neolithic revolution, as any intelligent person would agree; don't you?"

Faith slipped her foot behind Giuliana's ankle and Amanda gave her a shove. She hit the ground vituperating and crawled off in search of a pad and pen.

"What about us?" shouted Father William, running towards
the inexorably rising monolith of shadow. "Are you afraid to
give us weapons, demon?"

Priest, said the desert, the voice of Murakh. Priest, you shall
pray. You shall have reason enough for it, but never time
enough. I promise you that. I have come for my own.

The shaft of rock broke free of the desert and it was not a
rock, but the bloodthirsty black horn of Murakh, Murakh the
dragon, Murakh who ramped and slashed and thundred doom
and desolation from the scaly trumpet of his glittering throat.
Dr. Hack threw down his sword and grovelled in the sand.
Don Swann numbly nocked an arrow to his bow and let fly,
but it rebounded harmlessly from the monster's armored hide.
Claws grim as the sickle moons that used to witness ancient
sacrifices raked scarlet gashes through the living tissue of the
desert and reached out to seize their prey.

I will have you, the dragon gloated. In one killing I will
have you all.

He spread his wings of sorrow and took flight into the knott-
ing winds that shrieked a protest and fled at his coming. Storms
of ruin and chaos sailed before him, cleaving the air with blades
of lightning. The dragon laughed and fire seared the sky.

I will have you all.

The decimated news teams swarmed across the sand, following the flight of the dragon, cameras rolling, microphones
waving. If they had been afraid, they had either passed
through fear into lunacy or else had been taken over by their
own kind of battle-madness. As beserkers once threw themselves naked against the shields and spears of an advancing
army, these modern phrenetics flung themselves into the teeth
of the biggest story they had ever witnessed breaking, armed
only with mike, tape recorder, and camera.

It would have been a very grand and stirring gesture, but
somehow it reminded Faith more of coked-up lemmings than
blood-crazed barbarians. At least the barbarians would have
had a fighting chance.

Murakh looked down at them and laughed.

Sounds like the soft flutter of doves' wings nudged their
way through the reeling consciousness of the mortals and
disinherited demons who crouched on the sand, waiting for
death. The fluttering grew louder, stronger, and from the east
a wave of light like pearly seafoam drove the dragon's storms
from the horizon.

Turn, Murakh, said the angel.

The dragon wheeled in mid-flight, his tail whipping out to snap the newborn moon out of the heavens. Rage bubbled into as wide-mouthed scarlet roar. Bare-handed, the angel rose against the dragon's tempest, climbing the vaults of the sky. His feet left marks like stars. With a hell-shaking bellow, the dragon leaped upon him. The angel with Steve Ritter's face smiled grimly and joined combat.

The force of their impact shook the heavens and the earth. The angel's hand came up under the dragon's barbelled chin, snapping back the huge head. With a scream of pain and surprise, Murakh pushed away with all four paws, oaring his wings violently backwards. He protected his retreat with a lash of his tail. It just missed the angel, who hovered prudently out of range, still smiling.

Where is your sword? The dragon demanded.

I need no sword for the likes of you, Prince of nothing.

Murakh's beaked face showed all its teeth. It seems my prey are not the only ones contaminated by contact with mortal creatures, he said. Either you are filled with a fool's pride, or you imagine yourself capable of deeds great as dreams. Mortal failings both, and to be mortal means to die.

Or to have your dreams live forever, the angel replied.

The dragon's mouth gaped, his wings folded, and he dropped upon the angel without warning, a hawk's dive. Claws raked flesh that was not flesh, but that could bleed after its own fashion. The angel beat his wings strongly and dripped below the slashing fangs and talons, casting off the dragon with difficulty. He climbed the air for a better vantage in battle.

Murakh was amused. Run away, run away, you pitiful child of light. Fly to fetch a weapon, if you like. I will wait for you.

The dragon's neck swung low as he spoke. Little by little his huge body dropped toward the desert floor where the mortals swarmed. The camera crews ran back and forth like roaches surprised by a sudden kitchen light at midnight. They split into two groups, one tracking the dragon, the other the angel.

In front of their own tent, the Russian team gazed into the sky with hand-shaded eyes. Yuri's lips began to move over words he hadn't thought of in years.

"What are you saying?" Illya snapped. "Speak up!"

Yuri paused. "Why? Do you understand Hebrew?"

"He is praying," Sonia said calmly. She never took her eyes from the sky.

"Is that all you can say?" Behind his thick glasses, Illya's eyes bugged out and his face grew scarlet. "To tell me he is praying? *Praying!* Hebrew prayers, no less! Why aren't you taking notes? Why aren't you scribbling down the whole incident in triplicate the way you do every time *I* make one tiny misstep?"

"Why would she want to do that?" Yuri asked softly.

"Are you truly as much of a day-dreaming idiot as you pretend? Did you think that the glorious name of science had power enough to let us roam where we liked, free of proper supervision? Ha! What do you expect our own personal KGB effective to do with her spare time? Knit underw—oops."

Sonia patted Illya on the back and gently pried his hand away from his mouth. "Don't trouble yourself about it, comrade. I don't care if he knows." She looked back up. "We will discuss the matter later." Yuri's hand and hers linked in a firm clasp. "Pray for us all, my friend," she said. "Pray on."

Sunlight set the dragon's scales afire. He executed a taunting midair ballet before the angel's narrowed eyes. Winds of illusion blew from his wings. Sometimes he dwindled to the size of a gnat, sometimes he swelled until his awful majesty filled all the sky, leaving the earth a pebble on his flank to be shaken off at his pleasure.

The angel seized air and stretched it into a spear, cloud-white. It flew through the sky, scoring the crest of the dragon's back. Murakh roared with pain. His smile was gone.

You dare to strike against me? You know I am beyond death, and still you dare?

We are both immortal, Murakh, the angel replied. But death is not the worst defeat. How else shall I deal with you? You are not beyond pain.

Nor are you! And I am pain's master!

The dragon plunged earthward. It was too sudden for any hint of his intent, too swift for the angel to intercept him. The massed cameramen scattered, still filming. Geordie fit a stone to his sling and let fly, but it fell short of its target. Talons dug into the sand, split the earth. Molten fire filled the cracks, oozed out into the light.

Come, my pets, the dragon crooned. Come, my slavelings. Here is work for you to do. Here are easy victims.

The fire bubbled and seethed. Drops of liquid flame leaped out of the mass, took shape, grew wings, tails, claws, hungering faces. The hellmouth spewed out twoscore imps before the angel's second lance of frozen air struck the earth and sealed it.

They scampered across the sand, gibbering with glee. Loping on all fours, flapping razored wings, prancing on cloven hooves straight out of long-disbelieved stories, the imps raced to seize their promised prey. The mortals stood like headlight-taken deer, staring at the shrieking, cackling, howling wave of nightmares fast sweeping up to overwhelm them.

No! The angel formed a third spear in desperate haste. The dragon's satisfaction was too great to be contained. He looked up from the desert to where the angel hovered, the spear poised to throw.

Your last one, my foe. The last weapon you may forge in this battle. How will you use it? We have our limits in this world, you and I. We did not ordain the rules, but we must live by them . . . and fall by them. Think well on what you do! Use your last bolt to save those sorry worms and you will leave yourself weaponless indeed against me.

The angel never paused. He flung the spear well past the crouching dragon, into the midst of the excavation site. The clay huts shuddered and cracked.

The desert cracked, too. The earth itself inverted, turning inside-out. Sand burst upward, fell with a pattering like rain. The ground whitened, heaving up a layer of rag-wrapped bones.

Light poured over skulls and pelvises, rib-cages and thigh-bones. The air rippled with a host of phantoms. Ghosts rained from the air, soaked into their old homes. The bones linked, layer by layer putting on flesh and blood, skin and life. One by one they stood as men again, balding and bearded in their sackcloth robes. Some of the bones were too far gone to support returning flesh. These were quickly taken up as weapons. With a battle-yell in poor provincial Latin, the monks of Quintus Pilaster's monastery charged the creatures of the abyss.

The imps stopped and turned, distracted. Recognition made their faces even more hideous than before.

Yeeeaaagh! It is the old ones come back! one imp shouted. *Their prayers drove me off more than once. I remember them, may their bones rot!* another growled.

Obviously their bones have not done so, the first imp countered.

Then I will break them myself! Like a stampede turned by a single well-timed shot, in a body the imps wheeled away from the quivering mass of newsmen and attacked the monks.

Fools! the dragon raged, stamping his claws. The angel above laughed at Murakh's discomfiture.

"Hey! Hey, they're running away from us!" the young nothing from ABC yelled.

"Shit, just when I had a good angle on them," Sam complained.

"Well, what're we standing here like a bunch of jerks for, ha? Come on, guys! We're talking story of the fucking century!"

The newsmen pounded after the imps.

Oh, no, moaned the angel.

The dragon roared his joy and sprang into the air, exultant.

See them run, my foe! You cannot save those who desire their own destruction so ardently.

No, no, they mustn't, the angel protested, stooping towards the earth. He closed his eyes. His hands slowly rose, palms heavenward, as if he were elevating some invisible burden immeasurably heavy.

The earth humped and writhed. A small corner of time tore away. Gold and blue, flanked by winged guardian beasts, the ageless temple lifted her terraced walls to the winds. Massive stone slabs long buried erupted in the narrowing gap between the galloping imps and the pursuing reporters. The first ranks of camermen ran smack into gates of gilded bronze before they could backpedal.

The ponderous gates swung inward.

Oh, look, girls! Customers!

About time. I'm sooooo sick of backgammon.

Ooooooh, look at that one! He's got yellow hair.

Mine!

Touch him and I'll tear your earrings out. I saw him first!

Girls, please, there's plenty to go around.

And around, and around, and around! Whoopeeee!

In a torrent of scented skin, floating veils, hennaed feet, and gold-dusted nipples, the sacred prostitutes of the nameless temple streamed out of their gates to take the media by storm.

Ah, the angel sighed, wings slumping with relief.

Ah . . . the dragon purred, and struck in a thunderbolt from behind.

"Dr. Hack, what should we do?" Don Swann tugged timidly at his mentor's sleeve. He held his bow at arm's length, left the arrows where they had fallen.

"I—I'm not sure . . ." Dr. Hack surveyed the field. The monks were having the time of their second lives. A few veterans of the choir were bawling hymns as they cudgelled imps hip and thigh. The imps were smaller and quicker, but the monks had the reach and the muscle from long hours of digging a pointless garden plot for Quintus. Sparks shot up wherever bone made contact with infernal flesh, and the bruises stank of burning, but the desert holy men had smelled worse things in their time. They didn't look as if they wanted any help, although the imps might have appreciated some assistance. Their attempts at retreat and escape were blocked at every turn, their fire-hardened hides lambasted to a wisp-thin tissue of pain. Their yelps for mercy and pleas for their pummelers to forget old grudges were pitiful to hear. The monks broke into a four-part responsive chant on true salvation through suffering and laid on anew.

Across the battleground, on the far side of the revenant temple, things were at a similar pitch. The sacred prostitutes had not gone into their line of work to earn a little spare change for fripperies. They were strictly career-oriented, serious business women, and they resented having to interrupt their professional efforts just to answer a lot of stupid questions. They weren't about to explain how nice girls like them had first gotten into this line of work, or whether they had poor self-images or unresolved Electra complexes. Who in H'arish-ba'an was Electra, anyhow? They had a job to do, and by Sst'tyayim, they were going to do it! Microphones were tweaked away and flung to the wind's four quarters. So were jockey shorts.

"You can't do that with my light meter!" Sam hollered just before he was dragged down in a welter of arms, legs, oil of myrrh, and overexposed videotape.

"There's nothing we can do," Dr. Hack began as his remaining Marmota charges drifted nearer, all silently looking to him for guidance; even Geordie Burns. "I . . . don't think we're needed."

"NEEDED?" Hard hands tore Dr. Hack from the circle of his companions and spun him around. Atamar's inhumanly beautiful face was an inch from his own. The dung-stench was choking. "Look there and see where the need lies! He's losing! Do something! Help him! He is the one who needs all our help in this hour!" He pointed skyward.

It was true. Locked in the dragon's clasp, the angel was failing, falling, giving ground. Hellthirst and hate pressed him down from the heights of the sky.

Atamar bellowed, "No!" He shoved Dr. Hack away, seized the sling from Geordie's hand, and flung a stone hard for the dragon's eyes. The distance should have made the shot impossible, but there was something yet left to Atamar of his powers. The stone soared true, and the dragon screeched as its eye shattered.

That screech was the alarm that woke them all to action. Forgetting whether he had ever used a bow in his life, or if he had sight keen enough to aim one, Don Swann nocked and fired arrow after arrow. They were little more than gnats to scratch the dragon's side, yet Don still sent them flying. One lodged in the tender webbing between the monster's claws. Murakh shrieked and pulled it out with his teeth. Don did a war-dance of triumph.

Amanda and Faith threw their daggers, and fetched them when they fell, and threw them again. They were no common knives, but the mocking gift of a hellspawn. All that was wanted was the skill to aim them well, and they could fly higher than any dagger of human forging. Faith lacked the faintest touch of such skill. Her throws were too wild, too full of fury to do any good.

Amanda was more self-controlled. She gauged each throw before her dagger flew. The years of keeping unseemly public displays of emotion under wraps had finally paid off, but not in a way she could ever tell Mummy about. She saw her blade carve a superficial wound in the dragon's dangling tail and whooped her head off. Murakh squirmed, but his hold on the angel was unbroken. Amanda dove for the fallen dagger, got a grip on herself, and tried again.

Lura and Horgist rooted for stones to hurl, pelting Murakh as well as they could. Geordie grabbed his sling back from Atamar and scored a few hits of his own. Gerial brought him an unfailing supply of ammunition, grinning until his tusks ached. "Way to go, flyboy!" he bawled into the sun. "We're on your side! Whup his scaly ass!"

Fools! the dragon roared. *Do you think this will save you?*

I have stood against the hosts of Heaven! What is one child of light to me? You will not save him.

Murakh struck like a snake, driving his fangs into the angel's wing, tearing brightness to shadows. The angel sank earthwards still, in spite of all attempts to aid him. Tattered streams of brilliance trailed from his wings, like the clouds of sunset. His aura of light flickered feebly, frayed, dimmed.

"Oh, no." Dr. Hack felt wetness on his cheeks. "No. He came to help me. He cared about me. Please, no."

"Mount," said Atamar quietly. Dr. Hack wiped the tears from his eyes and stared at the demon as if he no longer understood language, any language. Atamar knelt at Dr. Hack's feet, presenting his broad back to the trembling archeologist. "You must," Atamar said. His voice was soft, calm, despairing. "He gave you the sword."

And Dr. Hack found himself linking his left arm around Atamar's throat and feeling the stiff desert wind in his face as the demon's flight ascended through the air to where dragon and angel battled. His right hand held the sword.

Steely clouds wrapped them from the light. Dr. Hack could see nothing. His head began to whirl. He had never been able to tolerate heights. He tried to look down and saw through a break in the clouds that they were not all that far from the earth. The course of battle was edging surely down the curve of the sky. Murakh was beating the angel earthwards, and the closer he forced him to the ground, the stronger Murakh's powers became, and the easier it was to force the angel lower still. The tip of one snowy wing nearly brushed the top of Ms. Ferrabosco's tent. Far below Dr. Hack thought he heard the thin, indignant wailing of a child.

Then Atamar dipped his wings and they were in the clouds again, but through the thick rolls of mist Dr. Hack saw a distant yellow glow, an evil luminosity towards which Atamar was flying as if nothing else on earth, or above it, or beneath it, mattered.

"Now," said Atamar. "Or never until the end of time."

"It's the dragon's belly," said Dr. Hack, simply as a child might say it. He let go of Atamar's neck and balanced precariously on the demon's broad back, his feet planted between Atamar's wings, both hands holding the sword. With one massive effort he thrust it upwards, deep into the shining flesh of the dragon, and into the heart of chaos itself.

Dragon and man, angel and demon, they tumbled down the

mountains of heaven in a hurtling mass of wings, faces, claws, hands, and penetrating every instant of that fearsome plunge through the void was Murakh's shriek of eternal agony.

Dr. Hack felt the jar of landing, a landing no worse than if he'd scooted down the kiddies' sliding pond at the park. A stone's-throw away, Atamar was shaking sand from his wings. Lura was already with him, showering him with kisses and tender words that were the closely guarded hoard of over a thousand years. There was no sign of the dragon and the black rock was gone. The angel that had once worn Steve Ritter for a mask was likewise nowhere to be seen.

Dr. Hack felt the earth shimmy. There was a gulping sound as the risen temple dropped back into its proper place in time and archeological strata. The imps, running for their skins' sakes from the Church Militant, leaped for the sinking structure and rode it back into the underworld.

One of the sacred prostitutes looked up from her work. *Uh-oh.*

Her sisters in service did not seem too upset by this turn of events. *Oh, stop worrying, Ghila. So the temple's gone. We'll be fine. Something will come up.*

It always does.

While the ladies withdrew to discuss their predicament, the newsmen crawled to shelter. Their female counterparts, understandably shunted to one side during the fray, waited to receive them. Pens were poised, smiles malicious, questions pointed. The words *cheap* and *used* and *exploited* were sprinkled freely throughout the ensuing interviews.

"Are you sure you didn't bring it on yourself by dressing in an overly provocative manner?" someone asked.

"Provocative? *This?*" The much-shopworn young nothing from ABC plucked at the moist shreds of his David Lee Roth T-shirt. He burst into hysterical laughter and bit the questioner.

"What do you mean, you didn't get any of it on film?" Sam gasped, and collapsed senseless.

Giuliana Caruso skimmed her notes, decided that this story might give less enlightened women some wrong ideas about career choices, and tore them to confetti.

At a little distance, the monks laid down their arms with proper reverence and dispatched one of their number to confer with their stranded fellow-fighters.

He addressed them in the lingua franca of the dead: *Fair ones, I am called Brother Petronius. Your plight has moved us. If it may bring you any comfort, we will offer up our insignificant prayers that your souls may find eternal rest.*

The fair ones in question giggled and whispered among themselves. A few ventured to wave and wink at the solemnly waiting monks. Their own immediately appointed leader ambled up and tucked her arm through that of Brother Petronius. *Oh would you? Just for little old us? Isn't that sweet! Why don't we all get out of this nasty old sunlight and give it a try?* Sackcloth and silk paired off and disappeared by twos into Ambrosius' unearthed hut. Muted sounds of very spirited ecumenicism in action soon echoed inside.

Father William and Father Lewis exchanged a look and ran to have a peek. They found the hut silent and empty.

"Just as well," the American priest sighed.

"A shame, though. In the interests of theological research, that is," Father Lewis added.

Someone tapped Dr. Hack on the shoulder. He turned and was nearly blinded by the sunlight reflecting off Illya's heavy glasses.

"I am sorry to trouble you at this time, Dr. Hack, but—"

"If it's about continuing the excavation, go ahead. It's all yours. I'm giving it back to you. You were here first, no argument. Take it up with Ms. Ferrabosco. Dig it in good health. I don't want anything more to do with it."

"Excuse me, please, my honored colleague. We do not wish to discuss excavating, thank you," Illya said with stilted courtesy.

"We wish to discuss defection," Sonia said, standing tall behind him. "Immediately, please."

"Defection . . . ?"

"We have had a religious experience," Yuri explained. He was still holding Sonia's hand.

Dr. Hack's head shook as it rose to push his spectacles back up his nose. "Please go away," he said. "Leave me out of it. Talk to the reporters. Talk to the kids. Talk to the nice demons over there. They understand religious experiences. I'm just not up to dealing with anything else today, so if you don't mind—"

"Ah, there you are, Dr. Hack," Ms. Ferrabosco called from her tent. "You might come in and see the baby, if you like. It's a little boy. Takes after his mother."

"With wings?" Dr. Hack sighed, obediently trudging to the tent-flap.

"Not so's you'd notice." Ms. Ferrabosco smiled. "You can all come, if you like. Mother and child are doing well, to use a cliché." She was beaming, satisfied with her impromptu midwifery. Behind her, Kent Cardiff held a small bundle with a lusty voice. The mortals were only that—mortal. They were drawn to the tent by the sound of the baby's cry. What mystery did they expect to see in that crumpled, scowling, indignant new face? Some answers didn't come in words.

"And what will become of us?" Lura whispered. There was lightless flicker in the air and Melisan was with them.

"The child?" Atamar asked. His perfect features no longer had the look of expertly chiselled stone.

"The child is well," Melisan murmured. "He will be of neither world, and of both. I wish I could stay with him to help him when the choices come, but I don't know where I belong myself anymore."

"Where can we go. Atamar?" asked Gerial pathetically. "Where can we go?"

"I don't know," confessed the bat-winged demon.

"You have to know!" Horgist insisted. "You're our leader!"

"No more!" cried Atamar. "I'm not your leader anymore!" His face was contorted with anguish and a shimmer of the fear they all felt. "We are the outcast of Hell itself, don't you realize that? Where is there for us to go? Where?!"

"Atamar," said the angel. The demons looked up and saw a tiny figure perched on the deep azure peak of a distant mountain, but the voice came strong and cool as a torrent of clear water. "Atamar, where you go now is bounded only by your own choice," the angel went on. "Hell is cast off, not you. Now choose. There is no end to your possibilities." A fresh mist crept up and veiled the mountain. It looked like a flight of milk-white wings.

"Wings," breathed Lura. "I always wanted wings."

"Then we shall go where you can have them, my love," said Atamar, and they stepped into the mist together.

"The Valley of Clouds!" gasped Gerial, transformed with all the joy of being able to go home again. His demon shape fell away like a husk and the winds took him.

"Sleep," mumbled Horgist. "All I really want are dreams." He sank contentedly into the sand.

"Mortal," said Melisan, alone. "Like you, my beloved." Her wings folded in upon themselves and vanished with her.

* * *

Inside the tent, weary but happy, Marguerite Gounod smiled at her new-found friends, her promised husband, and her recently arrived son and heir. Already Kent was quibbling about names, proposing some truly atrocious-sounding Old Germanic monickers merely because linguistically they meant Brave in Battle, Keeper of Treasure, or Terror of Virgins.

"Now out, all of you," clucked Ms. Ferrabosco. "You can take a rest, then we'll pack up and get out of here. Nothing's been the same since they found Ambrosius Minimus' scroll in the sarcophagus. The things that man revealed about Quintus! Not a saint by any stretch of the imagination. Not even a good theologian, and such a washout as abbot—! Poor man. He meant well."

Dr. Hack and Geordie walked out of the tent together.

"They're gone," remarked the older man. Geordie nodded. "I wonder where."

"I wonder, too," said Faith. "But I have a feeling they're all right."

"Listen to the optimist," Amanda teased. "With a name like Faith, what else did you expect?"

"Hey!" exclaimed Ms. Schleppey, hands on hips. "Let's not get allegorical about this."

Epilogue

THE WIND HAD blown since before time had a name and it would blow until time lost all meaning. It blew the dwindling sands of the desert across the encroaching greenness of the fields and forests, past the teeming cities with their needle spires, silver in the glaring sun. It sang a dirge for all the waste that once had stretched past the edge of imagination, and it moaned a lament for all who wandered, lost and outcast and alone.

The demon clung to the crumbled tooth of rock that the years had eaten away, the last refuge left him, swiftly waning monument to the failure that had toppled him from favor to serve out his days until the final shifting of things. On his belly was the mark of the sword, and his eyes were fixed on the brazen bowl of the sky where sometimes a rocket fell like a dying star, drowned in the ever-flowing tears of his searching eyes. The demon, the rock, and the wind.

All Sphere Books are available at your bookshop or newsagent, or can be ordered from the following address: Sphere Books, Cash Sales Department, P.O. Box 11, Falmouth, Cornwall TR10 9EN.

Please send cheque or postal order (no currency), and allow 60p for postage and packing for the first book plus 25p for the second book and 15p for each additional book ordered up to a maximum charge of £1.90 in U.K.

B.F.P.O. customers please allow 60p for the first book, 25p for the second book plus 15p per copy for the next 7 books, thereafter 9p per book.

Overseas customers, including Eire, please allow £1.25 for postage and packing for the first book, 75p for the second book and 28p for each subsequent title ordered.